STAR STRUCK

STAR STRUCK

STARLING LEGACIES
BOOK TWO

MEGAN MOORES

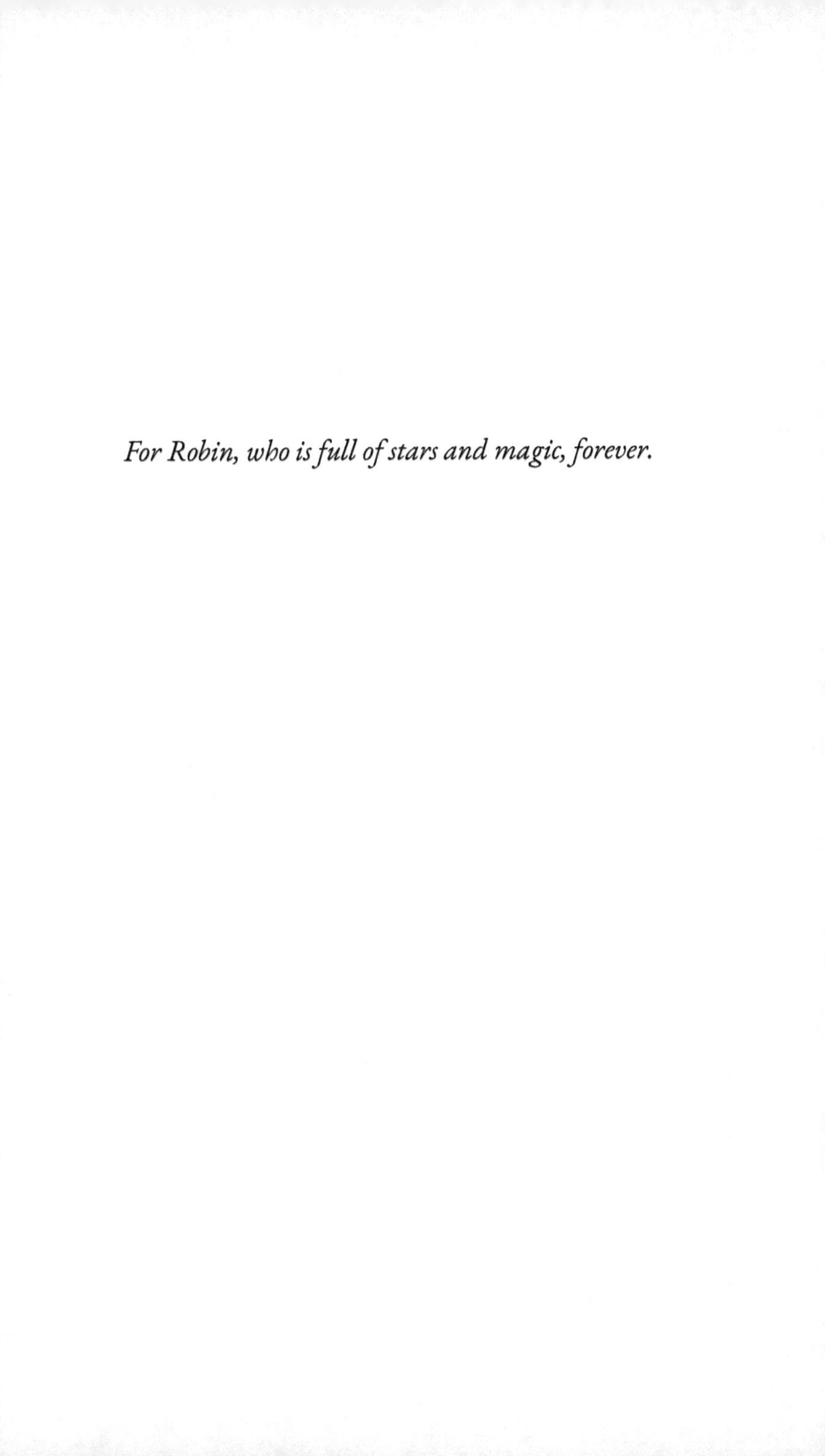

For Robin, who is full of stars and magic, forever.

1

ALICE

The phone rang, its red call button flashing impatiently like a tiny police car. *Answer me, answer me, answer me.* Why couldn't the light be green? Or yellow. Or even purple? Red was impossible to ignore.

I was already two steps away from my desk—two steps closer to the freedom of the weekend, not that I had any plans. I'd likely spend tonight slumped on my couch, binging classic Rom-Coms (my latest obsession), while devouring a large container of carry-out Cashew Chicken. After a few hours I'd thaw out from the over-air-conditioned office that often felt more like a walk-in freezer than a workplace.

Still ringing.

I froze, but not from the arctic temperatures. I froze because I couldn't bring myself to walk away from an expectation or obligation—I didn't want anyone to get upset with me, even if in this case the "anyone" was some unknown person on the other end of the line. Fine. Stupid phone.

"Starling Enterprises, Alice Goode speaking."

"Alice! Thank God you're still there!"

"Lacy?" I instantly recognized my co-worker's British accent. Usually, it made her sound refined and classier than the rest of us, especially me, with my slight Southern twang, but right now she just sounded panicked.

"Do you see the pile of black folders on my desk?" Lacy's whisper was bordering on a hysterical hiss.

"Just a sec." I set the receiver on my desk and jogged to Lacy's desk where about ten portfolio folders rested in a neat pile. I rushed back to the phone. "They're on your desk."

"I'm going to strangle Ryan's skinny little neck on Monday, that wanker. He promised that he'd bring them up to the boardroom, and the execs are about three minutes away from needing them and I'm going to look like an idiot. Is there any way you can run them up here? I'll buy you lunch for a week!" Lacy had burned her hand last weekend in a cooking class gone wrong, so she'd had people helping her out with tasks that required two hands.

"I can bring them, and you don't have to buy me lunch." Those of us on the executive clerical staff had to watch out for each other, even if we did feel like strangling one of our own sometimes. "Tenth floor, or twenty fifth?"

"I'm up top. Thank you so much, Alice. Just walk in with them and start passing them out. I'll stall until then. Cheers."

"Wait . . . Lacy? What do you mean, pass them out?" But the line was dead. Shit. I hung up the phone. The last thing I wanted to do was walk into some fancy executive meeting on the top floor. I liked the tasks that kept me invisible, and interrupting a meeting of the bigwigs was my absolute worst nightmare. For a second, I fantasized about going home anyway – my plan for the weekend involved watching as many Meg Ryan rom-coms as I could stand. Sure, the movies were made decades ago, but that was the point. I loved seeing how the romantic leads navigated "the course of true love" without cell phones, obsessive texting, and social media.

I felt like an outcast in the modern world of online dating, and I was pretty sure I was born thirty years too late. But no matter how strong the call to abscond to my solitary and anonymous apartment to hang out in an imaginary 1990s timeline, I couldn't bring myself to abandon Lacy in her time of need. I could, however, make her buy me lunch. I grabbed the folders off Lacy's desk and trudged to the elevator. The faster I got this over with, the sooner I could get home and hide out from the world for two whole days.

Twenty floors later, the elevator doors opened, and a gentle *ding* announced my arrival on the executive floor. *My* floor, the fifth, smelled like copy paper and perfume, but the top floor carried the scent of Italian leather and ambition.

Vivienne was at the main desk. Whenever one of the Starlings was in the office, there had to be someone at the desk, no matter the time. Also, everyone who worked on this floor was gorgeous. Not just pretty, or handsome, or good-looking, but knock-down, jaw-dropping, fresh off the model truck beautiful.

Vivienne was Korean, and she was a goddess. She pointed one expertly manicured finger in the direction of the boardroom and then used that same finger to smooth out the already impeccable line of her sleek black hair that ended bluntly at her shoulders in a perfect razor cut.

I was ridiculous in comparison. My usual selection of black slacks and a black sweater was meant to come across as professional and neutral, but in the presence of the divine Vivienne, I felt frumpy and boring. The dark color helped hide my curves —most of the other women in the office were thin and toned, and though most of us were the same age, around thirty, give or take, I felt like I looked older and softer. I tried to camouflage my ample boobs, full hips, and plump ass by wearing that same black ensemble every day, and every morning I'd wrestle my wild red curls into a bun in an effort to look sleek and professional. But, whatever. My general goal was to exist like a ghost—being seen could be dangerous, at least in my experience, so I'd leave the job of being eye-catching to people like the glorious Vivienne.

I arrived outside the boardroom and through the glass paneled wall, I spied nine people around the table, a mix of women and men. I recognized a few of them, like Mitchell Maddix Starling, sixtyish, handsome as hell, the CEO of Starling Enterprises, and my boss. Well, my boss's boss's boss. Then there was his brother, Miles Maddix Starling. Identically handsome, because the brothers were born in a set of identical triplets, though the third brother died years ago. Miles was COO of Starling Enterprises, but he worked out of a different office, and this was my first time seeing him up close. Also at the table was Simon Starling, son of Miles. He was CFO, and was tall, dark, and usually brooding. In my year of working at Starling Enterprises, I'd only seen him a handful of times.

I pushed open the door, and all heads turned to look at me. I had no doubt that my face was even redder than my hair, but surely they had more important things to do than to examine the errand girl. I stepped toward the table to pass out the folders, but Lacy sidled up to me, closed her hand around my elbow, and led me to the back corner.

"There's been a delay. They aren't ready for those yet," she whispered.

"Sorry." I was mortified and fought the urge to flee. I'd be more of a disruption if I plunked down the folders and high-tailed it out of there, so I stood off to the side, clutching the heavy pile, my arms aching. There was an empty seat at the table, next to Simon. I'd bet my whole collection of Hugh Grant DVDs (did it get better than *Notting Hill?*) that the lonely chair belonged to the absent Sebastian Starling.

Sebastian was the son of Mitchell and had the opposite reputation to his cousin Simon. Where Simon was known to be punctual, Sebastian was always late, or never arrived at all. Simon's clothing was impeccably tailored, but I'd seen Sebastian fly through the office in everything from fluorescent streetwear to a black and white checkerboard three-piece suit. His clothes were expensive, and somehow stylish, but they were not corporate culture by any stretch of the imagination.

Simon was quiet and cold, at least from what I'd observed, but you could often hear Sebastian and his hearty laugh before he even got off the elevator. He was known for being a playboy and apparently he only dated models. I refused to be starstruck by Sebastian, but that put me in the minority. A lot of the women on my floor talked about ways to catch his eye, but I'd rather speak in front of a thousand people than go on a date with Sebastian Starling, not that I'd ever catch his eye in a million years, so I guess I was safe from that nightmare scenario. Everyone knew that Sebastian Starling was "Look but don't touch," like some precious statue in a museum. Appreciate the beauty, but move on, girl.

I was pulled out of my daydream by a sharp poke in the ribs from Lacy. Everyone at the table was staring at me.

"I said, they're ready," Lacy muttered through gritted teeth and a fake smile.

I stepped forward and handed out the folders, starting with

Mitchell and Miles and moving around the table from there. After setting the last folder down in front of Simon, I returned to Lacy's side. I didn't know how to escape the room without being disruptive.

Lacy leaned close to my ear. "This is the last item on the agenda. Should just be a few more minutes."

"We've put this off as long as we can. Simon, have you heard back from your cousin?" Mitchell opened his folder and began flipping through its contents.

"Still going to voicemail." Simon's nostrils flared with apparent annoyance.

"Well, we can't get too far without Sebastian, but I'll give you the rundown. As you know, he's been wanting to take on more responsibility in the company—"

"Funny way to show it," Miles interrupted his brother.

Mitchell let out an audible sigh and his shoulders slumped. "I know. I'm giving him this one last chance to prove to us that he can do it. And it's no excuse, but I did just text him about this meeting a few hours ago. It was short notice." He lifted his glass to take a sip of water, but it was empty.

Another poke in the ribs from Lacy, who was holding up her bandaged hand to remind me of her injury. Just my luck that she'd hurt her dominant hand. Lacy nodded toward the refreshment table. Right. Water. I could do this. I retrieved the water pitcher from a side table and approached Mr. Starling. He handed me his glass and I filled it up, my hands shaking. There was a reason I'd never gone into waitressing: one wrong move and you could ruin someone's entire night. But I filled the glass without incident, leaned over Mr. Starling, and placed the drink back on the table without spilling it. My heart was pounding, and I took a deep breath to calm my nerves—but, at that exact moment, the condensation on the glass pitcher decided to betray me, and a single droplet of water dripped off the pitcher and plopped onto the top of Starling's head, right where his hair was starting to thin. Kill me now.

Mitchell's hand went to his head, and he patted the spot where the water had landed. "Anyone else feel a raindrop?" he asked, and everyone laughed.

I tried to laugh along, but tears rushed into my eyes. Mr. Starling looked back at me with a smile, but his face filled with concern when he saw my obvious embarrassment. "It was getting stuffy in here anyway; I appreciate the refresher!" He dipped two fingers into his full glass of water and flicked another drop of water onto the top of his head. "Ah, that's better."

Everyone laughed again, and I laughed along with them. I still wanted to disappear into nothingness, but at least I wasn't about to inappropriately burst into tears. I scurried back to my corner where Lacy gave my arm a reassuring squeeze.

Mitchell cleared his throat and guided the meeting back to the agenda. "So, this is about the Caluska Island property."

My ears started to ring, and my vision tunneled. Did he say *Caluska Island?* That's where I'd lived with my grandparents after my parents died. From age three to sixteen, I lived on that tiny island, and they were some of the best and worst years of my life.

"This is a chance to make some real inroads into the Southern market," Starling continued. "We have a few properties in Savannah and Hilton Head, but this one seems like it could be a special spot, or it could be a bust. It's a lower-risk negotiation because that's not really our area, so it might be one Sebastian can manage."

Simon huffed and rolled his eyes. "That remains to be seen. You're going to send him down there on his own?"

"Are you volunteering to join him?" Mitchell raised his eyebrow at his nephew.

"I most certainly am not. But you might want to consider hiring a handler."

"In what sense?"

"Someone to keep him on track. To make sure he's checking the boxes. You know, a corporate babysitter of sorts. Someone in junior management, maybe?"

Mitchell rubbed his palm along his jaw as he thought it over. "Might be a good idea. We'd need someone with tact. There's a sensitive situation brewing on the island."

"You're sending Bash into a situation where tact is paramount?" It was Simon's turn to raise his eyebrow.

"Not ideal, I know. The property we're looking at has been in one family for seventy years, but the younger folks have fled to the mainland and the remaining owners are elderly and in poor health. It's right in the heart of the island, but it's in major disrepair, and is close to being condemned."

Oh God, he was talking about the Scarlet Oaks Resort owned by the Blake family. My grandparents, who had both passed away in the last ten years, used to be very close to the Blakes, and I had a soft spot for them as well

Starling looked down at his notes. "Sarah and Edward Blake are listed as the current owners, though I'm not sure they even live on the island now. The resort has been shuttered for a few years and is right on the edge of needing major renovations if it's left abandoned for much longer. There's a big developer from Orlando who wants to take over the property, and that's who we'll be up against. We're seen as the underdog here, at least in real estate. Seems that the Blake family might hold a grudge against the big developers because of damage done in the past to the island's natural resources. It doesn't say here what happened, but I'm assuming they cut down trees or something—"

"Oysters." I was surprised as everyone else to hear my voice ring out in the room. Not only had I just blurted out *"oysters,"* but I'd interrupted the CEO of Starling Enterprises.

"Excuse me?" Mitchell Starling swiveled around in his chair to look at me.

Lacy took a step back like she didn't want to be associated with the brazen red-headed executive assistant who'd clearly lost her marbles.

"Uh . . . Oysters, sir. That's the natural resource that was destroyed on the island."

"Is that so?" Starling's face was open and curious. "And how do you know that?"

"I used to live there. Oysters were like gold on Caluska, back in the mid-twentieth century. Everyone made a good living, and people came from all over the world to visit the island. But about sixty years ago, a huge factory was built in Harborhollow, north of Caluska. Some developments in surrounding cities, too. All the new pollution flowed down the waterways and poisoned the island's oysters and they were unsellable. It's been downhill ever since. Sir."

Lacy's mouth had dropped open, and her eyes were wide. She'd probably never heard me say so many words at once to any of our supervisors, let alone the CEO.

"What's your name?"

"Alice Goode, sir."

"And where do you work?"

"Fifth floor, sir. Clerical pool."

Simon's phone buzzed, saving me from myself. He looked at the display and passed it across the table to his uncle. "It's Sebastian."

Mr. Starling swiveled back around, snatched the phone out of Simon's hand, and answered the call. "Son, get your ass to the office right now. I'll be waiting for you in the boardroom on the twenty-fifth." He hit a button to end the call. "It could be a while before my son makes an appearance, so let's wrap up. I'll have my assistant send out an update after I speak with Sebastian, and we finalize plans on Caluska. Thanks for staying late, and have a good weekend, everyone."

There *was* a god after all. I could go home and open that bottle of wine my co-workers had bought me for my thirtieth birthday last month—I might have to drink at least half of it to calm my nerves and stop myself from replaying everything in excruciating detail. I stepped toward the door, hoping to beat the executives to the elevator so I didn't have to talk to any of them.

"Ms. Goode." Mitchell Starling called out, stopping me in my tracks. "Not you. Have a seat. You've just been promoted to corporate handler."

2

SEBASTIAN

Talking to your father on the phone while a woman stuck her hands down your pants wasn't the sexiest of situations. Luckily, the call only lasted a few seconds. Unluckily, I'd been called into an emergency meeting, and even though I wanted to get ahead at work, I'd rather get head from Eva first. Or was it Ava? Shit.

Not that I was being selfish, or not entirely so. I wanted to pleasure Eva/Ava, too, but during the entire ride to the hotel she'd been groping my crotch while saying how much she wanted to get her mouth on me as soon as we got to the room. And who was I to disappoint a lady? I'd been distracted, though, because my driver kept glancing back at us, and my phone was buzzing as my cousin Simon called me over and over. It probably had something to do with the meeting I'd skipped out on, but hey, for all they knew, I never listened to the voice-mail about it in the first place.

I'd barely shut the door to my room when my date started unbuttoning my pants. "Hold on, just a second. I have to make a call." I didn't want my phone blowing up again while Eva/Ava was realizing her dream.

She'd ignored me and slid her hands into my underwear and cupped my balls. Wow, this woman got right down to business. I'd expected to hear Simon's voice on the line, since I'd called his phone, but it was my dad.

"Son, get your ass to the office right now. I'll be waiting for you in the boardroom on the twenty-fifth," he'd barked, and then hung up before I'd had a chance to respond.

Dammit. I had to cut this date short. "I'm sorry, I gotta go. There's an emergency at work." Whatshername had my pants pulled halfway down my thighs and was about to drag my underwear down, too. I was fully erect and didn't want her to stop touching me, but I knew that I wouldn't have time to concentrate on her, and that didn't seem right. She was beautiful—a model—and sweet. Though I'd only just met her a few days ago. We were moving pretty fast, but that seemed to be the norm for me lately.

"I think *this* is an emergency." She yanked on my boxer briefs and sank to her knees, putting her face right at dick-level.

"You really don't have to," I said, though my resolve was weakening. "I'd just have to leave right after and that isn't fair to—"

She pushed me against the wall, wrapped her lips around my cock and started jerking me off at the same time. Forget it. My resistance was gone. I closed my eyes and let the wall hold my weight as Ava (I'd decided to choose a name and stick to it) manhandled me. She was a bit rough, but I wasn't about to complain. Then she started moaning. A small moan at first, but then she got louder, and louder still. Ava was panting and keening and groaning like *she* was the one getting the blow job, and I was so distracted that I couldn't concentrate on my own pleasure. Her cries escalated and she pulled her mouth away from my dick and yanked on my shaft hard and fast while she threw her head back and gave a perfect orgasmic show, but why? Surely performing fellatio wasn't *that* exciting.

It wasn't working for me. And enough time had passed that I was starting to worry about my meeting, and that didn't do my erection any favors. I tried to stop her, but she was going wild, and was handling my penis like it was a cocktail shaker and she was making a martini. I'd rather be stirred, thank you very much.

"Hey," I said gently, but she couldn't hear me over her porn star imitation. I tried to pull her hands off me, but she had a death grip on my shaft. "Hey," I said, a little louder. No dice. Now it was getting painful. "Ava!" I almost yelled. That worked.

She stopped mid-yank and looked up at me, her moaning suddenly ceasing.

"I'm sorry, I really do have to go. I truly appreciate your effort here."

"Oh, that's ok." She dropped my dick like the director of our porno had yelled "cut!" and she was off the clock. She hopped up and put her hands on her hips. "Can I catch a ride to my friend's house? We're going to binge some old seasons of *The Bachelorette*."

Guess I wasn't the only one going through the motions. I pulled my pants up and ran my hand through my hair. "Sure thing, Ava."

"It's Eva."

. . .

Twenty minutes later, Eva was safely deposited at her friend's house, and I was riding the elevator up to the top floor of Starling Enterprises. I knew that I'd been the one who'd asked my dad for a chance to really do some real work at the company, but I was dreading the meeting. Over the last year I'd felt increasingly like a directionless loser. I had more money than I could spend, endless parties to attend, and could have any woman I wanted, but I felt empty. Ordinary. Lost. I hoped that a work project might be the direction and meaning I was looking for, but the idea of it also scared the shit out of me. What if I failed? I was almost out of chances as far as Starling Enterprises went, and I may've already fucked up by missing the initial meeting and dawdling with Eva after my dad called me. Maybe I was a master of self-sabotage.

I stepped off the elevator and Vivienne, who I'd taken to a few parties last year, gave me a slight nod, but otherwise ignored me. She was nice enough, but we didn't have much chemistry. I took a deep breath before entering the boardroom. *You can do this, Starling. You've got this.*

My dad was sitting at the table with a woman I'd never seen before. She had bright red hair piled into a messy bun that looked like it might explode into a cascade of untamed curls at any second. She was eating a salad when I entered the room, and she stood up so quickly at the sight of me that she knocked her fork off the table, which clattered to the floor. She dove under the table to retrieve it and popped back up, her cheeks flaming with embarrassment. I'd never seen so much red concentrated on one person's head. It especially stood out because the rest of her body was concealed beneath an entirely black outfit, leaving nothing for my eye to land on other than her pink cheeks, crimson hair, ruby lips, and sparkling blue eyes that regarded me with apprehension.

"Where were you that it took you an hour to get here? Your driver said you were just a few blocks away at the Concord." My father was not pleased.

"I had to drop off a friend and then I came as fast as I could." I actually never came, but that was beside the point.

My dad stood up, probably because the woman was still standing—she was looking at me like she was afraid I might pounce on her.

"Sebastian, this is Alice Goode. She's your new corporate handler and will be accompanying you to Caluska Island."

What the fuck was Caluska Island? I membered my manners enough to shake Alice's hand before unloading my questions on Dad. Her hand was cool and trembling. She offered me a weak smile, revealing a speck of lettuce stuck to a front tooth.

"You've got a little something," I said, pointing to my own front teeth.

"Oh God!" Her hand shot to her mouth and her face went positively scarlet. "Please excuse me for a moment!" She rushed out the door, probably to find the restroom.

"What the hell is a corporate handler?" I plopped down in the chair next to the one Alice had occupied before Lettucegate forced her from the room.

"Alice will be helping you navigate this project. I don't think you're ready to go it alone."

"Is she an account executive?" I looked around the room for some more food. Alice's salad looked good, and the rumble in my stomach made me realize I'd forgotten to eat dinner.

"Not exactly."

"Then exactly what is she?"

"She was a member of the executive clerical pool before this—"

"She's a junior secretary?" Wow. My dad really had zero faith in me.

"She's a business professional who happens to have intimate knowledge of Caluska Island."

"She's Canadian?"

My dad squinted his eyes and took a slow breath. He folded his hands in front of him. "Why would she be Canadian?"

"Isn't Caluska Island in Canada?"

"Did you not read the briefing I emailed you?" My dad pulled on his earlobe. Uh-oh, the earlobe pull was his tell when he was super pissed.

"Oh. Uh. I didn't realize you'd emailed something."

"Sebastian Maddix Starling." He'd used my full name. Shit was about to hit the fan.

"I can read it now!"

"That's a waste of my time. Read it later."

Alice shuffled back into the room. She'd taken her hair down in the bathroom, or it had finally burst out of that tenuous bun, and wow—that woman had a head of hair. No wonder she put it up. When it was loose, it was huge, and it seemed like it took up half the room. It was also pretty, in an untamed kind of way. "Sorry about that. What did I miss?"

"I was just explaining to Sebastian that Caluska Island is not in Canada."

Alice giggled, and for a moment her face softened and lit up. "It's *so* not in Canada."

I was annoyed that they were ganging up on me, and I felt

stupid. "Then where is it? I thought you had a resort project in Canada, so I just assumed—"

"I do have a resort project in Canada, but that's a premiere property. This one is in South Carolina."

"South Carolina?" South Carolina was hot. I didn't do hot weather. I was a cold weather kind of guy. Boston, where I lived, was the perfect climate for me. On vacation I preferred ski lodges, mountain tops, and ice fishing. I was not a beachy, steamy, warm weather dude.

"Correct." My dad was giving me the stare-down.

"But it's hot there." Speaking of hot, I was starting to sweat. I unbuttoned the top button of my shirt.

"Also correct."

"I don't do hot."

"Excuse me?" My father did not look pleased.

"Don't you have something that's up north?"

"Nothing you can handle. Alice spent her childhood on Caluska Island. She was filling me in on the island culture and history while we waited for you to arrive. You'll be in good hands with her, and if you actually read the briefs I emailed you, you should be prepared to fly down next Friday and get the ball rolling on negotiations."

My stomach dropped. This was really happening. "A week from today?"

"Yes, one week. Do you really want to do this, Sebastian? Because even though this is a smaller project, it's an important one. There are real stakes and it's going to take a lot of time and money to have a chance to make this happen. If this is just a game to you, then don't waste my time, or Alice's."

It was my turn to be embarrassed, and heat collected in my cheeks. "I want to do this." I did want to do it. That was true. I just wasn't sure I could do it well. What had I gotten myself into?

"Don't blow this, son."

Speaking of blowing, my rendezvous with Eva felt like it was weeks ago, not mere hours. That was the old Sebastian. It was time for a new chapter. "I won't. You can trust me. I'll make it happen." We both knew I was bluffing, but I had to start somewhere.

"We'll see. For now, you two have to start preparing. I've had Vivienne reserve a suite for you at the Concord, starting tonight."

Alice looked as shocked as I felt. "A suite?" Her voice was quiet and timid.

"You'll need to get as much prep time as possible before you get to the island. A driver will take you to collect your things, Alice. I'll assign someone to look after your apartment while you're gone. You said you have no children or pets, correct?"

"That's correct." Alice nervously twisted a strand of hair around her finger.

"Excellent. I'll let your supervisor know that you've been reassigned, and we'll set you up with a company phone and laptop, and you'll have a stipend for wardrobe, food, and travel."

Alice looked like she'd just been told they were sending her to the moon. "Oh . . . okay?"

"Let's meet Monday at 4:00 p.m. The two of you can update me on your progress. Anything else before we wrap up?"

My head was spinning. I'd gone from bachelor playboy to paired-up business bro in the span of an hour. I guess this was what I'd asked for, and I had to give it a chance. "Nope."

"Nothing from me, either," Alice said. She snuck a glance at me, and I thought I saw real fear on her face. Was she afraid of me, or of the task at hand? Or both?

"Great. Your mother's waiting for me at the pub over on State Street. Have a good night." Dad gathered up his things and left.

Alice and I sat in silence for a few moments.

"How do you feel about all this?" I asked her.

"Like it's a dog-eat-dog world out there, and I'm wearing milk-bone underwear."

Her humor hit me out of the blue and disoriented me. And why did that line sound familiar? "What's that from? It's ringing a bell somewhere back in the annals of my mind."

"I love ringing people's anals," Alice quipped.

A laugh bubbled out of me—I couldn't help it. "Annals, not anals!" Though I knew she didn't need the correction.

"If you're from Boston and you don't know that reference, I can't help you."

"Was that from *Cheers*? You know that show was on like, a thousand years ago."

"It aired from 1982 to 1993. Eleven seasons and—"

"Two hundred seventy-five episodes. I know."

She raised her eyebrows in a gesture of appreciation. "Ok, maybe you're a Bostonian after all."

"You can blame my mom—it's one of her comfort streaming shows, so I've seen more of it than I care to admit. That theme song is burned into my brain for all eternity."

"Making your way in—" she started to sing.

"Don't even start!" I demanded. "That one's an insidious earworm and you know it."

"Sorry," Alice's face blanched and her shoulders slumped, and she became suddenly small, like she was trying to disappear.

"No, it's ok. It's just if I get that song stuck in my head it'll be there for a month."

"Me too. I'm sorry." Alice scooped up her belongings and refused to look at me. She'd come out of her shell for a minute, but was definitely back in it. "See you at the hotel," she said as she dashed out of the room, leaving me wondering what the hell I'd just gotten myself into.

3

ALICE

My hands were on the wheel, but I was going nowhere. Literally. I hadn't even started the car because I didn't trust myself to not drive distractedly into a lamppost on the way home. The Starling Enterprises parking garage was mostly deserted, and I forced myself to take some slow, deep breaths. When I'd parked my car this morning, it was just another day of work: copies, errands, press releases, and small projects. And now, I was a "Corporate Handler" for the wild, handsome, and untamed son of the CEO.

Okay, maybe I'd been a *little* starstruck when he'd sashayed into the boardroom. While it was still true that he wasn't my type—I preferred the "boy next door" kind of guy—there was no denying that he was a breathtaking specimen of the male variety. He was a perfect six feet tall, so a good six inches taller than me. His dark hair had some kind of magical wave that made it appear impeccably styled yet totally casual, like he'd rolled out of bed looking like a god. When he wasn't being photographed with a new model each night at every hot party on the East Coast, Sebastian must've been working his personal trainer overtime—I'd spied muscles rippling in his forearms while he fiddled with his pen in the boardroom, and if he had muscles there, what did the rest of him look like?

His generous smile and that tiny gap between his front teeth —why? Why was a gap so damn sexy? And his green eyes—they were almost emerald, and the flecks of gold that sparkled like rays of morning sun peeking through a summer forest. What was wrong with me? I must've been ovulating.

The three knocks on my window scared the shit out of me and yanked me out of my daydream. My scream startled the knocker as well, and he backed up a few feet and put his hands up in an "I'm innocent and unarmed" gesture. I hit the lock button on the door, but it was already locked.

"I'm your driver!" the man said. He pulled an ID card out of his pocket, and it had the same Starling emblem on the corner that adorned my own employee ID.

"I don't have a driver," I told him through the closed window.

Mr. Driver held up a finger, as if asking me to wait and not peel out of the garage in a panic. He hit a button on his phone and held up the screen for me to see. It read: *calling Mitchell Starling*. The call connected and Mr. Driver spoke into the phone and then motioned for me to roll the window down. I tapped the button to start up the car's electronics and cracked the window a few inches. The man held the phone up to the window, and Mr. Starling's voice rang out through the speaker.

"Ms. Goode? Are you there?"

"I'm here," I said, two notches above an appropriate volume.

"I'm sorry for the abrupt nature of all of this."

I could hear voices and the clinking of glasses in the background. He must've been calling me from the pub. "That's okay."

"No, it's not, but it's what we have. The man outside your car is Nelson—he's one of my drivers. He tried to catch you in the office, but apparently you were too fast for him."

"I don't need a driver, Mr. Starling. I have a car." A nice, trusty, locked car.

"I understand. It's an excellent 2019 silver Honda Accord, and we promise to take good care of it. If you leave your keys with Nelson, he'll make sure it gets moved to the Executive Level of the parking garage where it will be washed, filled up, and we'll even see if it's ready for new tires or other scheduled maintenance while you're out of town."

"Oh," was all I could say. How did he know what kind of car I had? Also, this would be a genius way to carry out a successful carjacking ring. Would I get out of my car at gunpoint? Never. But get out at the promise of new tires? Sure, take it, it's all yours.

"Nelson will drive you to your apartment to get your things, and then he'll escort you to the Concord where you can get settled in your suite. If you have any needs or concerns, just let him know, and he will alert the appropriate person. I really appreciate what you're doing for the company, and for me personally, and I want to make this transition as smooth as possible."

I nodded but realized that Mr. Starling couldn't see me. I'd gotten this far. May as well jump in the deep end. "Alright. I'll go with Nelson."

"Excellent! I look forward to seeing you Monday afternoon

in our meeting. Thank you again, Ms. Goode." And then he was gone.

NINETY MINUTES later I was packed up, tucked into the backseat of a luxury SUV, and being driven through the late-night streets of Boson. The tinted windows dimmed the city lights, and I struggled to keep my eyes open as the soft leather seats of the car enveloped me. There was a lot of foot room, despite two suitcases and a backpack at my feet. I had no idea what I'd need, so I just stuffed everything I could into my bags and decided I'd figure it out later. Nelson had waited outside my door for me at my apartment, so it felt like he was half driver, half bodyguard.

I tried to let myself enjoy my fifteen minutes of this lifestyle of the rich and famous, but it was hard to fully relax knowing I was going to have to spend time with Sebastian Starling. I'd made a fool out of myself in the boardroom by singing that theme song. Mortification was my punishment for not staying invisible. I knew better.

We drove past the entrance to Concord Hotel, and I thought about asking Nelson why we hadn't stopped, but I figured he knew what he was doing. Thirty seconds later, he turned into a gated garage and used a key card to gain access. After a few more twists and turns, he stopped the car at an underground elevator staffed by two hotel employees. Nelson opened the door for me and one of the employees opened the other car door and extracted my suitcases.

"Where are we?" I asked Nelson as he guided me toward the elevator.

"VIP entrance. The elevator takes you right to the penthouse floor."

My clothes suddenly felt itchy, and I stifled the urge to bite my nails. I didn't fit in here. Not at this hotel, this VIP entrance, and certainly not in a penthouse suite.

"Ready, Ms. Goode?" asked one of the attendants.

Was I ready? Nope. "Yep," I lied.

"You have my number if you need anything," Nelson said right before I was ushered into the oversized elevator.

Seconds later, the doors opened onto a quiet and softly lit hallway. The wooden floors gleamed and wall sconces that looked like they were lit with real flames marked the locations of suite doors.

"Follow me." My attendant led me down the hall and around a corner where we came face to face with an imposing oak door. "This is the Starling Suite." He knocked, waited a few beats, and then used a key card to open the door. The suite must've been soundproofed because as soon the door swung open, we were hit with the pounding beat of music. The pulsing kick drum and baseline were familiar, but it took me a second to place it.

"Is that Billie Eilish's 'Bad Guy?'"

"I believe it is, Ms. Goode. Have a good evening." He pressed the key card into my hand and quickly exited the suite.

I was left alone in a palatial living room with obnoxiously tasteful furniture, a city view, and music loud enough to give me a headache if it went on much longer. Where was Sebastian? The lamps in the living room were emanating a low and warm glow, but I saw a brighter light coming from a bedroom off to the right—the door was ajar. "Sebastian?" My voice was drowned out by the song, so I went to investigate. I felt like I was in a movie and that the music was the score. Judging by the song, I was going to find something in that room—or someone.

That someone was Sebastian Starling. A naked Sebastian Starling, to be exact. With his back turned to me, and probably fresh from the shower, judging by the towel on the bed and by how his body glistened with moisture. For a second, I thought he was drunk. He was swaying—wait, God help me, he was dancing. His body found the beat and he moved—moved in a way that made me feel things highly inappropriate for a workplace situation. The bass thumped so loudly that it reverberated through my chest, and I couldn't take my eyes off him. He raised his arms and ran his fingers through his damp hair. If this was a thirst trap set-up, I'd fallen for it hook, line, and sinker. Sebastian let the rhythm of the song move through his shoulders, over his broad back, into his hips as they rocked back and forth, and his ass—Jesus, his ass. I'd never seen anything like it in real life.

He kept dancing as he lifted a pair of boxer briefs off the bed and stepped into them one muscled leg at a time and then (sadly, for me) pulled them over his bare ass. He slipped into some soft pants, and as the song came to an end, he turned to find his shirt and must've caught a glimpse of me in his peripheral vison.

"Alice!" He was startled and surprised, but did he yell? Hide behind his towel? Slam the door? None of the above. He laughed. A big, open, joyful laugh. A slower song came on next and he danced over to me like he was going to gather me into his arms and spin me around the room. This really *was* like a movie.

I stepped aside to avoid a collision between me and the shirtless Starling, but he would not be denied. He slipped his right hand around my waist and took my right hand in his left and led me across the room. Sebastian moved like he'd been training for Dancing with the Stars, which, if I thought about it, wasn't completely far-fetched. He gave me a twirl, pulled me back in, dipped me backwards, and pulled me in again. We were both breathless and our faces were so close to each other. For a moment he dropped his smile, and I may have imagined it, but I thought he leaned down just a little, like he was bringing his face closer to mine. The music swelled and I was painfully aware of the heat of his bare shoulder under my palm and of how our bodies were pressed together.

Then Sebastian let go of my hand and hit a button on the stereo, sending the room into sudden silence. "Thanks for being such a good sport!" He released me and walked toward the kitchen. "And sorry for the peep show! Didn't hear you come in. Want something to drink?"

"Water?" The word came out squeaky. I cleared my throat and tried again. "Water would be great."

"Sparkling or flat?" Sebastian was rifling through a massive refrigerator.

"Uh, sparkling?"

"Flavored or plain?"

"Plain."

"Topo Chico or Perrier?"

I had no idea. "Chef's choice?" How much water did he have in there?

He popped the top off a glass bottle and crossed the room to deliver it. "Have a seat," he nodded toward the couch. "You must be exhausted."

"I'm pretty tired." I sipped the water, and the bubbles stung my throat as I swallowed.

"I'll take your stuff into your room. It's too late to work, anyway." He slipped my backpack over his shoulders, and it looked tiny on his torso. He lifted my suitcases instead of rolling them. He may have done that just to show off his muscles, and I tried to avert my eyes, but I did end up sneaking a peek. *He* was the one who'd decided to forgo a shirt—it wasn't my fault. He returned to the living room and plopped down on the couch next to me. "So, Alice Goode."

"So, Sebastian Starling."

"How'd you end up as my handler?"

"Right place, right time?" I took another sip. I'd never noticed that he had a dimple, either.

"Think you can handle me? I hear I can be . . . a lot." Sebastian grinned as he ran his hands down his admittedly perfect abs.

I appreciated the show he was putting on, but I could do without the ego. "Oh yeah? Who tells you that?"

Sebastian's dimple disappeared as his smile faded. "Everyone."

"Is that so?" I sounded more confident than I felt. I took a final gulp of water.

He shrugged. "You might not have enough experience to handle a special case like me. I hear you're just an executive assistant?"

My stomach lurched and my face burned. Maybe he didn't mean to be rude, but his comment felt like a kick in the gut. I might've been shy, but I wasn't one to back down in the face of a bully. "Special case?" I stood up, straightened my shirt, and made a point to stare at him like I was checking him out. "You look pretty ordinary to me."

Sebastian went pale. His smirk faltered, like I'd stripped him bare. For a moment, he just stared at me, uncertainty in his eyes. I'd meant to sting him, not take him out at the knees. He opened his mouth to reply but then bit his lip and stayed silent. He stood and walked to his bedroom, and then paused in the doorway. His back was still gorgeous, but he seemed smaller. Deflated. "Goodnight, Alice." Without ever turning back around, he shut the door.

4

SEBASTIAN

I tossed and turned all night. The mattress was too hard, the pillows too soft, and the room was too hot, then too cold, then too hot again. Usually I could sleep anywhere: a concrete floor, a bathtub, a pool table—I'd had comfortable sleeps in all those places over the last month, though there was a fine line between being asleep and passing out, but whatever. Now I was stone-cold sober and wide-awake.

Why had I said that shit about Alice being "just" an assistant? That was more than I could say about myself—I was "just" a trust-fund baby. I had a degree in marketing but was no expert in that area. My dad was an accomplished businessman and the son of entertainment royalty—Sadie Starling and Quentin Maddix. My grandmother had been an iconic musician and entertainer, and my granddad came from one of those American families who ran a publishing empire and had more money than God. And what did I do? Nothing. Nothing but skate by on looks and my bank account. I was nothing special, that's for sure, unless you counted my special talent of being an asshole to unsuspecting corporate handlers.

The morning sun pushing through the cracks of the curtains found me groggy but wired. Screw trying to sleep—it wasn't going to happen. I threw on sweatpants and a t-shirt, hoping to redeem myself from last night's naked exhibition. I'd told Nelson to text me when Alice was headed up in the elevator, and he had, but I'd forgotten that I muted him earlier in the day when he kept texting me about that board meeting. So, I missed his text, and Alice got a real show. At least she only got the backside of me—not that my other side wasn't worth seeing, but a full-frontal greeting wasn't how I usually approached interactions with new coworkers.

The area rug was soft on the bare soles of my feet as I crossed the living room and headed for the kitchen. Maybe I could make breakfast for Alice, if she hadn't run away in the middle of the night. The lights that were on before I went to bed had never been turned off, probably because I'd stomped away like a baby and Alice didn't know where all the light switches were. I loaded up the coffee maker, started the brew cycle, and checked out the fridge to see what we had. Lots of beverages, some eggs and cheese, and some berries. Not enough. I texted a breakfast order to the kitchen—eggs benedict, French toast, a pastry plate, a side of breakfast meats, a fruit plate, oatmeal, and some yogurt. I didn't know if Alice had any allergies or restrictions, so I thought that should cover it. If not, I'd just order her something else when she woke up.

Laptop in hand, I stretched out on the couch and opened the email from my dad about Caluska Island. I'd tried to read it last night, but couldn't concentrate, and this morning was no different. There were all kinds of attachments: maps, lists, financial reports, contact sheets, proposal templates, historical documents, and some case studies. I'd been along for the ride with my dad on a lot of his business deals, but I'd never really engaged in the process, and I'd for sure never been in charge. I wanted to prove it to my dad and to myself that I could do this, but maybe it was a mistake. This stuff was over my head.

"You're up early." Alice's voice startled me.

I snapped my laptop shut and sat up. "Hey. Good morning. Couldn't sleep."

"Me either. Is that coffee I smell?" She wandered toward the kitchen. She'd also chosen sweatpants and a t-shirt as her morning outfit, but she sure wore it differently than I did.

I hadn't noticed her figure yesterday because she was shrouded in that all-black ensemble. I didn't want to be creepy, but I was having a hard time looking away from her as she stood in front of the coffeemaker, waiting for the last of the water to run through the grounds. I'd rarely seen curves like hers. The women in my orbit were usually long, lean, angular, and some-times sharp. Alice was all softness. Her breasts were full, her stomach slightly rounded, and her hips made me want to run my hands along them and see where I might be able to grab on. And the way her ass filled out her sweatpants, I could only imagine what she might look like if—

"How does this thing work?" She jostled the handle of the carafe, but it was stuck in a locked position.

I jumped up to help. *Get your mind out of the gutter, Star-ling.* "Should be ready." I found two mugs and set them on the counter along with a spoon from the utensil drawer. "How do you take it?"

"Do you have almond milk?" She peered into the fridge and pushed some containers around.

Shit, was she vegan? I'd need to order some from the kitchen. Along with avocado toast or something—the fruit plate wouldn't be enough. "I'm sorry. I think we only have dairy stuff. I can order you some, though." I pulled out my phone and started to text the kitchen again.

"Dairy's fine. I've just been on an almond milk kick lately."

"So, you're not allergic?"

"Nope. No allergies, no dietary restrictions." She located a carton of half-and-half and brought it to the counter as I poured coffee in our cups.

"Hope you're hungry, then. Our feast should be here soon."

She nodded but didn't make eye contact with me. Didn't smile. She took her coffee over toward the windows that looked out over the city. "How do you open this door? I tried to get out on the balcony last night but couldn't figure out the lock."

"Did I make you want to jump already? New record for me!" I joked, but she didn't laugh and still wouldn't look at me. This was no good. "Hey Alice?" Why did I feel sweaty? I hoped I wasn't coming down with something—this was not the time to get sick.

"Yeah?" she kept her back to me.

I approached her, but stayed a few feet away, giving her some space. "I apologize for what I said last night. That stupid 'executive assistant' remark."

Alice sipped her coffee and fiddled with the lock on the sliding door.

I moved closer and flipped the lock and disengaged the security latch on the bottom of the frame. "It was a dick thing to say. I'm absolutely sure you'll run circles around me, and I'm only a 'special' case because I'm such a pain in the ass to deal with." I slid the door open, letting in the cool morning air. "I apologize."

Alice stepped onto the balcony and the breeze lifted her red curls, swirling them around her head and into her face. She tried to sweep her wild locks out of her eyes, but the wind overpowered her and one thick curl landed in her coffee. "Shit. I should've put my hair up." She was trying to contain her flying tresses but was having trouble managing while holding on to her coffee mug.

Without thinking, I swept her hair into a ponytail, twisted it into a long snake, wound it into a bun, and secured it by tucking the end into the bun.

She patted her hair and turned to face me.She was flushed and her eyes fluttered. "Wow. Where'd you learn to do that?"

I shrugged. "I had long hair in college. And I've had a few girlfriends."

"More than a few if I'm to believe the gossip sites."

"Alice Goode, you don't waste time on those trash sites, do you?"

"Might take the occasional peek now and then." She reached out and placed a finger on my wrist, for just a second.

There was a knock at the door. Breakfast had arrived.

A HALF HOUR LATER, we were both stuffed. I didn't know about Alice, but I finally felt nice and sleepy. My eyes were heavy, and I needed a nap. Alice was not a big person, but wow, she could put away a lot of food! I mean, not as much as I could, but she gave me a run for my money. The only thing left over was one Danish, a container of yogurt, and a few sad grapes.

"Should we take a look at what your dad sent us? I went through it all last night, but we should probably review it together." She'd retrieved her computer from her bedroom and set it up at the table as I finished clearing our dishes.

"You don't feel like you need to pass out and digest that feast we just devoured?"

She tilted her head and narrowed her eyes. "Didn't take you for a lightweight."

I put my hands on my hips and was ready to shoot back a retort, until I realized that I couldn't think of what to say. *That'd* never happened to me before. Maybe I *was* coming down with something.

"Cat got your tongue?" Alice locked her gaze on me. Her eyes were almost ice blue when the sunlight hit them just right.

"Just didn't want to eviscerate you with my wit. Ok, we can look at this stuff. It's stressing me out."

"Which part is stressing you out?"

"I think I'm having trouble getting the big picture."

"Want me to give you a quick rundown, the way I understand it?"

I abandoned the dishes and sat next to her at the table. "That would be amazing."

"Alright." She took her hair out of the bun and shook it out. Then she smoothed it back into a ponytail again and twisted it right back into a bun.

"Hey, you ruined my work!"

"You did a great job. Just securing it so we can get down to business." She looked into the distance like she was gathering her thoughts. Her nose had a slight bump on the bridge, and might be considered slightly big by some, but I thought it was perfect. Her bottom lip was fuller than her top, which gave her a bit of a permanent pout. "Ok, it's like this. Caluska Island is small. Super small. Maybe 500 or so permanent residents. But there could be up to 75,000 tourists visiting a year depending on weather and housing availability. So, there's a lot of pressure on the islands and on the people who run things. But also, if things are well managed, there's the possibility for them to make a lot of money."

"Wow, ok." This was much easier to follow than my dad's reports and graphs.

"So, mostly there are a lot of smaller rentals available. Individual cottages and some newer duplex type homes. Those are owned by a few different companies. Mostly local. There's one larger hotel. It was originally owned by the Flannery family. But they were bought out by Oceanview, which is the developer based out of Orlando. Scarlet Oaks is the biggest resort on the island, but the Blakes haven't been able to keep it up, so it's been closed for a few years. Not having that place open and running hurts tourism. Oceanview wants to buy up more property, so it's probably them who we'll be bidding against."

"So, if they offer more money, they'll probably get the contract."

"Not necessarily." Alice absentmindedly pulled a curl loose at her temple and twirled it around her finger. "It's about relationships. Family and roots are really important to the residents of the island. And they don't want a faceless corporation coming to town and not respecting local culture and values."

"And you had family on the island?"

Alice's expression shifted and a few small lines appeared on her forehead. "Yeah, my grandparents. But they had to leave several years ago to get better medical care. And they've both passed away now."

"I'm sorry. You lived with them? And not your parents?"

"My parents died in a car accident when I was three. That's

when I went to live with my paternal grandparents. I left when I was fifteen because I wanted to go to a better school than they could offer there on Caluska."

Her words were matter-of-fact, but her expression softened just enough for me to know how much more there was to the story.

"God. That's awful. About your parents."

"Yeah. I don't really remember them, but I feel like I know who they were, thanks to the stories my grandparents told me." Alice got up to refill her coffee. "Anyway."

I took that as a sign to change the subject. "Isn't Starling Enterprises just as faceless as Oceanview?"

"Maybe. But we don't have to be." She came back to the table. "If we can show the Blake family that we understand the history of Scarlet Oaks, and that we respect their vision for the future, they might see us as stewards of their hopes and dreams instead of thieves in the night."

Damn. She was impressive. "Then that's how we'll approach it."

"Good. I think that's the way to go in."

"I do have an important question for you, Ms. Goode."

"Let's hear it."

"Is it actually hot down there? I don't like hot weather."

Alice's eyes twinkled and her lips twitched as she tried to suppress a smile. "Buckle up, pretty boy. It's blazing."

5

ALICE

Never leave your buns unattended around Sebastian Starling. Especially sticky buns covered in cream cheese icing and sprinkled with pecans. I'd walked away from the table for less than a minute and he'd gobbled up the last breakfast pastry. All our strategy sessions about Caluska Island had made us hungry, and over the last twenty-four hours we'd hunkered down in the suite and worked and ate, worked some more, and ate again. I think we both slept pretty well last night, and nobody did any naked dancing, so things were trending in the right direction.

"I was saving that for last, you know." I pointed to the crumbs and the one sad pecan Sebastian had left behind when he stole the pastry.

His eyebrows raised in mock surprise and his mouth was so full he could barely talk. "I'm frorry," he mumbled. He chewed and swallowed. "I thought you were done. I can order more."

"Don't worry about it. I'm not really hungry anymore. It just looked so good."

"It *was* good."

I tossed my pencil at him, and he swiped it out of midair and tucked it behind his ear.

"Let's review the financials one more time and see if there's anything we missed." I dug through my bag looking for another pencil, and Sebastian's phone started wildly vibrating against the table. It'd done that for hours yesterday until I finally told him to turn off vibrate mode or put it in the other room.

"Sorry. Turned it back on when I went to bed and forgot to disable it this morning." He'd been evasive about all the notifications yesterday and I hadn't asked. But today was a new day.

"Is someone texting you?"

He swiped through a few menus on his phone and then put it face down on the table. "No, it's just an app." He stood to collect his work materials from the counter. He avoided eye contact with me, which was unusual for him. I'd only known him for a day, but he was intense, looking right into my eyes when we spoke, so I noticed the difference.

"What app?"

Sebastian shrugged and sat back down with his open laptop. "So, financials. Where do you want to start?"

Now I was extra curious. "What app?"

He shut his laptop and sighed. "Just some dating apps. No big deal."

"Some? How many?"

He shrugged again. "Two or three? Sorry about the buzzing."

"Show me."

Ah, we were back to eye contact. I'd surprised him, and he regarded me with a puzzled expression. "Show you what?"

"Your dating apps."

He picked up his phone, glanced at the screen, and put it face down again. "Why would you want to see those?"

"I've never used online dating before. I want to see how it works. And see what kind of selection you have on there. Of women. Or men. Or just people. Whatever you like."

"Women for me," he said. He rubbed his fingertips across his cheek, which had a nice layer of stubble since he presumably skipped shaving that morning. "But I thought you wanted to look at the financials."

"It's Sunday morning. We're supposed to take it easy, right?" I got up from the table and made myself comfortable on the couch, which was the most comfortable piece of furniture I'd ever encountered—I was already plotting ways to take it home with me. "Let's have a look." I had a weird brazen side that came out around the Starlings, and it didn't feel entirely familiar or comfortable to me, but I was trying not to censor myself. Speaking out of turn had gotten me this new job, and who knew where else it might lead me.

Sebastian ran his hand through his wavy hair (there was no way he hadn't practiced that in front of a mirror a thousand times—he was picture perfect when he did it, making me remind myself that he wasn't my type, and this was a business relationship anyway). "Ok. Just for a minute."

"Yay!"

He laughed at my cheer and joined me on the couch. "Ok, which one do you want to look at?" He opened a folder called "Ladies."

"Your folder is called 'Ladies?'"

"Hey, no judging, or I won't let you look."

I crisscrossed my legs underneath me and pulled a throw blanket over my lap. "Fair enough. What are my options?"

"Let's see. We have SparkMate, Amourly, and Vibe."

"What's your favorite?"

Red spots appeared on the apples of his cheeks. "Well, that depends on what I'm looking for."

"What do you mean?" I knew what he meant, but I was curious to hear his explanation.

"If I want, uh, no strings attached, I try Amourly. Vibe has a lot of young professionals who like to meet up at bars or restaurants, and SparkMate is usually for people looking for something more serious or steady."

"Which one do you use the most?"

There was that cheek scratching again. Maybe that was his tell that he was uncomfortable.

"Show me Vibe." I didn't need to embarrass him anymore than I had.

He opened the app, and a grid of photos showed up. "You can choose a photo and go from there."

"Choose one."

He clicked on a stunning blonde, "Phoebe, 25," who surely had a modeling contract. Thank God I wasn't on this app—no one would ever click on me with women like Phoebe around.

"You can like, love, or skip." He showed me the different spots to click.

"What happens if you like or love?"

"It sends her a notification. Some women have it set up where only they initiate the messaging, so they don't get blasted from creeps. So, she'd see that I liked her photo, she could check out my profile, and then she can message me if she wants." He went back to the main page and scrolled through the photos. So many women, who all looked perfect. This was depressing.

"When your phone's buzzing, what's coming through? Messages?"

"Sometimes. Or hook-up requests from Amourly, or just notifications that someone liked my profile."

"Isn't that distracting? How do you get any work done with all those pop-ups?"

He raised his eyebrows and shot me a knowing look.

"Oh, you *don't* get work done."

"Correct." He flipped through some more photos and sighed.

"How many women have you gone out with through these apps?"

"Uh," he opened up Amourly. "This one has a record of my chats. Went out with a lot of these women." He turned his screen so I could see it and I watched as he flipped through photos of over thirty women before I stopped him.

"You went out with all of those people?"

"Pretty much."

"In the last ten years?" There were so many women. My stomach churned—glad I didn't eat that sticky bun after all.

"No, last six months."

Yikes. "How regularly do you get tested for STIs?"

He rolled his eyes and closed the app. "I don't have sex with all of them!"

"One is enough!"

"I get tested every six months, and my latest test was last week." He bit his thumbnail, which was a shame, because that thing looked perfectly buffed and manicured.

We needed to change subjects, at least a little. "Here, show me those photos one more time. I'll be nice."

He chewed on his lip, but he honored my request and opened the app again.

"That one." I pointed to a brunette with giant pouty lips. "Who's that?"

He squinted at the photo. "Um—Emily, I think." He clicked on the photo so her image filled the screen. Either Emily was an AI alien, or she was using a seriously intense filter. "Yeah, Emily."

"And you went out with her?"

"Yep."

"What did you like about her?"

Sebastian looked at me, and then looked back at the photo. "I'm not sure. I think she spent most of the time on her phone, texting her ex."

"Oh, shit. Ok, pick a different one."

He scrolled past a few faces and landed on another blonde.

"Who's that?"

"Riley."

"And what did you like about her?"

"She was funny, I think. Drank too much, though, and threw up in my car."

I was starting to see a trend. "Did any of these women make you feel good? Or happy? Or special?"

Sebastian cocked his head to one side. "You mean sexually?"

I slapped his arm. "No! Not sexually. Like, just regular. When you're into someone, you feel good around them."

His brow furrowed and his mouth settled into a subtle frown. "Oh. I don't know. I mean, they didn't make me feel *bad*. Or not usually. I guess I felt neutral? Had some fun? It's a way to pass the time." He shut off his phone and leaned back on the couch. He tucked his hands behind his head and closed his eyes. "It's depressing when you look at it like that."

I felt guilty. "I'm sorry. I shouldn't have asked about it."

"You know what? I'm going to delete them."

"Delete the apps?"

"Yep." He brought his phone to life again and held his thumb down on the "Ladies" folder.

"Wait!" I pulled his hand away. "Don't delete them because of this conversation."

"I'm not. I'm deleting them because I'm going to be working for the next few weeks anyway, and I don't need the distraction. And if it's taking me this long to come up with a name of a woman who made me feel good, then maybe I don't need them anyway." He deleted the folder. "And besides, I can always reinstall them if I get desperate." He smiled, and his dimple appeared, making him look boyish, naughty, and too handsome for my own comfort. "Your turn," he said, tossing his phone to the other end of the couch.

"My turn what?" I felt myself heat up under the intensity of his gaze.

"You really don't have any dating apps?"

"Nope." Thank god. I'd be mortified if I had to pull up an empty chat history, which was probably what would happen if I had a profile on Amourly.

"Then who was the last person you went on a date with?" Sebastian kept staring at me and I squirmed a little.

"Uh—" I couldn't remember. How long had it been?

"Are there so many that you can't remember who was most recent, or have you had a dry spell?" There was that dimple again.

"Todd!"

"*Todd*?" Sebastian spoke the name like he'd just spit a frog out of his mouth. "I didn't know people were still named '*Todd*.'"

"He's from HR. We met at the company Christmas party."

"Of *course* he's from HR." Sebastian rolled his eyes so hard I thought he might give himself a headache. "And how did *Todd* make *you* feel?"

"You don't have to say his name like you just tasted a lemon, you know."

"Was *Todd* a good lover?"

I swatted him again. "It didn't get that far."

"Oh yeah?"

"Yeah. Todd was a little—" I tried to remember. It'd been several months. "Well, Todd was more into Todd than he was into me."

"Then *Todd* was an idiot."

I knew my cheeks were flaming because I could feel the heat, and Sebastian stared at me as I probably turned six shades of red.

He lifted his hand to my face, and he softly touched the backs of his fingers to my cheek, just for a second. "Speaking of blazing," he said.

I turned my head away. "Were we speaking of blazing?"

"We were yesterday." He studied my face. "Your face turns a cool shade of red when you're embarrassed. But the color's not as pretty as your hair." His phone vibrated from the end of the couch with a different pattern than it had emitted earlier, and he reached back for his phone. He looked at the screen and then answered a call. "Hey, Cuz." Sebastian was quiet on the line as the caller relayed some information, then he spoke again, "Ok, sounds good. I'll let her know." He ended the call.

"Your cousin Simon?"

"Bingo. There's been a change of plans."

6

SEBASTIAN

I was taking a woman to meet my family. Kind of. Simon had called to tell me that I was expected at Starling Manor at 5:00 that evening for a surprise party for our cousin Susana. It felt wrong to leave Alice behind at the hotel, so that meant she'd be tagging along and would get thrown right into the Starling Family Three-Ring Circus. She'd see my dad again, along with Simon and my Uncle Miles. My mom and my aunt wouldn't be among the partygoers because they'd gone to Paris for their annual Spring trip.

While I was notorious for always having a date when it came to my public appearances, among my family I was famous for never, not even once, bringing a girl home to my family. Alice wasn't my girlfriend, not even close, but her presence would attract some attention.

Though in a weird way, after just a weekend of working together, I felt closer to Alice than to any of the women on those dating apps. My collaboration with Alice was strictly business, but something about it felt . . . different. I wasn't her boss, even though at first glance, someone might think she was my assistant. If anything, she was the one in charge—or maybe she was more like my guide—as she explained to me all the aspects of the business deal, the whole thing became less abstract and more real. Before Alice, it was just words on paper, and intimidating words at that. But now I had some working knowledge of Caluska Island and of the project I needed to tackle. My anxiety over the assignment had gone way down and I even felt a spark of confidence. If I was being honest, all the credit had to go to Alice.

And our chat about online dating kept echoing in my head. In that one conversation she'd made me laugh, she'd challenged me, she'd charmed me. Why had I never stopped to think about how any of my dates made me feel, or, conversely, how I'd made them feel? It's like we were all just robots going through the motions of hook-ups and social appearances. Was everyone as numb as I was, or was I just a freak?

"How do I look?" Alice walked slowly out of her bedroom and tugged at the sleeve of her dress. It was long and black with a scoop neck and plain front. She looked like she was headed to a funeral instead of a birthday party.

I paused to choose my words wisely. "Elegant. But . . ."

"I know. It's awful."

I guess my face had given away my reservations about her dress. "It's not awful. I'm sure we can brighten it. Let me think." It was hard to make suggestions when I didn't know what she'd brought.

Alice slumped down in a chair and put her face in her hands. "I don't have much other than my black work outfits and then my house lounging clothes. I'm not cut out for this."

We didn't have time to go shopping, which was a shame—shopping always cheered *me* up, at least for a few hours. I used to have a stylist who dressed me in outlandish suits, and the media ate it up. They plastered my photo on all the gossip and fashion sites. I learned some of the tricks of the trade and now I did most of my shopping and styling for myself. Wearing wild things always gave me a confidence boost. It was hard to feel ordinary in vintage psychedelic velvet pants, a turquoise button-down topped with a moss-green blazer, plus an orange and white checkered ascot, which was my outfit for a night out on the town last weekend. I didn't want to dig through Alice's bags, but surely she had something a little less . . . morbid. "Do you have anything that's not black?"

Alice's eyes shifted up as she mentally reviewed her wardrobe. "When I packed my stuff, I didn't know I'd be attending a private party at Starling Manor. I have one dress, but I was saving it."

"Saving it for what?"

"For the island. It's kind of a sundress."

It was April, and the days were warming, but the nights were still cool. She'd be chilly in a sundress. "Have any sweaters you could put on top?"

"I might. Let me look."

WHILE ALICE WAS in her room, I texted my former stylist who was currently working for my cousin Susana.

SEBASTIAN: Will I c u at the party tonight

INDY: I'll be there. And at some point, you need to use real words in text. And punctuation.

SEBASTIAN: rude

INDY: Unless you don't text clients like that. But still.

Indy had always been sassy with me, so I wasn't sure if they were joking or serious, but they had a point about clients. I was so used to texting and messaging with a casual shorthand, and that probably wouldn't translate into the professional world. I'd keep it in mind if I had to text anyone on the Caluska Island project. I responded to Indy but thought I'd practice my complete sentences.

SEBASTIAN: My apologies, my dear Indy. I am writing to inquire about your styling services. I know you are currently employed by my lovely cousin, but if you had a spare moment, my business associate desperately needs some new clothes for our endeavors later this week. Sincerely, Sebastian Maddix Starling.!?...!;

INDY: How many brain cells did you kill to write that?

SEBASTIAN: 1,272,894

INDY: Thought so

SEBASTIAN: Think u can fit in my partner? She'll b there 2 nite.

INDY: Partner??

SEBASTIAN: Alice. My "Corporate Handler" but that makes me feel like I'm a show dog.

INDY: Wait. You're not a show dog?? Also, good use of punctuation.

SEBASTIAN: 

INDY: Slow week coming up, so I can probably help. Are you at the suite?

SEBASTIAN: yep

INDY: There's a measuring tape in the linen closet. Have her take bust, waist, hip, inseam. And send me a picture so I can start thinking, and we can talk more tonight. Just clothes for meetings? Any events?

SEBASTIAN: Meetings, yes. But on some tiny island down south. casual. hot as balls.

INDY: Island is hot as balls or Alice?

SEBASTIAN: Island, but Alice is pretty

INDY: Cool. Send picture.

Alice rushed out of her bedroom and did a little twirl. Her face was much brighter with this dress, and it wasn't just because of how the green warmed up her skin tone. She'd topped the dress with a pink cardigan. "How does this look? Do these colors clash?"

"I don't think any colors clash as long as you wear them with attitude." I offered her my hand and she took it, and I spun her around once to inspect her outfit from all angles.

She completed her full circle and turned to me with an

open and expectant expression. She hadn't put on any make-up yet and I realized I was staring at her. I hadn't realized how expressive a face could be, close up, especially when there wasn't any concealer, contouring, or Botox to contend with. Her hair was back in a thick braid, which made her face look even younger than she probably was.

"I think that outfit will be perfect for the party. May I take a photo of you? Your new stylist wants one. You'll meet them tonight at the party."

"What stylist?"

"Their name is Indy. They used to work with me, but now they mostly style Susana, but I think that work is getting slow. They're going to get you some things for our trip."

"Did you ask them to do that?" Alice's expression was unreadable.

Shit. Maybe I'd offended her. "You seemed disappointed that you didn't have the right clothes. I thought I could help. Oh, and they need your measurements. Bust, waist, hips, and inseam. There's a measuring tape in the closet by the front door." I wouldn't mind taking those measurements myself. Alice's curves were inviting, and I imagined running the tape measure across her hips—

"Does this work?" Alice jutted her hip out, raised her chin, and framed her face with her hands like she was posing for a dramatic photo.

A wave of relief rushed over me. She wasn't upset with me. I took her picture and quickly texted it to Indy. I couldn't get over how young Alice looked. How real. Had I never really looked closely at a woman? I was starting to think there was something seriously wrong with me. "How old are you?"

"My grandmother said you should never ask a lady her age." Alice curtsied and pretended to hide behind an invisible fan.

"You're not a lady, you're my handler."

"I'll try not to take that as an insult," she said. "I'm thirty. And I don't know what earrings to wear." Alice set a small pair of pearl earrings on the counter next to a pair of silver oversized dangle earrings shaped like feathers. She held up the pearl to her left ear and the feather to her right and checked out her reflection in a decorative wall mirror.

"Wear the feather earrings," I blurted out.

She caught my eye in the mirror and her glance lingered on my face, and then she looked away. "Thanks. I'm not great at accessorizing. Do you think Gabriel Green is as good looking in real life as he is in the magazines?"

Annoyance sparked in my chest. Gabriel Green was Susana's husband, and he was one of those dudes who looked rugged and handsome without even trying. "You'll find out for yourself in a few hours."

"Is he nice?"

"You know he's married, right? To my cousin?"

Alice rolled her eyes. "I don't want to date him. I'm just curious about who'll be at the party and what I should expect."

"Gabe is a good guy. You'll like him. Nicer than my cousin Simon."

"Simon doesn't seem mean," she said as she sat on the couch and stretched out her bare legs.

"He's not mean. He's just . . . Simon."

"Are you two close?" She pulled a blanket over her lap, and I was sad to see her legs disappear underneath it.

"Very. Like brothers. Simon, Susana, and I feel more like

siblings than cousins, probably because our fathers were identical triplets. We are biologically siblings, in a way."

"I knew that, I guess, just from the Starling lore, but it still kind of blows my mind."

"What Starling lore?" I sat on the other end of the couch and stretched my legs out toward hers. "Don't be a blanket hog."

Alice shifted the blanket so my shins were covered. "You know, all the stories everyone tells about your family."

"Everyone?"

"People at work, stories online, in magazines, stuff like that. You know you're famous, right?"

I averted her eye contact and picked at the open weave of the blanket. Why did I feel embarrassed? Of course, I knew I was famous. That's really all I had going for me, so why did it feel so strange to hear Alice say it? It's like she'd seen me naked —well, ok, she'd already seen me in my birthday suit, which had felt less awkward than this. "Yeah, I know. But to me, I'm just, you know . . . ordinary."

Alice barked out a laugh that was so sudden and loud it startled me. "We've been over this once, you know."

My face burned at the memory of Alice calling me ordinary on our first night in the Starling Suite. "Oh yeah. See, you already said I was ordinary, so it must be true."

"I was wrong."

I lifted my eyes and saw that she was looking at me directly and intensely. She wasn't flirting or putting on a show. Her words were as honest as her face and something about it made my stomach feel funny. "Oh," was all I could manage to squeak out. My phone buzzed and I picked it up to check the notification. A text from Indy about the photo of Alice.

INDY: You didn't tell me I'd be dressing a
goddess!

"Why'd you ask how old I was? You're thirty-one, right?"
Alice pulled her cardigan closed against her chest. The pink of
the sweater made her hair seem even more intensely red.

"Thirty-two in October. I just asked about your age because
when your hair's back like that, you look so young."

Her hand went to her head as if she had forgotten that she'd
put her hair in a braid. She patted the crown of her head.
"That's how every woman wants to look, right? Young? Either
that or like some kind of frequent flyer at the plastic surgeon's
filler station. At least that's my impression after seeing the
photos on your dating apps." She stood up abruptly and the
blanket fell to the floor.

I jumped to my feet. She turned her back to me and bent
down to retrieve the blanket. She tossed it back on the couch
and I couldn't resist the urge to run my finger down her braid
where her gregarious curls had been trapped in a tight plait.
Wait until Indy saw Alice with her hair let loose.

"Do you ever wear it down?"

She spun around. "What, my hair?"

"Yeah. It was so wild and amazing out on the balcony the
other morning. But it seems like you usually put it back."

There were those pink cheeks again. Alice was one of those
people who blushed easily. I bet it was annoying for her, but I
found it endearing.

"I wear it down at home, but not out."

"Why not?" I moved to touch her braid again, but she
jumped out of my reach.

She crossed the room and opened up the door to the linen

closet and pushed a few baskets around until she found the measuring tape. "It doesn't matter. I just don't. I'm going to take my measurements and check my make-up. Let me know when it's time to go down to the car." She bolted into the bedroom and closed the door behind her.

That was a pop-up storm. Note to self: don't mention the hair.

7

ALICE

High-rises gave way to interstates, which morphed into strip malls and ended in rolling hills. The shifting landscape was a giveaway that we'd left the city and were entering another world. Sebastian and I sat silent in the back of the company car as we were driven toward Starling Manor. The atmosphere was chilly, and it was my fault.

He'd only touched my braid, and I reacted like a schoolgirl who'd had her pigtail yanked by the playground bully—which had actually happened and was probably why I freaked out— but I had to do better. I hadn't minded when he put my hair up in a bun, but something about the risk of him taking my hair down hit different.

It was becoming apparent how living in a solitary bubble had impacted my social graces. I did fine at work, but maybe that was because I avoided people there, too. I tried to pick the tasks that I could do without interacting with my colleagues, and I was sorely out of practice with how to react, converse, and engage with other human beings.

"How much longer?" I wasn't great at small talk, and it felt especially forced with someone who I'd been having real conversations with, but I had to try to get us back on track.

"Almost there. Ten minutes. Maybe not even that." Sebastian had his phone balanced on his leg and he was tapping his fingertips absentmindedly against the screen, like he was playing a tiny piano. The rest of his body looked still and calm, but his fingers seemed to betray a restlessness. Maybe he was sorry he'd deleted those dating apps—his phone was very quiet.

"And you said it's a surprise party?"

"Yep. We get there at 5:00 and I think Gabe will be bringing Susana over at about 6:00."

"I'm sorry about the hair thing." I said the words so quickly that they came out sounding like *"sorrybouthairing."*

Sebastian's phone buzzed and he snatched it off his knee to check the notification. He set it back down and leaned forward to get closer to the driver. "Just got a text from Simon. He said that it's best if you drop us off in the maintenance driveway behind the stables and don't pull up all the way to the house."

"No problem." The driver made a right turn onto a county road.

"Your hair is none of my business. I—" Sebastian's phone vibrated again, and he stopped talking as he read the text that had popped up. A long, slow sigh made his chest rise and then fall. He rubbed his eyes and let his head fall against the headrest.

"Everything alright?"

Sebastian looked out the window and seemed almost pensive, which didn't strike me as one of the moods in his emotional toolbox. "Yeah. Just my dad."

I waited a beat and when he didn't add more, I pushed it. "Is he okay?"

Another sigh from Sebastian. "He's fine. Just telling me not to be late. Treating me like I'm an irresponsible little boy."

I checked my phone. 4:50 p.m. "Do you usually run late?"

He rolled his eyes. "I guess so. If I show up at all." Pensive Sebastian at the helm again as his brow furrowed.

"So, 'irresponsible little boy' isn't a total stretch?" Where the hell had my filter gone? So much for being a better conversationalist.

But a smile broke through Sebastian's cloudy expression. "Okay, fine. You're not wrong."

Relief washed over me and before I even realized what I was doing, I brushed my fingers against his wrist to reassure him. "You're not running late today. You're right on time." I thought he startled when I touched him, but maybe I imagined it.

"You're a good influence." He winked at me.

I didn't know that winking was still in the modern facial communication repertoire— I'd assumed it had gone out of fashion, but there it was, in present-day usage and for some reason it didn't creep me out. In fact, it was bordering on attractive—maybe because it was in the middle of Sebastian's annoyingly handsome face.

It was *my* phone's turn to buzz as text notifications flooded my screen.

"Who's spamming you?" Sebastian leaned over to get a look at my phone.

"It's just Lacy."

"Who's Lacy?"

"My friend. Coworker. Coworker friend. She likes to text in batches." I opened my messaging app and the texts were still pouring in.

LACY: OMG

LACY: I just got an email from Donna

LACY: It said you've been assigned to a special project?

LACY: And that we have a temp coming in tomorrow to help while you're out

LACY: You said you would text me after the meeting

LACY: And you did NOT

LACY: Where are you? Have you been kidnapped???

I TURNED TO SEBASTIAN. "I haven't signed any non-disclosure agreements. Is our partnership confidential or anything like that?"

"I don't think so. I mean, the pending terms of the deal and all that aren't for public knowledge, but us working together isn't a secret."

"And what about this party we're going to?"

Sebastian squinted and cocked his head to the side. "Well, it's a surprise party."

"Lacy just wants to know where I am. Is it ok to tell her?"

"Is your friend someone who goes immediately to social media with stuff?"

"No, she never posts. Just lurks and obsessively watches reels about political astrology and 'a day in the life' videos posted by Japanese housewives who have the most amazing kitchen gadgets."

"That's weird. But I think you're fine to tell her."

> ALICE: Sorry. Been locked up in a Starling penthouse suite with Sebastian Starling and now I'm in a company car with him being driven out to Starling Manor. Next week we're going to an island together.

I didn't tell her it was my old hometown of Caluska Island. Just saying "island" made it sound more glamorous.

> LACY: Right. Cool. Did they reassign you to the mailroom for dripping water on King Starling's bald spot?

> ALICE: Do we have a mailroom?

> LACY: WHERE. ARE. YOU.

"Would you mind taking a photo with me?" I felt shy about asking, but I couldn't resist the level of shock value I'd achieve if I sent Lacy a selfie of Sebastian and me.

"Sure. Scoot over."

I slid as far toward Sebastian as my seatbelt would allow. We still weren't close enough, so Sebastian unbuckled and closed the gap between us. He slid his arm behind my head and gripped my shoulder with his finger. Tingles shot across my skin. He tilted his head toward mine as I raised up my phone to take our photo. I gasped when I saw our faces on my screen. It was deeply uncool to be as caught off guard as I was, but my "smile, you're taking a photo with a famous sex-god" skills were rusty. Sebastian was gorgeous enough in the flesh, but holy shit, he turned it to overkill in front of a camera. I took the photo and started to untangle myself from Sebastian, but he pulled me back.

"Take another one."

"Why?"

"Look at it."

We looked at my phone together as I pulled up the selfie. "Oh god!" I started laughing. Sebastian looked perfect in the photo, just like he had on the screen, but *my* face? My mouth was half open, my eyes were buggy, and I looked like I'd just seen Jesus himself pop out of my phone.

"Let me do it." Sebastian took my phone from me and fiddled with some settings on the camera. He held it up, higher than I had. He smiled this time, and I hadn't thought he could look any more handsome than he did in the first selfie, but I was wrong. "Alice," he said like a mother gently reprimanding a child, "fix your face."

Crap. I was staring at him again. I tried to contort my features into a version of what Sebastian was putting out, but I just looked frightened and constipated. I pushed his wrist down. "I don't look good in photos. This is a waste of time. We can send the other one."

"Not true." Sebastian put the phone back up. "You just need some pointers. First, look at the camera, not yourself." He pointed to the glowing dot, and I shifted my eyes. "Chin down a little. Tilt your head to the side." He put his head against mine and I tried not to notice how good he smelled. Like cinnamon, clover, and burnt sugar. "Now think about how jealous Lacy's going to be when she sees this picture."

The thought of Lacy's reaction zapped me with pleasure and Sebastian snapped the photo right when the sly smile must've crossed my face.

"Wow." In the second selfie we looked like a couple who had a private joke that only the two of them knew, and they'd never tell a soul. "You know how to take a photo, that's for sure."

He smiled and pulled his arm away as he settled back into his seat and refastened his seatbelt. "It just takes some practice."

The driver turned off the highway and onto a paved lane that meandered through lush hills bordered by a green forest. I texted the photo to Lacy with no commentary attached.

"Lemme see what she says." Sebastian craned his neck so he could see my phone.

We watched as three dots appeared on the screen, letting us know that she was writing a response. The dots disappeared. Then reappeared. Then disappeared again. "She's taking long enough." Right as he finished his sentence, her next batch of texts rushed in.

LACY: WHAT

LACY: THE

LACY: ACTUAL

LACY: FUCK

"Yes!" Sebastian raised both fists in a gesture of triumph as the car rolled to a stop. "Perfect timing. We're here."

8

ALICE

This isn't a date, this isn't a date, this isn't a date, I told myself as Sebastian led me into the converted stable on the grounds of one of the most iconic estates in the country. I didn't have romantic feelings for Sebastian—I could appreciate his handsomeness and goofy charm without wanting to date him—but I couldn't figure out why my stomach was doing clumsy somersaults like a toddler at her first gymnastics class.

Maybe it was because I was going to meet the famous Susana Starling and her husband Gabriel Green. I'd gotten over my "Starling Stargazing" phase with Sebastian, Simon, and their fathers. "Starling Stargazing" was a term we had for anyone new at the office who went into a kind of shock when any of the Starling men were near. Usually, it only happened to people early on in their employment, but there were a few die-hard fans who still got tongue-tied any time one of the Starlings approached.

But I'd never met Susana Starling in person, and her husband checked all my "boy next door" boxes, so I was hoping I wouldn't sweat through my dress. The only flaw in the story I was telling myself was that the butterflies in my stomach seemed to take flight every time Sebastian put his hand on my elbow, brushed against me, or smiled at me. Pure coincidence, I was sure.

"They're going to lock us in here for the next hour or so," Sebastian told me as we entered the barn. Or, it used to be a barn. Now it was something magical. Instead of smelling like animals and hay, it smelled of aged wood and lilacs. The vaulted ceiling was adorned with silk scarves of every color hanging from the walls and rafters, and as the fabric quivered when the air moved.

"They're like bird feathers fluttering in the wind," I said to Sebastian.

He stopped walking and looked up, taking a moment to watch the scarves dance against the inside of the barn. "Huh. They are."

"You must be Alice." I turned around to find someone with an enthusiastic smile, a nose-piercing, cropped bleach-blonde hair and wearing a black jumpsuit and one feather earring not dissimilar from the ones I'd chosen for the evening.

"Alice, this is Indy. They're the stylist I was telling you about." Sebastian put his hand on my arm when he made the introduction, and why did that give me goosebumps?

Indy was looking me up and down, but in a way that felt professional, not weird. "That picture Sebastian sent was gorgeous, but it didn't do you justice."

"No one's ever said that about a photo of me before. I think Sebastian might have a photographer's eye."

"Bash does have an eye for things he cares about, but usually that's just himself. I'm about to fight one of those kids for some cake. I forgot to eat today and I'm starving!" Indy sauntered over to the refreshments table where several kids were guarding a tiered cake like their lives depended on it.

I was glad Indy escaped before they could see my face blush. Surely Sebastian didn't care about me—he'd only known me for a few days. He did care about impressing his dad, and I was a means to an end.

"'Bash.' Is that what they call you?"

"Some people. 'Sebastian' is more than a mouthful." He stared at me with a naughty smile as he waited for my reply.

"You know I'm not going anywhere near that joke, right?"

"I don't know what you're talking about. Get your mind out of the gutter, Alice."

"You're the one in the gutter, Baz."

"Baz? Where'd you get that?"

"I think Bash is too . . . I don't know. It reminds me of one of those crazy kids who's wildly hyperactive and smashing against the walls."

"That's exactly why they call me that." Sebastian scanned the room. "I think we beat my dad here! Let's find a drink."

I couldn't let the nickname thing go. I was starting to recognize that feeling when I was about to speak out of turn around one of the Starlings. It was like thunder in my belly that shifted into lightning in my chest and throat. "But you're not a hyperactive kid anymore." I tugged on his sleeve to stop him from walking away.

He stopped and turned toward me. His eyes settled on my face and lingered. "You've never seen me three-tequilas-in at the family Christmas party."

"You're right, Baz, I haven't."

"You can't just make up a nickname for someone."

"What other way would someone get a nickname, then?"

Sebastian threw up his hands in defeat. "Fine. But if you call me Baz, I'm going to call you . . ." He pursed his lips as he thought.

I couldn't handle the intensity of his stare, and I felt the heat rising again. God, was there some kind of pill I could take to prevent this absurd blushing problem?

"Blaze," he said quietly.

"Did you say 'Blaze?'"

"Yes, I did."

I huffed and crossed my arms. "I'm not a horse."

"I know you're not a horse. You're a woman." He reached out his hand and ran his finger along my temple, followed my hairline behind my ear, and then trailed away by tracing my jawline. "A woman who throws off some fiery color."

I needed that prescription for Blush-Be-Gone ASAP. I had no doubt that my face currently matched my hair. I fought the urge to lean into his hand.

"Ready to find a drink?" Sebastian swiveled on his foot and collided with his cousin Simon.

"Why are you here so early?" Simon asked Sebastian.

Sebastian put his palms up to show his confusion and exasperation. "You said 5:00. We were only five minutes early. And most everyone else is here, except my dad, who—"

"When I tell you 5:00, that means I expect you at 5:45 Sebastian time."

"Sebastian time?"

"You're always late, so we subtract a half hour or so in hopes that you'll be somewhat on time."

"Who's 'we?'" Sebastian stood up taller, and while he was burlier than his cousin, he couldn't reach the height of Simon, who had to be almost six foot six.

"Everyone?"

"Come on, Alice. Let's get a drink."

Simon stepped between us. "Bring one back for her. I need a minute with my colleague."

Since when was I Simon Starling's colleague?

"Asshole," Sebastian muttered. "Alice, what would you like to drink?"

"Whatever you're having."

"I'd be careful with that," Simon said.

I'd always respected Simon Starling, or at least his professional reputation, but he was starting to get on my nerves. As Sebastian headed off to the makeshift bar that was operating out of a former horse stall, Simon motioned for me to follow him to a quieter corner of the barn.

When we got away from the other partygoers, Simon held out his hand. "I don't think we've officially met. I'm Simon Starling."

I shook his hand. He had a firm grip but didn't linger.

"Alice Goode. Nice to officially meet you."

"Thank you for taking this job on such short notice. I'd like to give you my cell phone number in case you need to reach me for anything."

There was that feeling of thunder and lightning moving through my torso. "Why would I need to reach you?"

Simon's expression didn't change as he regarded me from his lofty vantage point, but I sensed something shift in his affect. "Sebastian can be . . . challenging, and I thought it might be helpful for you to have an additional contact in case you run into any problems." He fished out a business card from his lapel pocket and extended it toward me.

I plucked the card from his slender hands and tucked it

away in my purse. I wasn't kidding myself that I knew Sebastian better than Simon did, but maybe Simon knew him too well, and wasn't open to seeing his cousin in new ways. "I appreciate it."

A smile threatened to cross Simon's face, but he pulled it back quickly as Sebastian approached with a glass of white wine in each hand. "Wine? That's a new one, cousin."

"I'd like Alice to meet some other people. Are you done here?"

"We're finished. It was nice to speak with you, Alice." Simon bowed slightly and then left us alone.

"Is he from the seventeenth century or something? So formal." I took a sip of my wine. Delicious.

Sebastian shook his head. "He's a good guy underneath that attitude. Don't let it get to you." He took a sip of his wine and made a face.

"Not a wine guy?"

He peered into his glass. "It's not my regular drink. But I thought you might like it."

"I love it. Thank you."

"Sure thing." He started to raise his glass to his mouth but then lowered it, like he thought better of that plan. He pulled out his phone to check the time. "Susana and Gabe should be arriving soon."

"Is it one of those 'hide and shout surprise' kind of parties?"

"I don't think so. I think at some point they'll raise the bay door, and they'll come in from the pasture." He stared at his drink.

I took the wine from his hand. "Would you mind if I had this one, too? Parties make me nervous, and I could use another."

Sebastian's face lit up. "Of course! I'll just get something different from the bar." He moved so fast he nearly tripped over one of the kids who was peeking through a crack in the wall.

"I see them out there!" the boy whispered. He skittered back to the cake table where he and his friends giggled with nervous anticipation.

"Did you happen to get your measurements? Sebastian didn't send me those along with your photo." Indy was back with a cookie in hand. I guess they'd lost the fight over a slice of cake.

"Oh! Yes, I have them on my phone."

"You can text them to me." Indy recited their phone number, and I sent the measurements. "Got it. Perfect. I'll have some deliveries for both of you in the next day or two."

"We're leaving tomorrow," I said. I really wanted to see what Indy had in store for me, but there might not be time.

"No problem. I can have the clothes sent to Caluska Island if I have to."

"You know about that?"

"I checked with Mitch Starling about the project. I had a hunch that Sebastian might need a few new looks of his own. The man has style, but he might need a little *less* style on the island, if you know what I mean."

I felt a surge of relief. I'd been worried about Sebastian making too much of an impression on the island, but I thought it was my own insecurities bleeding through. I *never* wanted to stand out, but apparently, I wasn't alone in thinking that my business partner might need to tone things down to play the part. "Does he know you're sending him things? He didn't mention it."

"Let's keep it between us for now. I don't feel like dealing with the pushback from Giorgio Armani Junior over there." Indy's phone vibrated. "I have to take this call. Text me if you need anything!" Indy waved as they went to find a quieter spot.

"Thirsty?" A man about my age approached me, beer in hand.

I raised both of my glasses to him. "Saves me some steps when I'm ready for a refill."

"Smart woman. I'm Tyler."

"I'm Alice. I work with Sebastian. And Simon, I guess." I hadn't been lying when I said that parties make me nervous.

"I used to live here. My dad was married to Susana's mother." Tyler looked hesitant and even took a step back as if he was used to people yelling at him after he introduced himself.

"Oh, nice. So, you're Susana's stepbrother?"

"Uh, yeah."

Why was he so nervous? "What's your last name?" He looked familiar, but I couldn't place him.

"Hardin." He'd answered so quietly that I barely heard him.

"Oh! Harry Hardin's your father!" He was Tyler Hardin. I'd read about his dad in the news. He was in jail for some long list of offenses, including stealing money and abusing women.

"Yeah." Tyler hung his head and looked at his feet.

We could stand there in awkward silence, or I could try to change the subject. "Do they keep animals in here? It looks too clean to house any livestock."

Tyler glanced up at me with relief. His shoulders relaxed and he took a sip of his beer. "No, they use this for events and meetings now. There's a functional barn next door where the horses live."

"There are horses?"

"There are as of," Tyler checked his watch, "two hours ago."

I heard someone shouting from outside the barn and then the words, "Open the doors!" rang out. Several men pushed open the doors and there in the field stood the breathtaking Susana Starling, her even more breathtaking husband, Gabriel Green, along with two horses and a pony. Was this real life?

"Stop ogling Gabe," Sebastian whispered in my ear. "He's married. Come with me." He held my hand and pulled me along until he got right up to Susana. He let go so he could throw his arms around her.

His aggressive affection touched something in me, and I almost teared up like a weirdo.

"Happy birthday, cousin! I was getting claustrophobic in that barn, and those kids wouldn't let me eat the cake!"

"It's for her, so she has to go first," one of the kids chimed in.

"He's impossible to control," I added.

Susana turned to me with an expectant look on her face. Of course she had no idea who I was. More blushing for me. Great.

"Susana, meet Alice. Dad hired her as my handler." He reached over and squeezed my arm which sent a warm tingle up the skin of my arm, over my shoulder, and into my chest.

"As if anyone can handle you, Sebastian," I said, a little too loudly. Hopefully at some point I'd outgrow my nerdy phase. "It's nice to meet you, Susana."

Susana smiled at me and wow, she was gorgeous. I felt frumpy next to her glamor, but she pulled me in for a hug, making me feel less awkward.

"Likewise," she said. "Thank you for coming. And my apologies in advance for anything my cousin says or does."

Sebastian backed away to make room for Simon who

wanted to wish Susana a happy birthday. "Hey, do you want to grab some food and dash?"

"We've barely spent any time here!"

"If you want to stay, Blaze, we can stay."

I punched him softly in the ribs, but to him it probably felt like I'd just brushed his abs, which were quite firm, not that I'd let my hand linger or anything. "Let's wait for them to cut the cake, Baz, and then we can escape."

"Cake! You're speaking my language." He grabbed my waist, lifted me into the air, spun me around, and set me back down on Earth.

I wobbled on my feet, but more from surprise than dizziness. "What was that for?"

A warm flush settled on Sebastian's cheeks, like he'd gone for an easy jog. "Just felt like it."

I "just felt like" staying in his arms for a few moments more, but the moment had passed. We returned to the barn, and the pasture was bumpy and soft under my feet. Sebastian noticed me wobble and gripped my elbow to keep me steady. When we were back inside, I found my wine glasses were right where I'd left them. I drained the last drops out of the first glass and took a sip of the second. "What time do we leave tomorrow?"

"Flight's at 2:00 tomorrow afternoon. You ready for this?" He captured the end of my braid with his hand and tugged, ever so slightly. His gaze was soft, like he was thinking of something else and wasn't entirely present. Then he dropped my hair like it was on fire and had singed his fingertips. "I'm sorry. I forgot."

"I didn't mind," I said, and I wasn't lying. This time it didn't bother me. Maybe the wine had softened my hard edges.

Sebastian looked different in the romantic lighting of the barn. Strands of twinkle lights sliced through the darkness and shadows deepened the hollow of his cheekbones and intensified the chiseled edge of his jaw. His green eyes had shifted from emerald to more of a mixture of slate and moss with flecks of firefly gold. His dark hair was mussed and almost falling into his eyes, making him look boyish and nearly innocent. But I knew better—this man had bedded half the models on the Eastern Seaboard. I turned away from his too-handsome face and took another sip of my wine. "Ready as I'll ever be."

9

SEBASTIAN

"Did we just land in a swamp ogre's armpit?" As soon as I stepped off the small plane, the air slapped me in the face like a hot soggy washcloth.

"Swamp ogre?" Alice was playing it cool, but I could tell the heat was affecting her, too. Not ten steps from the aircraft and she'd peeled off her black cardigan and was clad just in her silk tank top and dress pants. Her hair was up in a tight bun, but sweat beaded on her neck.

My blazer was already off, and I was down to a t-shirt, jeans, and boots, but there was a fair chance I might expire before I got to the air conditioned car that was waiting for us outside the private airfield. At least I wasn't wearing black like poor Alice, who was back to her mortician get-up. "You know, big green stinky thing. Sweats a lot."

Alice stopped walking and I almost bumped into her.

"Hey, use your brake lights next time—" I started, but the look on her face shut me up.

"This is where I grew up. We've been here less than five minutes and you're already insulting this place?"

"Technically this is fifteen miles away from your island. I usually institute a ten-mile radius for my location-related insults."

Not even the tiniest smile from Alice. "Your job is to convince the owners of Scarlet Oaks, and the people of Caluska Island, that you respect them and this place. Next time you have the urge to say something stupid, which I'm sure will be any second now, keep it to yourself."

Her comment stung. Alice's mood had been fine this morning, but as soon as we boarded the company plane, she'd gone quiet. I thought she might be nervous or tired, but I had no idea she was this angsty. We'd had a good rapport, and I was getting used to using humor to communicate with her, but now she'd flipped the script, and it felt like a betrayal. I was annoyed with myself for even caring.

"Got it," I snapped as I pushed past her and picked up my pace. I forced myself not to look back and see if she was keeping up with me. My stomach was knotted up and I wanted to kick something. I heard her footsteps smacking against the steaming tarmac as she scurried after me. The car was in sight, and I sped up. Alice didn't have a chance at keeping up with me unless she broke into a jog, which, judging by the panting sounds behind me, she just might've done—but I still refused to turn around. I was acting like an asshole; I mean, I probably was one, but she'd gotten under my skin, and I didn't want to look at her until I calmed down. I reached the car, and the driver stepped forward to take my bags. I reached toward the handle to open the door, but I got shoved into the side of the SUV by a set of angry hands against my back.

"What the hell, Starling?"

I swung around and saw a very angry and very red Alice

huffing and puffing with her hands on her knees. "What's *your* problem, Blaze?"

"You're my problem!" She was almost shouting.

Our driver snatched her bags, tossed them into the back of the vehicle, and quickly got back into the car, probably to give us some privacy.

"Do you need a juice box or something?"

Alice barked out a half-laugh, but it came out strangled and tight, like she was holding back a sob. She squared off with me and moved in close so she could yell at me from point-blank range. "You're talking shit about my home, you didn't prepare for the weather, and you think you can just say anything that comes to your mind and vomit it out there. You're going to make us both look bad, we won't get the sale, everyone will hate us, and all of this will be for nothing!" Now she *was* shouting.

"Alice—"

"Don't 'Alice' me. I haven't been here in over ten years, and we aren't prepared and YOU—" she raised her fists and was about to bang them into my chest when I caught her wrists and stopped her. "Let go of me!" She squirmed and tried to pull away.

I spun her around. Now *her* back was against the car, and I moved closer so there were only a few inches between us. "No."

"Sebastian—"

If she told me to let go a second time, I'd release her. But something told me she wanted to be held. To be contained. To be heard. "What's wrong, Alice?"

She wiggled some more, but she didn't ask me to let go. She'd also pressed her body against mine and I was trying to ignore how her breasts were now smashed into my chest. I was hot enough out here without her added body heat and the infusion of lust that had shot straight to my dick, causing it to swell.

"Nothing's wrong." She looked down at the ground but wasn't struggling against my hold.

I lowered her wrists but kept my grip tight. I shifted her arms behind her back like I was about to handcuff her, and I leaned down so my mouth was close to her ear. "We're going to get in the car, and drive to the dock. We're going to cool off. I'm not going to say anything stupid, and you're going to believe me when I tell you that I care about making a good impression. I respect your home, and the people here." I released her hands but kept my face close to hers. "I promise you that we're going to make this deal, Alice, and it will all be worth it." I stepped back.

"Sebastian—"

"Let's talk in the car."

"Ok." She used the back of her hand to wipe sweat off her brow and she moved so I could open the door for her. "I know I told you it was steamy down here, but this is hotter than normal." The air that rushed out of the SUV was like an artic breeze compared to the air outside the car. Alice climbed into the backseat, and I followed, making sure to keep a safe distance.

A HALF HOUR later we were bouncing through the waves on a private boat that was ushering us to Caluska Island. It was still hot as balls, but we were sitting on the soft seats in the bow of the boat, and it was cooler once we were moving on the water. Alice was finishing a protein bar and an orange juice (not a juice box, but close enough) and her mood was improving.

"I'm sorry," she said. She stuffed the wrapper into the

pocket of her flowy trousers and tendrils of her hair whipped about in the breeze. "I didn't eat much this morning. I'm nervous. It's been a long time since I've been here and I'm not sure what to expect."

I thought back to our breakfast at the suite. Alice had picked at some toast and a hard boiled egg, a far cry from her usual feasting. She must've had a robust metabolism—she was so much smaller than me and had soft edges, but she was beautifully shaped, and her appetite easily kept up with mine. "So you're one of those people who get hangry?"

"Guilty as charged."

"We'll keep snacks on hand, then." I could see the island in the distance, and it looked densely wooded. A few homes peeked out between the trees, and there was a swath of light sand around the perimeter, but mostly, I saw green. "What kind of trees are those?"

Alice shifted in her seat to look at the island, making me realize that she'd had her back turned for the whole ride. What was she scared of on that island?

"There are different kinds. Live oaks are what people think of when they think of the island. Those giant old trees that have the Spanish moss hanging from their branches. But there are so many other beautiful trees. Lots of oaks—scarlet oak, that the property is named after, red oak, willow oak. There are magnolia trees, tulip, maples, and hickories. I love the loblolly and longleaf pines. And those are just the big trees. Want to hear about the smaller ones?"

"Maybe later." I liked trees, but my head was already overloaded with information. "No palm trees? That's what I think of when I think of island life."

"Oh yes. You can see some there, right along the shoreline."

Alice pointed to the beach where a row of tall palm trees lined up and loomed like sentinels keeping watch over all who dared to step onto Caluska's shores. She faced me again and rode backwards as we approached the island.

"Do you know anyone who still lives there?"

"I think so. No one my age, though. Any kids I grew up with have moved away, and if they come back at all, it's just to tend to their properties or to the older members of their families who still live on the island."

"Are you looking forward to visiting?"

She shrugged. "I have a lot of feelings, but I'm having trouble sorting them out."

"I'm looking forward to honing my golf cart skills. I'm not at my best when I'm limited to those manicured paths on the links. I finally get to realize my dream of driving on the open road!" Apparently, there weren't many cars on Caluska Island. If you wanted one, you had to send it over on a barge, and we'd be fine with a golf cart. We were closer to shore, and I could see the spot where I assumed we'd be mooring the boat. The wooden dock was my first big clue, but it was especially hard to miss the woman who was standing at the end of said dock, waving at us like we were her long-lost relatives. "Is everyone here this enthusiastic?"

"What do you—" Alice's sentence stopped short like someone sliced through her words with a sword. Her eyes bulged and all the color had drained out of her face. I'd heard people describe that before—"she turned as white as a sheet" or "he went pale–" but I'd never seen it happen in real time. It was like someone drained all the blood out of her face in about five seconds flat.

"You ok?" I touched Alice's shoulder but she was in a trance or something. "Do you know that person?" It was a woman. An attractive woman, from what I could tell. Once we pulled in I could get a better look. About our age. And still waving like a maniac. "Alice?" I shook her shoulder.

"What?" She spun around, pushed past me, and dashed toward the boat's cabin. "Have to get something," she called out. Her disappearance left me alone as we approached the shore. Guess I was going to have to deal with the rabid waver all on my own.

The boat pulled alongside the dock and a deckhand eased the vessel into its spot. The woman on the dock started talking to me before the captain had turned off the engine.

"Sebastian Starling, as I live and breathe." The yapper was tall. Thin. Big boobs, but probably not ones that were part of her original operating system. Pretty, with chestnut hair that fell in waves to her shoulders and big brown eyes. Unlike Alice and me, she was dressed for the weather in a form-fitting tank top, linen capri pants, and strappy sandals.

"Have we met?"

She held her hand out for me to grab as I got off the boat, but I pretended like I didn't see and just used the railing.

"I haven't had the pleasure, but I sure do recognize that handsome face of yours." Great. A superfan. Her voice had a Southern lilt, but different from the one that Alice fell into from time to time. Speaking of, where the hell was Alice? "I'd love to show you around the island!"

"And who are you?" I didn't mean to be rude, but this was a weird conversation.

"Where are my manners? I'm Tristan Taber. Caluska Island born and bred and part of your welcoming committee."

"Nice to meet you. I'm waiting on—"

"Little Alice B Goode?" Tristan said with a sugary smile, but her tone was less than sweet. I thought Alice's middle name was Elizabeth.

"Yes, I'm waiting on Alice. You know her?"

"I surely do. Well, there's the little spitfire!"

Alice appeared, wrestling with her bags as she exited the cabin. The deckhand jumped down to the boat to assist her and she reluctantly handed over the bags. She took a big breath, exhaled it slowly, and finally looked up at Tristan and me. She looked different. Smaller. Her face was closed off, closed down. Like the sparkle of her personality was an ice cream left out in the heat and had melted all over the sidewalk. "Hello, Tristan."

"I heard you were coming back to Caluska, but I had to see it to believe it. And here you are!" Tristan didn't offer to help Alice up as she'd done for me. Instead, she clutched my hand like she was my girlfriend and tried to pull me away from the boat. "Did you forget how hot it is down here? You must be boiling!" Tristan kept a weird smile on her face as Alice looked down at her all-black outfit. "We'll meet you at the golf carts, ABG!"

"Don't call me that," Alice said. She was still standing in the same place on the boat, like her feet were glued to the floorboards.

"It's just a nickname, silly." Tristan turned to me. "Alice was always such a goody two-shoes that we—"

"No, I wasn't. You didn't really know me."

Tristan clicked her tongue. "Of course I knew you, *Alice*." She emphasized Alice's name. "We grew up together." Tristan pulled on my hand again, but I untangled myself from her grip and jumped back onto the boat. Something had triggered Alice, and she was frozen.

I put my hand on the small of Alice's back and gently pushed. Still stuck. "You ok?" I asked through closed teeth.

Alice shook her head almost imperceptibly. I didn't know who or what Tristan was to Alice, but something about it didn't sit right.

"I've got you. Just stay with me."

"Y'all ready to go to your cottage? Your ride is ready." Tristan pointed to a couple of golf carts parked on the grass next to a crooked palm tree.

"Let's go, Alice." I pushed a little harder and she finally moved forward. I got her off the boat, down the dock, and across some sand before taking my hand off her.

"I thought I could drive y'all. It's been a long time since you've been here, Alice, and you might get turned around." Tristan sidled into the driver's seat of one of the carts and the deckhand sat behind the wheel of the other, with our bags stacked in the back seat. "Sebastian, you can ride with me. Alice, hop in with AJ," Tristan said, pointing to the second golf cart.

"Why are you here?" Alice's voice had an edge to it.

"Ruuuude!" Tristan teased as she rolled her eyes dramatically. "I'm just here to welcome you! I—"

"You don't live here anymore." Alice looked a little more like herself, but still guarded.

"Correct," said Tristan. She ran her fingers through her hair, fluffed up the ends, and then shook out her mane like she was auditioning for a shampoo commercial. She checked the parking brake, put the cart into neutral, and started the engine. "I'm down by Orlando now. But I come back sometimes to see my pappy, and my work brings me—"

Alice interrupted her. "You work for Oceanview."

Tristan's smile fell away and was replaced by a smirk.

"That's right. And you work for Starling Enterprises. Looks like we both found our way to the top after our start on this little island. Though, I hear you were just an admin until a few days ago."

Fuck this. "AJ," I said, "will you lead the way to our cottage?" I hopped into the passenger side of the cart and slid across the leather bench. I bumped into Tristan's hip, shoving her to the left. "I've been dying to get behind the wheel of one of these puppies. You don't mind if Alice and I drive ourselves, do you? I told her she's required to give me a tour."

"Uh, I mean, sure?" Tristan reached her left sandaled foot out of the golf cart, and I bumped her hip again, pushing her all the way out.

"Wanna ride with me?" AJ asked her.

"Come back and get me. I have some calls to make."

"Ready, Alice?" Alice, looking like a sweaty and moody goth teenager, plopped down on the seat next to me. I disengaged the parking brake and slammed my foot on the gas, causing the golf cart to lurch forward, and more importantly, causing Tristan to screech and jump aside. "Catch you later, Taber!" I hit the gas again, this time less violently, and we bumped over the uneven ground as we made our way through the sandy grass.

AJ caught up with us and took the lead in our golf cart parade as we headed to our rental.

"You okay?" I asked Alice, who was looking back at Tristan standing abandoned on the shore.

A grin lit up her face. "I am now."

10

ALICE

Sebastian drove the rest of the way in silence, which I appreciated. I'd had too many memories unlocked at once, and I needed a few minutes to equalize. Nowhere in the world smelled like Caluska Island.

The salt, the pine, and the heavy air that ferried the musk of the trees across the island and let it settle over the place like one of my nana's handmade quilts. The scent of it all brought me right back to my childhood. To my grandparents, our island bungalow, the ocean, and the love I felt here. The safety.

But then there was Tristan and the obnoxious timbre of her voice—I knew every cadence and it all came back to me like the music of a song I'd listened to on repeat but hadn't heard in years. I knew when she was putting on a show. That's when her accent went a little more Southern and when her smile got a little too big. Tristan's right eye twitched when she was "putting on airs," as Nana used to say, and it was super twitchy today. That's when I realized she was hiding something. I'd heard she was working for a developer in Florida, and it'd hit me why she was probably in town.

She moved here in seventh grade. Rumor had it that she'd gotten kicked out of her school in Georgia, and her parents sent her to live with her grandfather. She was new blood and all the kids at school wanted to be her friend. She was tall, had perfectly smooth brown hair, and was brash and confident; in other words, everything I wasn't, and everything I wanted to be. We all tried to win her over, but she didn't let any of us in. I knew that she was destined to be my best friend—she had to be. Everyone else had a bestie but I didn't have that one friend I could tell all my secrets to. It was *my* turn.

In eighth grade I found Tristan smoking behind the maintenance shed during our lunch hour. I'd smelled the smoke and followed the trail, but I wasn't the only one. Our head teacher, Mrs. Moss, smelled it too and poked her head around the corner of the shed. I jumped in front of Tristan, hiding her and the cigarette behind me.

"Who's smoking? You know that's an automatic suspension. Or expulsion, if you're on a last strike." She glared at Tristan. Tristan had already been suspended twice since she'd arrived, and another suspension meant she'd get kicked out. This was the only school on the island, and if she got expelled, I'd never have the chance to make her my best friend.

I'd wiggled my fingers behind my back and Tristan slid the cigarette into my hand. I brought it forward where the teacher could see it. "It was me, Mrs. Moss. Not Tristan."

"Is that so?" She totally didn't believe me. "Where'd you get it?"

Where did one even get cigarettes? I wasn't old enough to buy them. My mind raced for an answer. "I stole it from my grandpa."

Mrs. Moss's eyes narrowed. "Hank doesn't smoke."

That was the problem with everyone on the island knowing each other. "He found it on the beach and brought it home on one of his walks. I stole one before he threw out the pack."

"You sure you want to take the fall for this, Alice?"

"It's my cigarette, Mrs. Moss. I don't want Tristan to get in trouble for my mistake." I still remembered how my heart was hammering and I felt like throwing up. I wasn't a great liar, and I didn't have much practice.

"Then take a puff." Mrs. Moss crossed her arms and stared me down.

A few curious kids peeked around the shed to see who was in trouble. They expected Tristan, but not me. "Over here!" one of them called. Within seconds, half the middle school was gathered around us.

I didn't know what to do with the stupid cigarette which was stinky and growing some kind of precarious looking ash snake on one end. I'd seen people drop them and smash them under the toe of their shoes, and that seemed like my best bet. I looked for a safe spot to drop it (it'd been a dry season, and I was scared of starting a fire) but Mrs. Moss was on to me.

"Don't you dare drop it. If it's yours, let me see you smoke it."

I glanced at Tristan, who shrugged and motioned toward the cigarette. "Go ahead," she said. "Like you did before."

I was regretting my life choices, but there was no turning back. I assumed I should put the non-ashy side in my mouth, but I wasn't sure. I tucked the filter between my lips and sucked in a breath like I'd just come up for air after swimming the length of a pool. Bad idea.

"You can stop coughing," the school nurse told me, ten minutes later when I was still hacking up my lungs in her office.

"There can't be any smoke left in your chest, and you'll make yourself vomit. I had a barfer in here this morning—don't need another. And, your grandmother is here to pick you up."

From that fiasco I ended up with a one-day suspension and with the nickname "Alice B. Goode" because it was obvious that I'd never smoked a day in my life. But it was a small price to pay for friendship. Or so I thought.

I still remembered that ride home with Nana, where she was mostly silent, much like Sebastian was today. I thought it was because she was angry with me, but looking back, she was probably more worried than anything. "Just be careful of the company you keep," was all she'd said. If only I had listened. All I cared about that day was if I'd done enough to win over Tristan. It turned out that I had. From that day forward, we were inseparable . . . until that night on the beach a few years later.

"THIS MUST BE IT." Sebastian turned off the engine. I'd been so caught up in my memories that I'd barely looked at him since we got to the island. That was stupid. Or smart, depending on your point of view. His sweat combined with the humidity had turned his hair into a curly, sexy mop. It was longer on top, feathered above his ears, and snaked in waves almost to his collar line. He'd gone a few days without shaving and his stubble was coming in dark and rough. His dark eyebrows framed his lighter eyes and, hell, I needed to stop staring at him. "Ready to go in?"

AJ carried our bags up the steps of the front porch, handed Sebastian a card with his contact info, and zoomed off in his cart. He went in the opposite direction from which we came, so I hoped that Tristan had to walk back to the town center in this heat. Just a twenty-minute walk, but enough to deflate her precious hair.

Sebastian entered a code on the front door, and I followed him into the living room. It was nice, but the temperature inside was warmer than we'd hoped it would be, and Sebastian immediately started hunting for the thermostat. I wandered around the cottage to inspect the rooms. Two bedrooms, one bathroom. Not a perfect set-up, but it would do. A full chef's kitchen with stocked shelves and, I found when I opened the refrigerator, enough perishable food to feed a family of ten.

"Sebastian?" I called out.

"In here! Just found the thermostat. It was set at 78 and I lowered it to 70 degrees."

"Are we in the right place? There's so much food here."

"Oh, yeah!" Sebastian popped into the kitchen. "Simon sent me an email about that. Let me read the whole thing." He opened his email app and scrolled until he found the note from his cousin. "Ok, says here that this place was booked as the hub house for a big bachelorette party, but it got canceled at the last minute and all the food was already here. 'Along with some other party favors but the bride-to-be says she'll just buy new stuff, so feel free to use whatever's there in the cottage.'"

"If we find t-shirts that say 'BRIDEZILLA,' I'm making you wear one."

"I'd be proud to do so!" Sebastian stuck out his chest and I resisted the urge to touch his pecs. I'd seen them that first night in the suite, and I'd had trouble shaking the memory of their beauty. "Did you pick a bedroom?"

"Not yet. Doesn't matter to me." I was more interested in the back porch. The front of the house faced a wooded path, but I knew the other side of the house backed up to the ocean, and there was probably a killer view. The hottest part of the day was over, so maybe we could enjoy a drink on the back porch.

"Oh Alice," Sebastian called. "I found your room, and you have presents!"

I headed toward his voice. "If it's a t-shirt that says, 'Sun's Out, Buns Out,' I'm not wearing it." I found Sebastian standing next to a bed where six shopping bags were lined up. "What's all that?"

"Indy's been busy."

My clothes! I didn't realize how much I'd been hoping Indy hadn't forgotten me until I felt a weight lift off my chest when I saw the bags. Especially after our run-in with Tristan. My self-image was not at its highest point, and I needed to be confident, cunning, and poised if I was going into battle with my former best friend as the opposing party. My city uniform of black on black wasn't going to cut it. "I can't wait to go through these."

Sebastian pulled out a sundress. "This is nice. It suits you."

"Does it?" It gave me a thrill that Sebastian thought about me enough to think that something "suited me." "What about you?" I asked.

"What *about* me?"

"Any presents in *your* room?"

He squinted at me with suspicion. "Why would there be anything in my room?"

"Oh, you never know."

Sebastian went to find his bedroom while I sorted through the bags. Indy had thought of everything. There were a few dresses, some tops, skirts, shorts, and sweaters, plus two bags, a hat, sunglasses, sneakers, and sandals. Tears pricked my eyes. I wanted to dump everything on the bed, climb on top of the pile, sob for a half hour, and then fall asleep. That probably meant that I needed a good meal.

"Ugh!" Sebastian grunted from his room.

"Find anything?" I called as I put my clothing back in the bags. I'd sort through it all later.

"Nothing good!" he called back.

I found him with clothes strewn all around his room. Beautiful clothes of linen, cotton, and even a silk shirt or two. Some sandals and a pair of gorgeous brown loafers.

"What's wrong?" I picked up a black linen button-up shirt with a tiny starling embroidered on the hem. "This stuff is amazing."

Sebastian's mouth dropped open. "Are you kidding? Just look at it!" He picked up a pair of khaki shorts and let them fall back to the bed.

"What am I looking at that you're not looking at?"

"The colors! Or lack thereof." He held up a stunning light gray cashmere sweatshirt in one hand, and a pair of white linen pants in the other. He shook them at the ceiling like he was angry with God. "Monotone monstrosities! That's what these are! I should have fluorescents. Bright greens and blues. Maybe some pink."

"First of all, Jimmy Buffet, this isn't Miami."

Sebastian rolled his eyes and tossed a tan t-shirt at my head. "Take that back. I didn't ask for a shirt covered in parrots."

"Why, because you already have one?"

He crossed his arms. "Maybe I do. Maybe I don't."

"Second, as your handler—"

"I wondered when you were going to start rubbing that in," he huffed.

"I haven't had the chance. Mostly you've been handling me, for which I'm very grateful."

Was that a blush on Sebastian Starling's face? Hard to tell with the stubble, but it might've been.

"As I was saying, as your handler, I think you need to have a more conservative wardrobe for the task at hand. Believe me, you'll still reek of style. It just oozes from your pores."

"I'm not sure about all this reeking and oozing." He sniffed one of the sandals. "I suppose this is nice Italian leather."

"Has Indy ever done you wrong?" I asked, not having any idea if Indy had ever done him wrong *or* right, but it seemed like a good thing to ask.

"Fine," Sebastian sighed. "No, they've never done me wrong, but these many neutrals aren't good for anyone." He sighed again. A big, fat, dramatic sigh.

"Got that out of your system?"

"I guess I should hang all this up." He opened his closet and plucked a few hangers from the rod. "Do you want the first shower? I need to wash this day off."

"You can take it. I'm going to see what we can put together for dinner."

"Sounds good. I'll be quick."

I left Sebastian to his task and continued my quest for the back porch. It just took ten seconds to find, and it was glorious. The porch was huge and screened in and it looked out over a grove of trees, and grass beyond that, white sand after the grass, and then there was the perfect churning Atlantic Ocean that stretched as far as I could see.

For a moment I didn't care about the deal, or about work, or about Tristan, or even about Sebastian (ok, I still cared about Sebastian a little). Mostly I cared about the ocean. That body of water that was full of mystery and hope and fear and calm and every emotion I could hold in my body—the ocean could hold more. Seeing the water here, framed by my island, it was truly a homecoming.

A bucket in the corner of the porch caught my attention. A bucket filled with . . . no. It couldn't be. Surely not. I moved closer. Yep. That's exactly what was in there. "Sebastian?" I yelled.

"Yeah? You ok?" he called back.

"We have a situation!"

"What kind of situation?" His voice was closer, but I still couldn't see him.

"A special situation!"

"What the hell is a 'special situation?'" He'd appeared in the doorway of the porch with nothing on but the towel that was wrapped around his waist. For a second, I forgot all about the bucket, but Sebastian saw it and his eyes widened. "What *is* that?"

"Exactly what it looks like," I said.

"No way." He took a tentative step forward.

"Yep."

"Holy shit." Sebastian leaned over the container. "Is that a—"

"A bucket of boners? A container of cocks? A pail of peckers? A depository of dongs? It sure is."

11

SEBASTIAN

"Why would somebody need that many dildos?" I wondered what kind of bachelorette party included this many fake phalli, but I refused to let my imagination go very far down that road.

"You mean a flotilla of flesh flutes?" Alice picked up a green wobbly silicone penis and shook it at me.

"I've never heard that term but I'm sure that I never want to hear it again." I was so distracted by our find that I'd forgotten I was standing there nearly naked. I only rushed out because I thought Alice was dealing with a snake or something. Well, I guess she was, in a manner of speaking. "I need to find a robe."

"Go take your shower." Alice was digging through the bucket and pulling out one dick after another. There had to be at least thirty dildos of all different shapes and sizes. "I'll be fine out here with . . . 'Little Richard.'" She squeezed a pink one that was short but fat. "And 'Richard the Twelfth.'" She pulled out a purple dildo that was at least twelve inches and textured with nubs dotted all along the shaft. "And this one is just 'Dick.'" She held up a flesh-colored dick that was too realistic for my tastes—it even had veins and balls.

If I stood there much longer watching Alice on her knees handling a bunch of cocks, my own dick was likely to jump to attention. "Don't forget about the food. One can't survive on schlongs alone."

She waggled a giant purple dildo at me. It was so long and so thick that there was no way that could go inside someone without a lot of lube and a lot of effort. "This one is insane." She dumped the dicks back in the bucket one by one. "I'd need some alcohol in me if I was attending *this* bachelorette party."

"How so?"

"Let's just say after one drink, I can be the life of the party. Speaking of, I'll get started on dinner, and I think I saw a bottle of wine in the kitchen." She looked at the flesh-colored veiny dick for an extra second before tossing it in the bucket, and my dirty mind imagined what her lips would look like wrapped around it.

Too much. My dick stiffened and I spun around so she wouldn't see the growing bulge under my towel. "Have fun. I'll be back in a few." I escaped to the bathroom and ran the shower hot, even though I'd probably be better off with a cold shower. Alice needed to rinse off, too, so I couldn't take too much time, but if I'd been alone in the house I might've taken a few extra minutes to take care of my own "special situation" which was that I couldn't stop imagining Alice with her mouth around that dick. Maybe the shower alone would reset me, and I'd stop with the inappropriate thoughts, and the even more inappropriate erections.

I stopped the water, dried off, and wrapped the towel around me again. Why had I not packed a robe? I cracked the door open to make sure the coast was clear and heard Alice banging around in the kitchen, so I made my way to my bedroom and closed the door behind me. Getting back to the real Alice in the kitchen (rather than the one running around in my imagination) had a stronger pull than my need to jerk off, so I decided to get dressed.

I almost fished something out of my own suitcase but changed my mind. If I had to wear the stuff that Indy got me, maybe it was best to get used to it now. I slipped into a pair of black shorts—they were soft, light, and of course fit me perfectly. I picked out a white linen button-up shirt and tried it on, expecting to hate it. But I didn't hate it. The white looked good against my skin, and it was almost weightless against my torso. If I had to suffer in the blistering heat of Caluska Island, these were the clothes that would make it survivable. Damn it, Indy. Why did you always have to be right? I inspected my reflection in the full-length mirror on the inside of the closet door. I looked fucking amazing, if I did say so myself. I rubbed my jaw. One more day of not shaving and I'd have moved from stubble to light beard. Usually I kept my face clean-shaven, but I felt like trying something different. I'd ask my handler what she thought.

"What's for dinner?" I startled Alice who had her head stuck in the fridge.

"Jesus, Baz, are you part cat? That was a silent approach." She straightened up and started unloading food onto the counter.

"The fog comes on little cat feet. It sits looking over harbor and city on silent haunches and then moves on." She'd reminded me of one of my favorite poems.

Alice stared at me. "Was that a poem?"

I snagged a handful of grapes from a cluster she'd placed on a cutting board. "Carl Sandburg. Heard it before?" The grapes tasted amazing, and I realized how hungry I really was.

"I haven't." She kept staring at me.

"Why are you looking at me like that?"

"Sorry. It's just—" She plunked down a bottle of wine. "I didn't expect you to be the poetry quoting type."

"No?" I ran a hand through my hair.

"And also, you look great in those new clothes."

"Thanks. They feel pretty good, at least."

Alice had pulled out a random assortment of food. Olives, canned peaches, rice, spinach, cheese, salami, pasta, green onions, crackers, grapes, mustard, and a bag of shelled pista-chios crowded the countertop.

"Do you cook much?" I asked her.

"Uhhh. I work a lot. So I usually do take-out or have a sand-wich or something."

"Why don't you take your shower, and I'll put something together in here." I wanted to put her out of her kitchen misery, or we might end up eating an olive pistachio casserole with a cracker-crumb crust. Also, I wanted to cook for her.

A look of relief passed over her face. "That would be great! Can I have a glass of that to go?" She pointed at the wine.

"Of course. Find a corkscrew anywhere?"

She opened a drawer and retrieved one. "I've got this skill mastered." She uncorked the wine while I looked for a stemless glass that wouldn't tip over if she bumped into it in the bathroom.

I found a glass and held it while she filled it with wine.

"Want one?" she asked me.

I'd seen a bottle of gin on the liquor cart in the living room and thought I'd go that way instead. "No thanks. I'll have something ready to eat by the time you get back."

"Cheers!" She raised her glass and took a sip. "Damn, that's good." She took another sip. A big one.

"Don't drink too much before you eat. Wouldn't want you making any regrettable decisions on an empty stomach."

"Cheers to that, too!" She drank again. She'd tried to slick back her hair in that bun, but the weather had done a number —it was frizzed and fuzzy and red tendrils escaped left and right.

"Get out of here, Blaze."

She rolled her eyes but headed back to the shower, wine in hand.

After some rummaging I decided to make a simple pasta dish. I slow-sauted some garlic in olive oil and butter and let that simmer while I cooked the angel hair. It only took five minutes to boil, and in the meantime, I grated a wedge of parmesan cheese and found a jar of crushed red pepper in the spice drawer.

I mixed some spinach and romaine, whipped up a vinaigrette, and topped the salad with chopped tomatoes and roasted sunflower seeds. I heard Alice turn off the shower and close her bedroom door, so she must've been getting dressed. I filled a glass with ice and visited the drink cart where I found all the ingredients to make a nice gin and tonic, save the lime, which I found in the fruit basket. Perfect.

I plated the food and set it out on the bar. I was about to take my first sip of my drink when Alice stepped into the kitchen. Now it was *my* turn to stare. She wore a white sleeveless dress that hugged her breasts and flowed into a loose skirt that hit just below her knees. Free of all the black, her skin was rosy with a peach undertone. She was barefoot and her fingers tapped nervously against the glass of wine she held in her hand. A warm blush had settled on her cheeks, but one I hadn't seen on her before—it might be because of the wine. But the part that I couldn't look away from was her hair. It was down and stretched below her shoulders in fat damp curls. Because it was wet, it was darker, which made her eyes look lighter—almost translucent. She had no make-up on other than maybe a touch of lip gloss that made her mouth look soft and extra kissable. *Fuck, Starling, don't think about kissing your coworker.*

"Does this look alright?" Alice asked, spinning around, and causing her skirt to twirl and flare.

"You look lovely." I managed to sound casual, but I was having less than casual feelings all of a sudden. "Ready to eat?"

"More than ready." She perched on a barstool and gazed at her plate. "You made all this when I was in the shower?"

"It's easier than it looks. Do you like spicy? I wasn't sure how much red pepper you wanted on top."

"I love spicy. The hotter the better."

Great, there went my dick again. Maybe I should've taken care of that when I had the chance. "I'll let you put on as much as you want. I don't want to take the blame if your mouth catches fire."

"I wouldn't dare blame you, Baz. Unless you forced something hot into my mouth."

Shit, we were doing this now? Her wine glass was almost empty. That was a lot of alcohol to drink in just twenty minutes, not to mention that she hadn't had much to eat. I took a big swig of my G&T, trying to catch up, and I also slid the wine bottle toward my plate. I'd be doing the refills if she let me, just to slow her down a little. I ignored her comment, or at least pretended to. "Dig in. And there's more if you need seconds."

She shoveled a forkful of pasta into her mouth and moaned with pleasure as she chewed. I wasn't sure if I was going to get through this dinner without having to deal with a constant hard-on. "May I have some more wine, please?"

I poured a small amount into her glass and set the bottle back out of her reach. "So what kind of drunk are you?" I asked her.

"Hey, I'm not drunk!"

"I didn't mean to say you are." I took a bite of my own pasta. Delicious, thank you very much. "I just meant, if you *do* get drunk, what does it do to your personality?" I really wanted to touch her hair. Why did I want to touch her hair? *Keep your hands to yourself, Bash.*

"Hmmmmm." She thought it over while she took several more bites.

I waited her out and finished my first serving. I was famished.

"I'm not sure. What about you? You said something about being nuts at a holiday party?"

Oh, she'd remembered that comment. "I suppose it depends. With beer, I'm likely to get tired. Sweet. A little slurry. With whisky or scotch I get rougher. Not mean, but loud. Gregarious. Mouthy. Tequila makes me hyperactive and chatty. That's what I had at that Christmas party."

"What are you drinking tonight?" She nodded toward my beverage.

"Gin and tonic." I lifted the glass and swirled the liquid around and the ice clinked like tiny chimes.

"And what does gin do to you?"

I debated whether I should be honest with her. Gin had a specific effect on me, which I hadn't explicitly thought about when I poured my drink. "Gin makes me less inhibited and a little quieter. I feel things more intensely with gin."

"What do you mean?" She drained her wine glass. Maybe she wouldn't ask for another refill.

"Gin makes me horny." So much for beating around the bush.

Alice threw her head back and laughed. It was a beautiful sound. "All alcohol makes me horny! That's so funny that one kind makes a difference for you." I was relieved that she'd just laughed off my stupid confession. She hopped off her stool and passed behind me. She grabbed the wine and brought the bottle with her and poured some more for herself. A small amount, thank goodness. "I'm going to get seconds. Do you want to take this out to the porch? We could eat at the little table out there."

"You take our drinks and I'll get more food for both of us."

"I'll meet you on the penis porch!" she teased. Was this the "life of the party" version of Alice?

I filled our plates and brought them to the porch where Alice was sitting with her feet up on one of the extra chairs at the round patio table. The ocean was loud, and wind pushed through the screens, cooling us even though the night was balmy.

"It's perfect out here." She took a small bite of her pasta and set her fork down. "I didn't realize how much I'd missed it."

"Care to tell me about Tristan?" It'd seemed too risky to ask her earlier, but with the wine lubricating her courage, maybe she'd be open to talking.

"Ugh, Tristan is booorrring," Alice said.

"You seemed upset to see her."

"I don't think I'd say 'upset.' Maybe surprised?"

"You grew up with her?" Maybe if I just asked small specific questions, I could get her to divulge the basics of her relationship with Tristan. The more I knew, the better prepared I'd be to deal with Tristan when it came to Scarlet Oaks. And, the more I'd know about Alice, which was the most interesting thing to me right now.

"I was three when I got here, but she was twelve. We were best friends until we were seventeen."

"What happened?"

"It's a long story. I'll tell you later. Right now I don't want to think about her or her stupid perfect hair."

"Perfect hair? Nobody has more perfect hair than you."

Alice let out a sound of disbelief. "Don't make fun of me, Baz, or I'll stick those dildos in your bed while you're sleeping. It will make The Godfather's horse's head look like child's play."

"I'm not making fun of you! I adore your hair!"

"You do?" She touched her tresses absentmindedly. Her hair was drying and the curls were tightening up.

"I do. I wish you wore it down all the time."

Alice looked confused, like she was trying to make sense of what I'd just said. "But it gets all big and poofy."

"Great. The poofier the better!"

"Really?"

"Really."

"Huh." She picked up her wine and then put it back down

without taking a sip. "I'd like to go for a walk. On my own, if that's ok with you."

"That's fine," I told her, though I was a little worried about her safety.

She read my mind. "I won't drink any more wine. I can really feel it and shouldn't have any more anyway. I'm just going to sit down on that bench. Can you see it? Right on the beach beyond the tree line." She pointed and I spotted the bench. "I used to love to go for night walks with my grandparents, and I'd like to sit out there and think about them for a few minutes. It sounds stupid, but sometimes I talk to them out loud, and I don't want you to hear me."

"It doesn't sound stupid at all. I'll stay back and babysit the cock collective."

She laughed again. "In case you want to try any out, there are several mini bottles of lube at the bottom of the bucket."

"What the fuck? I thought those were just photo props! Were they actually going to use them?"

"I don't know, and I'm not sure I want to find out." She stood up, wobbled a little, and then steadied herself.

"You sure you're okay?"

"I'm fine. I'll grab a bottle of water." She went back into the house, and I followed.

"I'll only stay out there for a half hour. Forty-five minutes, tops. If I'm gone longer than that, I give you permission to come get me."

"Ok, and don't go into the water, even to put your feet in. Not in the dark, and not when you're alone and you've been drinking."

"Just the bench. I promise."

"Take your phone."

"Got it right here." She held up her phone which she was grasping in her fingers. She sounded a little drunk. This made me nervous, and maybe she could see it in my face. "You can check on me every few minutes. You can see me from the porch, or the living room windows."

"Alright. Be careful. I'm setting the timer on my watch, and if you're not back in forty-five minutes, I'm coming to get you."

"Deal!" She clomped out onto the porch (how could someone make so much noise in bare feet?) and the porch door creaked as she pushed it open. It slammed shut with a bang.

I watched her walk all the way to the bench where she sat down, exactly as she'd promised. I went back inside to pour myself another drink while I waited for her to return. I noticed that she'd left her water on the kitchen counter, probably when she grabbed her phone. I considered delivering it to her but wanted to respect her privacy.

It was fully dark out and I dimmed the lights in the living room. I'd just enjoy this drink and then I'd clean up the kitchen. That would put me at the forty-five-minute mark and Alice would either be back, or I'd go get her. I poured another drink and sunk into an easy chair that had a matching ottoman. It felt great to put my feet up and stretch out. I could hear the waves crashing behind the house and I could've fallen asleep right there. Except part of me still remembered Alice with the dildos, and Alice in the dress, and Alice moaning over her pasta, and Alice saying that alcohol made her horny. That part of me was fully erect and demanded my attention.

I unbuttoned my shorts and lowered my zipper. I slid my hand inside my shorts and wrapped my fingers around my dick. This soft clothing meant way easier access—maybe these monotone monstrosities had an upside. This would only take a minute—Alice was safely away from the house, and there was a box of tissues on the table next to me. There was no way Alice could sneak up on me because I'd hear her coming through that squeaky porch door and walking over the creaky floorboards, and she was a bit clumsy right now anyway because she was drunk. A spot of precum was already beading on my tip and I spread it around the head of my cock. I let myself imagine that it was *my* dick that Alice was about to wrap her lips around instead of one of those silicone shafts. Yep, this wouldn't take long at all.

12

—————

ALICE

Shit. I'd left my water at the house. I'd just settled onto the bench and went to take a sip, but all I had was my phone. Maybe I was more drunk than I thought. The wine had made my mouth awfully dry, and I thought about toughing it out, but had to have something to sip on.

I'd just grab it and come back. I thought about texting Sebastian and asking him to bring it to me, but then I might try to convince him to stay on the bench with me, and that wasn't a good idea considering the state I was in.

I hadn't been lying when I told him that drinking made me horny. I'd left out that wine made me doubly so, and Sebastian —freshly showered and decked out in linen—he was like some kind of beachy sex god. Add the salt air, good food, and the drinks—it took everything I had not to tear off his clothes and fuck him right there next to that bucket of dildos. Wine made me crass and brave and reckless, which is why I rarely drank. And was also why perhaps I'd misjudged how much alcohol I could handle on an empty stomach. Water. I just needed some water, and I'd be fine.

I made my way across the sand, which felt so good between my toes. I didn't even mind stepping on sharp blades of grass or ragged sticks. It all reminded me of when I was a kid, and I could walk barefoot over any terrain and the soles of my feet were tough and trusty. I approached the steps to the porch, but my feet were sandy, and I didn't want to track that all over the house. Where was the foot shower? All these houses had one, I just had to find it.

I walked along the outside of the porch, turned the corner, and saw a spigot sticking out of the wall about halfway down the house next to a side door I hadn't noticed before. It must've led into the little mud room off the kitchen. There was a cement pad to stand on and even a fancy electric foot dryer. I washed and dried my feet and tried the door, which had a keypad just like the one on the front. Locked. Shit. What was the code to the doors? I tried to remember what it said on the house info sheet. 8-1-7-2? I usually had a good memory for numbers, and I gave it a shot. Bingo!

The door opened quietly, and I stepped into the mudroom. The lights were on in the kitchen, but the living room ones were off, or dimmed. I walked softly across the tile floor. Maybe Sebastian had gone to bed. I felt a twinge of disappointment. I'd kind of hoped that he'd come out to find me on the bench, but maybe that was the wine talking.

My water was on the kitchen counter. I unscrewed the cap and took several sips. I put the cap back on and stood silently in the kitchen, listening. Sebastian's bedroom door was ajar, and no lights were on, and I didn't think he'd pass out that quickly, so he wasn't in there. Maybe he'd gone out the back door as I was coming in the side one.

I heard a soft sound in the living room. Like ice tinkling in a glass. He must've been in there, relaxing with another drink. I'd tell him that I came back for the water before I returned to the beach. When I stepped into the living room, it took me a second to register what I was seeing—the lights were dim and my eyes had to adjust. Sebastian was in a chair with a drink next to him, just like I'd predicted. What I'd not predicted was that he'd have his dick out of his pants and that he'd have his eyes closed as he roughly jerked off.

I must've made a sound because Sebastian's eyes shot open, and he yelled out.

"Alice! Fuck!" He tried to cover himself with his shirt, but I could still see the outline of his very ample cock under the thin material.

"Oh god. I'm so sorry!" I *was* sorry. I hadn't meant to interrupt his private moment, but I also noticed that I hadn't left the room. Nope. I was still standing there. Still staring at the outline of his dick. Which was still hard. It was like I had two brains. My rational, polite brain, which was shouting at me to leave the room and give the poor man his privacy and his dignity; and a second brain, which wasn't in my head—it was in my gut, or maybe between my legs, and it was telling me to sit down and stay awhile.

"I didn't hear you come in. How did you—"

"There's a side door? Off the kitchen?" Why was I ending every sentence with a question?

"I'm sorry. I should've gone into my bedroom. I just thought you'd be gone for a few minutes, and—"

"You don't have to explain. It's my fault. I left my water here and I was just coming back for it." Yep. Still standing there. Staring at poor Sebastian Starling and his cock.

"Could you excuse me for a second?" he asked. "I'll just put myself together here and go into my room. I'm sorry you had to see that."

"Yep." My rational brain told me to leave the room. The other brain told me not to move.

Sebastian looked at me and crossed his hands in front of his belly. He was still hard, and he couldn't tuck himself back into his pants without exposing himself again. "Alice?"

"Yep?"

"Could you step out for a second?"

"Yep."

"Thank you."

"Yep," I said again. Drunk me didn't have a very nuanced vocabulary. Rational brain finally got me to move my feet, and I turned around and took a step. Gut brain muscled its way in and pushed rational brain out of the arena. I turned back around, just in time to see Sebastian's glorious dick as he stood up and was trying to fit it back into his pants. "No." I said. Louder than I intended.

Sebastian jumped. "Shit, Alice. Why are you still there?"

"I don't want to go."

Sebastian froze, his hand down his pants. "Ok, I can go. I'm sorry about that." He snatched a throw pillow from the couch and put it in front of himself. "I'll clean the kitchen in a bit. Don't worry about that."

"No," I said.

Sebastian looked thoroughly confused and I didn't blame him. I didn't even know exactly what I was doing. What I *did* know was that I had that fiery ball in my stomach, which popped up when I was about to say or do something out of character.

"What?" he asked.

"Don't go. Sit back down."

"Okay . . ." Sebastian fell back into the chair but kept the pillow on his lap.

"Move the pillow."

"Uh." He did not move the pillow. "Are you feeling ok?"

"I'm feeling fine. A bit drunk, but fine."

"Maybe you should—"

"Sebastian." I said his name clearly. With confidence. With poise. With cunning? Cunningly? Whatever. I said his name like I meant business.

"Alice," he replied.

There was the ball of fire, growing, pushing, up, up, and . . . "I want to watch you." The lights were pretty dim, but I could still make out the shocked look on his face.

"You want to *what*?"

"I want to watch you touch yourself." I sat down on the couch across from Sebastian's chair. "Go ahead. Show me what you were doing."

"I'm not sure this is a good idea."

"Ok, listen, Starling," I started, and he laughed. "It might not be a good idea. It could be a terrible idea. Or it could be the best idea I ever had. I think we have about thirty seconds for you to decide if you want to go along with my plan. If you don't, I totally understand. It's unprofessional. I mean, it's hot, but it's unprofessional. I'm a little drunk and a lot attracted to you, and I want to see you hold your dick in your hand and make yourself come. Are you in, or are you out?" Huh. Guess drunk me had access to a vocabulary after all. Sebastian sat silently, and I started to count to thirty in my head. If he said no, or didn't say anything at all, I'd plead amnesia in the morning. *One, two, three, four, five, six—*

"I'm in." Sebastian's voice sounded like it came from a different place than his usual voice. Maybe *his* gut brain had been activated, too.

I'd set this game in motion, and I refused to let myself chicken out. And I *did* want to watch him touch himself. "Don't move. I'll be right back." I ran to the kitchen, uncorked the wine, and poured myself half a glass. I might need some additional liquid courage. And speaking of liquid, I went to the bucket of dicks and extracted a mini bottle of lube. Because I had an idea. I returned to the living room and hoped against hope that Sebastian was still there. He was. Right where I left him. "Where were we?" I asked.

"*We* weren't anywhere," he said. "But I remember where *I* was." He tossed his lap pillow to me, and I caught it and hugged it against my stomach. He unbuttoned his shorts and slowly unzipped his zipper. He slid his hand into his shorts but didn't bring anything out for me to see.

"I want to raise the lights."

"No. Leave them low," he said. I guess he had to have some say in how this went down.

I was hungry for him. For the sight of him touching himself. Seeing him before had been such a shock and thrill, and I wanted more.

"Tell me what to do," he demanded.

Shit. He'd turned the tables. I'd been bossy and now he wanted me to keep being bossy. I took a big gulp of my wine. *Speak your mind, Alice. What do you want him to do?* "Pull your dick out of your pants."

Sebastian slid his shorts and boxers down in the front, exposing his hand, which was clutching his dick. He wasn't as erect as he'd been earlier, but he was hard. Full. He untangled his cock from his clothing and pulled it out. "Now what?"

I cleared my throat. I'd never done anything like this, ever. My heart was pounding and there was a hot and heavy pulse surging between my legs. "Run your fingers up and down your shaft."

He did as instructed, and softly caressed himself with the fingertips of his right hand, up his shaft, down, and back up.

"Now play with the head."

Sebastian teased the head of his cock and dabbed a finger at his slit and then ran it around the tip. Maybe he had some pre-cum.

That reminded me. I picked up the small container of lube. "Catch this," I said. I tossed it to him, and he caught it easily with his left hand.

He examined the bottle and raised an eyebrow. "What would you like me to do with this, Alice?"

The way my name sounded in his mouth made me want to put my hand in my own panties and join the party. But I had a mission, and that mission was to see Sebastian Starling bring himself to orgasm. "I'd like you to fill your palm with lube, Sebastian. And then rub it all over your cock."

He let go of himself, flicked the lid open and squeezed some lube into his open palm. Then he transferred it to his dick, covering himself in the lubricant.

"Stroke yourself. Slowly."

He slid his hand up and down his slippery shaft, around his tip, and back down toward his balls. He moaned softly.

"Close your eyes and put your head back."

He obeyed.

"Touch yourself however you want to. I'm going to watch. I want to watch you come."

He groaned and grabbed his dick firmly in his fist. He rotated his wrist back and forth and then started sweeping up and down again. Slowly at first and then faster. Harder. His breathing quickened and I watched his chest rapidly rise and fall, and with a sharp inhale, he held his breath. He slowed his hand and used just his fingertips to massage his cock and then he expelled his breath and cried out. His body jerked and he spilled onto his belly as he continued to pump his dick until he had nothing left. His stomach, hand, and cock glistened in the low light. He stilled but kept his hand on himself and kept his eyes closed. I waited and watched as his breath slowed and his chest rose and fell evenly and softly.

"Open your eyes."

Sebastian opened his eyes. He looked at me. No one had ever looked at me like that. The power of his gaze almost knocked the wind out of me, and my limbs felt weak.

"Thank you, Sebastian." I didn't know what else to say, but I did feel true gratitude for what he'd just done. For what he let me witness.

He pulled a few tissues from a box on the table and cleaned himself off. He left himself exposed, though he was no longer engorged with desire. There was something in the confidence of that act—how he let me see him after his climax— that was sexier than anything I'd ever experienced. I needed to go to bed. Not to sleep, but I had to relieve the pressure of the intense desire that built up in me as I'd watched Sebastian pleasure himself.

He adjusted himself and fixed his shorts so he was back to being covered and fully clothed. He took a final sip from his glass, draining the last drops of gin and tonic. He held the glass up and out, like he wanted me to collect it from him. It was the least I could do after the show he'd put on. I let go of my emotional support pillow and crossed the room to where Sebastian sat. I took the glass from his hand, but as soon as I had a grip on it, Sebastian grabbed my wrist.

"Where do you think you're going?" His voice was throaty and dark, and I wasn't sure I could keep standing if he spoke to me again like that.

"To bed?" I'd meant it to be a statement, but it came out as a question.

"Like hell you are."

13

ALICE

His fingers were on my pulse point—he had to feel my blood thrumming and throbbing under his grip. My first instinct should've been to pull away. He'd grabbed me, after all, and it was just common sense that you'd have an urge to flee if you were under threat. Or maybe I should've tried to shove him away. Fight or flight, right? Though some people, like me, usually froze when faced with fear or peril.

But that was the thing, I didn't freeze, either. I leaned in. I wanted him to seize my other wrist. I wanted him to push up my skirt, pull my hair, and consume me entirely. Which meant two things: first, I wasn't under threat—he meant me no harm; and two, I might be developing feelings for Sebastian Starling. I should've known this would happen. It's always the ones who "aren't your type" who sneak in and steal your heart. Or maybe I was just drunk and horny and that's all it was. I wouldn't know until morning, but until then, what was the harm in riding the wave?

"Unhand me, kind sir." I didn't want him to let go, but I couldn't admit it out loud.

Amusement sparkled in Sebastian's eyes. "Are we doing the Victorian thing?" He plucked the glass from my hand and set it back on the table. He stood up, letting go of my wrist, but capturing me in his arms. "Pray, good lady, if I may be so bold—"

I laughed, but it was nervous laughter. He was so close. He was holding me so tightly.

"Might I ask you to settle on the sofa and await my return?" He released me and I wobbled.

"Where are you going?" I clutched his forearm which was solid and warm.

He guided me to the couch and pressed on my shoulders until I sat down. He unbuttoned his shirt and slid it off and God, there was that chest again. He clutched the tail ends of his shirt and whipped them around a few times until his shirt was wrapped like a snake—just the right weapon if you wanted to snap it like a whip. But Sebastian hadn't made his shirt into a whip. He'd constructed a blindfold. He covered my eyes with the soft linen and tied it in a knot at the back of my head, being careful not to pinch my hair in the process. "Stay here," he commanded, and he sounded so serious, so strict, that I had no choice but to obey.

I heard him leave the living room, pass through the kitchen, and walk across the creaky boards of the back porch. Something scraped against the wooden planks, and I heard Sebastian's footsteps as he retraced his path. He exhaled as he set something down on the floor next to the couch. My toes curled in anticipation as I waited for him to speak. All I could hear was his breathing and the muted crashing of the surf.

"Alice." Sebastian's voice was rough and low and so close.

"Why am I blindfolded?" My hand fluttered up to the shirt wrapped around my head, but Sebastian pushed my fingers away from my face and held my wrist down against my lap.

"Do you want to take it off?"

Did I want to take it off? Not really. I liked being in the dark. So to speak. And also literally. I shook my head.

"Good. Now it's *my* turn to tell *you* what to do."

Oh god. Any coherent thoughts that were trying to form in my mind were obliterated, and all I could focus on was Sebastian's voice and the heat between my legs.

"Is that okay?" he asked.

"Yes," I tried to say, but the word came out in a half-whisper.

"Any time you want to stop, or take off the blindfold, that's fine."

I gave up on speaking and just nodded.

"I want you to pick one." Sebastian moved my hand off my lap.

"Pick one what?"

"One of these." He placed my hand on something plastic, cool, and hard.

It was the bucket. The bucket of dildos. Were we really doing this? I dipped my fingers into the container and felt the pile of shafts. Some were smooth, others nubby, some bendy, and a few were rock hard. "But I can't see them."

"Exactly. Luck of the draw." Sebastian trailed one fingertip up my arm, and his touch sent shivers throughout my body. "Don't think too much. Just pick one."

I burrowed lower in the bucket, grasped a dick, and pulled it out. It was heavy.

"Maybe not that one." Sebastian laughed. "Put both hands around it and tell me what you think."

I brought the silicone schlong to my lap and wrapped my hands around it—oh shit, it was Richard the Twelfth. I wasn't about to do anything with that one in front of Sebastian Starling. "I'll pick again." I went for one on top this time, cheating a little by squeeze testing the girths, and came up with a medium-sized textured member. "How's this?"

"We'll find out. I want to watch you, Alice."

"Watch me?" Did he mean what I thought he meant?

"Like you watched me. Turnabout's fair play, right?"

I swallowed and my mouth had gone dry. "Watch me touch myself?"

"Yes." Sebastian stood up and I heard the chair creak under his weight. He'd gone back to where he'd been sitting when I watched him pleasure himself. "Pull up your skirt, Alice."

I paused. I was either doing this all the way, or I was stopping now. Regular Alice never would've gotten herself into this situation. But drunk uninhibited Alice had just made Sebastian Starling jerk off in front of her, so nothing was in regular territory any longer. And I wanted to touch myself. So badly. And I wanted him to watch me. I set the dildo next to me on the couch and I pulled my skirt up to my waist.

"I want you to rub yourself with that dick next to you. Over your underwear."

I'd never, ever done anything like this. And it was so hot that I wondered if I might come just by doing what he'd asked. One way to find out. I picked up the dildo and gently touched the head against the fabric that covered my folds. I was already so sensitive that I shuttered and arched my back. I heard Sebastian get out of the chair and sit down closer to me. "Did you move?"

"I'm sitting on the floor. Needed a better view. Open your legs more, Alice."

This man would be the end of me. Was it possible to climax just because of someone's words? I spread my legs a little.

"May I try something?" he asked.

"Sure," I said, though I had no idea what he meant.

"Let me hold that." He scooted closer and took the dildo from my hand. "I'm holding it close to your body. If you scoot down an inch, you'll feel it."

I shifted on the couch and felt the touch of the toy between my legs.

"I'll hold it here, and you do what you want."

I wanted that pressure against my body again. I needed to touch myself. I rocked my pelvis up and then arched my back, and rocked up again, so the head of the toy ran up and down the crease of my sex. I arched again so the cock was against my clit, and I shifted left and right so it rubbed against me just right. I wanted to pull my underwear to the side and slide the shaft into my pussy and I wanted to rub my clit until I exploded, but I couldn't do any of that with Sebastian watching me so closely. I started to move my pelvis in a circle and Sebastian pushed the dildo against me a little harder so there was more pressure on my clit.

"You're soaking your panties, Alice. You're so wet. Does that feel good?"

His words sent a surge of desire through me that was so strong it was like he'd just run his tongue over my skin. But he hadn't touched me. "So good," I tried to say, but it came out breathless. I was panting.

"How about this?" Sebastian must've reached into the bucket and grabbed another toy because I felt one press lower, right against where my wet opening pulsed under the thin fabric of my underwear. He pulsed in and out of me with the second dildo, or as best as he could without having full access, while he started moving the other toy against my clit in a circle, giving my hips a rest.

"Oh god," I moaned. I spread my legs further and squirmed and shivered and Sebastian taunted my covered pussy with the two cocks. I stopped thinking. I stopped everything but feeling pressure and heat build in the deepest part of me and bloom outwards like a flower on fire. I gripped the couch and squeezed the fabric as I bucked and writhed, and I cried out as I came. The climax crashed down on me like the rough surf of the ocean, and I was swept out to sea by the pleasure of it all. I was making noises that I didn't recognize, and I didn't care. And Sebastian was making noises, too. Murmurs of approval. Of appreciation.

"Yes, Alice. God, yes. That was beautiful," he said as the aftershocks quaked through me and I closed my legs to push away the probes and protect my sensitive areas.

I felt him lean over me, and he pulled the blindfold off my eyes. I blinked a few times as my eyes adjusted to the dim light in the room. His face. Oh wow. Sebastian's face. There was no way I would've had the nerve to let this happen if I'd had to stare at that spectacular face. It was distracting. His lips were swollen, and his cheeks were flushed. I wanted him. I wanted him to want me. I wanted everything.

"Thank you, Alice." Sebastian brushed his lips against my thigh, planting a small and gentle kiss against my skin. He pulled on the hem of my skirt, covering me back up. "I'm going to clean up the kitchen. You get some rest." He took the two sex toys with him, maybe to wash them, and left me alone in the living room. I felt too relaxed, too sleepy, too filled with expensive red wine to move from that couch. I closed my eyes. *Just for a minute,* I told myself, then I'd move to my bed. *Really. Just for a minute.*

14

SEBASTIAN

I slammed a pillow over my face to avoid the morning light streaming in through the window. It worked to block the brightness but did nothing to block my memories of last night. Not that I wanted to forget, but I wasn't sure I'd behaved well. I sure as shit hadn't acted professionally.

And Alice had consented, but she'd had more to drink than I did, and I had no idea what she'd think about it all when she woke up from her night on the couch. I'd cleaned the kitchen and checked on her a few times—I even tried to wake her up and get her to relocate to her bedroom, but she was unmovable. So I'd covered her with some blankets, put a fresh bottle of water on the table next to her, and turned off all the lights. And I'd put that bucket of toys back on the porch, so she didn't wake up to a bunch of dicks in her face.

Watching her climax like that was the hottest thing I'd ever witnessed. And the most intimate. I'd never felt that close to any of the other women I'd dated, and Alice and I weren't even dating. Or were we? Fuck. Not only was I confused on a personal level, I was worried about the professional angle. I'd try to talk to Alice about it when she woke up, but maybe I could gather some information before I talked to her.

I came out from under my pillow—Christ, this southern sunshine was bright. I unplugged my phone from the charger on the nightstand and called Simon.

He picked up after just the first ring. "Why are you calling me?" Simon's voice was flat but suspicious.

"Good morning to you, too, cousin."

"It's 7:30. Why are you up this early?"

"7:30 isn't early."

"It is for you," Simon said.

"I'm a working man now."

"Right. So, what do you need? Speaking of work, I'm at the office and I have some things to take care of."

"I might have a small problem."

There was silence on the other line, and then Simon sighed. "What kind of problem, Sebastian?"

"Well. I may have—" I didn't know how to tactfully say that my coworker had gotten drunk, asked me to jerk off in front of her, and then I blindfolded her and got her off by rubbing her with two silicone dicks.

"Go on," Simon prodded.

"I may have maybe hooked up with Alice. A little."

Simon sighed again, but this time in an exasperated way. "And this was consensual?"

"Of course it was consensual. She started it!"

"Right."

"No, really!" Why did I sound so desperate? I tried to tone it down. "We had some physical intimacy last night, but—"

"I thought you respected her," Simon replied. "You seemed different around her than you do around other women."

"What the fuck, Simon. Of course I respect her. A lot. Which is why I'm calling you to figure out what to do."

"You've never come to me for romantic advice."

"I don't need romantic advice. At least, I don't think I do. I need some professional advice."

"What do you mean?"

It was my turn to sigh. "I mean, like, if she and I like each other and maybe want to start dating, shouldn't I tell HR or something?"

Nothing from Simon, other than silence.

"Simon? Are you still there?"

"I'm here."

"So, do I need to speak to HR?"

"You like her." It was a statement, not a question.

"I like her."

"You want to date her."

"I might? Like, if she wants to date me?" I said.

"Have you spoken to her about this?"

"She's still asleep. So, no."

"You're serious. This isn't a joke."

"Why would I joke about this?" I asked.

"My apologies," said Simon, "this is just new territory. I'm standing outside the HR suite right now, actually. I can ask Todd what the policy is on—"

"Do NOT ask Todd!" I said, a little too loudly.

"Why not?"

"If you do, leave names out of it for now, please."

"Fine," Simon said. "I'll speak to him and get back to you."

"Thanks," I said, but he'd already disconnected the call.

"Is he gonna ask Todd?" Alice said from the doorway of my

bedroom. She startled me so badly that I jerked, and my phone flew from my hand and crashed against the floor.

"Somebody's jumpy," she said as she collected my phone and handed it to me. She was sipping water from the bottle I'd left her, and she perched on the side of my bed. She was still in the white dress that she'd slept in, and her hair was big and wild and fucking sexy, if you asked me.

"You surprised me," I pulled the blanket up to my stomach and covered my lap with the pillow. I was only wearing underwear, though I suppose she'd seen more last night.

"Sorry. So, is Simon going to talk to HR about us possibly dating?"

Shit. "So, you heard that?"

"I did."

I was mortified. Not only was our partnership in the Scarlet Oaks deal probably off, but I'd most likely blown my chance with the only woman who'd really intrigued me in my whole adult life. Way to go, Starling. "I'm sorry. I was just . . . concerned about what I did last night and thought that maybe —" I stopped, not sure how to finish the sentence.

"What *you* did?" Alice took a long swig from her water bottle. "You mean what *we* did. And you might be right about me starting it. Or maybe the wine started it. Anyway." I couldn't read her face. Was she happy? Pissed? Still drunk?

"How do you feel about last night?" My heart was pounding, and my stomach flipped as I worried about how she might answer.

"I feel—" she started, and then she stood up from the bed and stepped closer to me. She touched a finger to my shoulder and slid it down my bicep, across the crook of my elbow, over my inner forearm, and it ended up in my palm where she drew soft ticklish circles on my hand. I was glad for the pillow over my lap because my dick had jumped to attention at her touch. "I feel sad that I'm going to miss seeing the look on Todd's face when Simon reports us to HR."

"Sad how?" I still couldn't tell how she felt.

"If he hears that I have a thing for Sebastian Starling—"

"Wait." I interrupted. I heard her words, but I was having trouble processing what she meant. Did she have a thing for me, or did she just want to make Todd jealous? I wasn't one to beat around the bush, so I just asked. "Do you have a thing for me?"

"Do *you* have a thing for *me*?" she asked in return.

"I don't like it when people answer questions with questions." I wanted her to answer me. I wanted to make sure I understood. I wasn't great with the unknown.

"Too bad, Baz. Do you have a thing for me?" She drew another circle in my palm.

Did I? I might. But I didn't want to say it out loud. "Are you hungry?" I asked. "Or are you feeling sick from last night?"

"Ah, the 'change the subject' technique."

I noticed that she wasn't wearing a bra under her dress. Her nipples were hard and pushing at the fabric. How had I missed that last night? Or maybe she took off her bra in the middle of the night? Was she still wearing that underwear that she'd soaked with her arousal? Fuck, there went my dick again. Silence landed between us for a few more beats before Alice spoke again.

"I feel ok. But yes, I'm hungry. You made dinner, so I'll make us breakfast." She pulled her warm fingertips away from my palm and I craved her touch as soon as she'd stopped. She stood up. "Let me know what Simon hears from HR. I'm good to go on the record that maybe we, how did you say it?" Alice rolled her eyes upward and raised her chin and stroked it like she was thinking hard about something. "Oh yeah, that we 'like each other and maybe want to start dating.'" And with that, she exited the bedroom, leaving me with an uncomfortable erection and an even more uncomfortable fluttering feeling in my chest.

After a few minutes spent pondering our impending meeting at Scarlet Oaks and running through all the non-sexy scenarios of how I could possibly fuck up the deal for Starling Enterprises, I was no longer at risk of pitching a tent in my boxers and I got out of bed. I threw on some of my new clothes from Indy—this time a pair of black linen pants and a gray t-shirt. Boring in hand, but when I checked myself out in the mirror, I didn't look half bad. Ok, I looked good. And professional, I grudgingly admitted, even though I was still bare-footed. I smelled good things coming from the kitchen.

"You've got this, Starling," I said to my reflection in the mirror. Jesus, I was giving myself a pep talk just so I could walk into a room where a woman was making breakfast. I'd dated supermodels, been on talk shows, and even did a brief stint on reality tv (which was a memory better left buried in the vault), so why did the simple act of being near Alice Goode make me feel unnerved and jittery?

Sure, I was attracted to her, interested in what she had to say and *maybe* I had a few feelings brewing—but I'd had feelings for women before, I'd even been in love. Like with . . . ok, no names were popping right to the surface, but . . . I adjusted the collar of my shirt and stroked my cheek which had officially passed stubble territory and had arrived in beard land . . . why couldn't I name a woman I'd been in love with? Faces of former girlfriends flashed before my eyes, but none of them had given me the stomach tugs I was getting just thinking about Alice last night. Alice blindfolded. Alice with her skirt up, Alice—

"Where are you?" Alice yelled from the kitchen.

"Coming!" Wrong choice of words. Now all I could think about was Alice coming last night as I—*no, Starling. Focus.* I headed toward the smoky smell of maple bacon and that aroma of coffee brewing that made me feel more awake before the elixir even passed over my lips.

15

ALICE

"Coming!" Sebastian had replied when I'd called out. Our breakfast of pancakes and bacon was almost ready.

Wrong choice of words on his part. Now all I could concentrate on was the memory of Sebastian coming last night, his dick in his hand as he pleasured himself in the low light—and how watching him turned me on so intensely that I felt dizzy just remembering it.

"Like your bacon super crispy?" Sebastian raised an eyebrow at the now overcooked bacon as he opened a cabinet to find a coffee mug.

Shit. I turned off the heat and raced to get the slices out of the hot pan. It was all Sebastian's fault. If he hadn't been so damn sexy last night, I would've been able to concentrate on the task at hand. Hand. His hand. Wrapped around his thick cock—

"You sure you're ok?" Sebastian brushed his fingers across my shoulder, knocking me out of my trance.

I'd been standing there while the hot bacon grease pebbled my knuckles with burning spit, and I hadn't even fucking noticed. "Yes, sorry. Just nervous about today." That wasn't a lie. I *was* nervous about today. At noon, Sebastian and I were scheduled to meet with the realtor and the representative of the Blake family to officially tour the Scarlet Oaks property. It was part of the deal that the prospective buyers visit the property a final time in person before submitting the official proposal. Starling Enterprise inspectors had already done an assessment, so this was a formality, but I was nervous for personal reasons.

"Should we talk about last night?" he asked.

I felt my stomach jump and twist. "Probably. But can we talk about it later?"

"We can. But I don't want either of us feeling weird about what happened."

"I'm ok with what happened. Are you ok?"

"Very ok," he said. "Also, don't be nervous. I'm so up on this Scarlet Acres shit that all you'll have to do is stand there and look pretty. The Drake family is gonna love me." He pulled a piece of charred bacon out from the tongs I held and gobbled it down in one bite.

I felt sweat tingle against the skin of my underarms and my mouth went dry. "Sebastian Maddix Starling—"

"Uh-oh, full name alert!" He took a whiff of the coffee in the pot before pouring some into a mug printed with the phrase: "I'm the IDGAF Bridesmaid!"

"It's not the 'Drake' family! And it's Scarlet *Oaks*. And I'm here to make sure you get everything right, not to be your arm candy! In fact—"

"Alice." Sebastian placed his mug on the counter and rested his hands on my hips. He was close. Too close. "I'm kidding. It's Sarah and Edward Blake. Married in 1966. Parents of Michael Blake. They currently live in Riverview Heights retirement home in Harborhollow. Inherited the land for Scarlet Oaks in 1975, developed the property and opened the resort in 1981. Enjoyed its heyday from 1985 to 2000. Hurricane Julian hit hard in '04 they never fully recovered. Place has been shuttered for almost three years now and is at risk of further deterioration. One option on the table is tearing down and starting over." He gave me a little squeeze and went back to his coffee. "And any success we have here, I owe to you. Also, do you think I'd give the title of 'arm candy' to anyone else but myself? I mean, look at me in my stunning neutral palate." Sebastian swept his arm down his body and spun around.

I didn't think he had any idea how gorgeous he was in his new attire. In his preferred wardrobe, Sebastian was certainly eye-catching—his bright clothes made it impossible to look away from him. But in the more understated hues of his Caluska Island apparel, it was Sebastian you noticed, not his clothes. I was trying not to let it distract me, but there was probably a sixty percent chance that the moment he walked out the door he'd be offered a modeling contract. This morning his dark hair was damp and wavy and his 5 o'clock shadow from the first day we'd met had turned into a scruffy beard, a look I'd never seen him wear before in any of the photos I'd seen of him over the years. It suited him.

He wore a silver t-shirt that clung to his chest in all the right places, and his black linen trousers were masculine but looked achingly soft, and I just wanted to reach out and run my hand along—*no, Goode. Focus.*

"You going to eat or just stand there? Might need some food to soak up any extra wine in your system." He grabbed another coffee mug and offered it to me; this one said: "I'm the LAID-BACK Bridesmaid!"

"They really went all out with this bachelorette weekend stuff. I can't believe they canceled at the last minute." I accepted the mug and Sebastian filled it up. I lifted the cup to my lips to take a sip. Black coffee sounded good to me this morning.

"I heard from Simon that the groom was injured in a horrific skydiving incident, and his fiancée couldn't bear to have the party while he—"

I spit out my coffee in surprise, and Sebastian jumped back.

"Hey, watch the threads, lady!"

"Did he die?" I squeaked out between coughs. I didn't give a shit about Sebastian's shirt when some poor guy had slammed to the earth a few weeks before his wedding day.

"My jokes aren't landing well this morning," Sebastian said. "Think I'll stick to playing it straight until lunchtime, at least."

"God, you're an asshole!" I reached out and pinched the skin of his bicep between my fingers, or tried to. I wanted to pinch other parts of his body but restrained myself.

"Takes one to know one!" he teased. "Now give me a pancake."

BREAKFAST WAS FINISHED and it was only nine o'clock. Three hours until our appointment, and I felt restless. Sebastian washed the last dish and handed it off to me.

I dried it and put it back in the cabinet. "Want to walk on the beach for a few minutes? Then I'll shower and get ready for our meeting."

"Sure. Let me find some shoes."

"No shoes needed."

"What if my precious toes step on something sharp?"

"Let's go, Princess Starling." I headed toward the back porch and motioned for him to follow.

"It's about time you used my official title."

I couldn't help but let a laugh escape. Sebastian Starling, worried about his toes, obsessed with his outfits, but not getting his feathers ruffled when I teased him or called him a princess. Sebastian came across as secure in his masculinity, in his clothes, in his skin. It was part of what made him impossible to shake from my thoughts and now my fantasies. But part of his allure was also that he was contradictory: his confidence existed next to a kind of softness; his assuredness was tinged with a hint of questioning; and I wondered if his bravado masked a wound that he kept hidden away in a dark, secret place.

Sebastian and I crossed the sandy lawn behind the house, which gave way to a beach littered with pine needles (some sharp, but Sebastian didn't seem to notice) and ended up at the shoreline where waves swept over the clear sand.

"Walk with me in the water?" I asked him, and held out my hand for him to grab. I don't know why I did it. It just seemed natural, and before I knew it I was standing there with my arm outstretched while water lapped at my toes. Sebastian Starling was staring at me and my empty hand, and I wanted to disappear into the ocean, but I had too much ego so I kept standing there with my hand left hanging, like a comedian who bombs a joke, while the audience goes silent.

"If this is a ploy to toss me to the sharks, you're in trouble." He took my hand.

Ok. Maybe I was an overthinker. We walked for several minutes on the empty stretch of beach. It was early, but I still expected to see some other beach goers. I'd need to check tourism numbers and see if they were trending downward. Was the island dying? These were the things I was thinking, because if I stopped filling my head with facts and figures and questions, all I'd be able to think would be "I'm holding hands with Sebastian Starling like he was my boyfriend!" *Was* he my boyfriend? Why did I ask him to hold my hand? Shit, I was spiraling again.

"Do you ever think about how many creatures there are in the water within 1000 feet of us that could kill us right now?" he asked.

"I didn't until right now."

"Motherfucker!" Sebastian shouted out and he dropped my hand and clutched his right foot.

"What happened?"

"I don't know. I think something bit me!"

"There's nothing to bite you—" I watched as blood started to seep out through Sebastian's fingers. "Oh shit!"

Sebastian dropped down on the sand and inspected the sole of his foot which had a bloody slice across the heel. I searched for the source of the injury and found it in the form of a broken beer bottle. No glass on the beach was a rule for a reason.

I sat down next to him. "I'm sorry. You can say 'I told you so.'"

"It's not your fault some asshole had too many Coronas at his beach bonfire." Sebastian nodded toward a circle of burnt-out logs. "And it was only my precious toes I was worried about. My heel is completely dispensable." He poked at the wound and winced. It was still bleeding. He reached into his pocket and pulled out a beautiful white handkerchief that had an embroidered starling in the corner. He moved to put it across his wound until I stopped him.

"Wait!"

"What?"

"You'll ruin that!" I could tell by the way his eyes squinted that he was in pain, but he was taking it in stride.

"Would you prefer that I bleed out?"

"I don't think it's *that* deep," I teased, but I realized I was being stupid about the handkerchief. It was just so lovely, and I wasn't used to men my age carrying those around. I took it from his hand and pressed it against his foot.

He winced. "Thanks. And I have an endless supply of those, so it's ok to sacrifice it for the greater good."

"You shouldn't walk back on that. We need to wash it out and see how deep it is."

"If only I'd brought some shoes!"

I couldn't argue with that. "I'll run back and get the golf cart. Will you be ok?"

"Alice, if I expire from this cut before you get back with the golf cart, there was no saving me to begin with." He started scooching down the sand toward the water.

"What are you doing?"

"I'm going to rinse it off."

"That's salt water!"

"Nature's saline."

"Oh, no you don't, mister." I stood in front of him to block his path. "The ocean isn't sterile, and who knows what's flowing downstream from the bigger cities. Remember how I told you that all the oysters got polluted?"

"But you swim in these waters, right?"

"I used to. But not with open wounds!"

"Fine." He stopped his crab walk to the water and shuffled back to the softer dry sand.

"You stay there. I'm going to get the golf cart and come back for you."

"I'll try to hold on, but if I don't make it, tell my family to auction off all my clothes and donate the proceeds to the Save the Oysters Foundation."

"Smart ass." I retrieved a piece of driftwood from the nearby firepit and drew a circle in the sand around Sebastian.

"Is this some kind of witchcraft thing I should know about?" He poked the line with his toe.

"You stay inside this circle. I'll be back."

"Hurry up, high priestess. I'll be protected from demons until you return."

16

SEBASTIAN

I enjoyed watching Alice jog the quarter mile back to the house. I was mourning the moment when she'd change out of that dress. I wasn't ashamed to watch her full hips and luscious ass swish and sway as she hurried to get the cart. And it took my mind off my foot, which really throbbed. I'd wanted to dip it in salt water even though it would sting.

Something about seeking more pain to erase the initial pain made sense at the time, but I didn't need some pathogen seeping into my bloodstream and making the situation worse than it already was. So, I sat there in my time-out circle like a good boy.

The beach was empty. It was a Tuesday morning, and it wasn't high season yet. Our house was on the Southern tip of the island, and most of the rental properties were on the north side, so it was quieter here. The day was heating up already and I was uncomfortable with the sweat that ran down my back. I hated being hot. I mean, not sexy hot, but temperature hot. There was no stopping my intense attractiveness, if I did say so myself.

But the breeze off the water cut the weight of the heat and I found myself taking a deep breath and letting the salt air fill my lungs. For a moment I felt lighter—like I'd gotten out of my head and my body and my annoyance with the heat and my worry about fucking up the deal and I was just there. On the sand. Breathing.

The buzzing engine of the golf cart brought me out of my Zen moment. Damn. Alice had changed clothes. I was disappointed until I saw that now she was wearing a tight t-shirt and short shorts that really hugged her curves. I worried that I was enjoying the sight of her a little too much. Either I was becoming a real letch, or I was into Alice. "Over here! SOS!" I waved my arms like I was trying to signal a passing airplane while stranded on a desert island. My antics made Alice smile as she pulled up in the cart. Mission accomplished. I liked making her smile. Making her laugh. Making her feel pleasurable things like—

"I'm glad to see you stayed in your circle." Alice parked the cart and stood outside of my sand spot.

"It's a good thing you drew this. The onslaught of water demons was incredible, but I stayed safe."

Alice rolled her eyes. "Let me help you up."

"Wait!" I put out my hand and Alice jumped back. "If you cross the line without the proper incantation, you'll curse us both!"

She put her hands on her hips. "Baz, we don't have time for this. Is your foot still bleeding?"

I held it up for her to see. It didn't look great, but the cut wasn't too deep. "Stopped a few minutes ago."

She huffed out an exasperated sigh. "Fine." She knelt near me, making sure to stay outside the circle. She closed her eyes, and her long eyelashes kissed the top of her cheeks. She scooped up some sand in each palm, spread her fingers, and let it trickle out and fall back to the beach. "Goddess of the island, hear our call. Guide us as we walk your shifting surface and let our hearts expand to accept the ebb and flow of your tide. Use your salt to soften our rough edges and to expose our wounds. Let us explore your boundaries between earth and sea and help us be brave enough to swim in your deep waters and return safely to your shore once our wanderlust is satisfied. We now break the circle." Alice opened her eyes and broke my circle in the sand by dragging her finger through the soft grains.

Something in her voice made the moment feel sacred. Who was this woman and how did I find myself alone with her on a beach, sliced up, bleeding, but entirely enchanted? "Did you just make that up?"

"Yep. Ready cowboy?" She helped me stand and I hopped over to the cart on one foot while Alice held on to my elbow. She drove us to the side of the house where a low spigot waited just for the purpose of washing feet. I noticed a first aid kit, soap, and a towel waiting in a basket on the side steps. "Did you put that out there?"

"Wanted to have the supplies ready for you." She ushered me out of the cart, which I didn't need, really. I could've made it just fine on my own, but I didn't mind the extra attention.

I sat on the step and extended my injured foot. Alice rolled up my pant leg and her fingers lingered on my shin—I was sure of it. The pain barely registered now, and I was almost glad to have stepped on that stupid bottle if it meant this kind of TLC from Alice.

"It doesn't look too deep. Let's wash it and go from there." My personal nurse cleaned my wound with soap and water, then used some kind of antibacterial wipe, then doctored it up with some other stuff she'd found in the kit.

I stopped paying attention to the details—even going as far as blocking out the pain—because I was laser focused on Alice instead. Alice and her furrowed brow and the serious set of her mouth as she disinfected my foot. Alice as she chewed her lip in concentration, leaving me to wonder how that lip would feel between my teeth instead. Alice swiping away wisps of hair that had escaped her bun—I wish she'd just let it down and embrace the wild look. I liked *wild* on Alice. It was a nice contrast to her more serious personality.

"Ok, done. Except for the bandage. Do you need to shower or anything, or can I go ahead and put this butterfly bandage on it? Then I'll cover that with something bigger. I don't know if it's going to hurt to walk or not."

"I showered last night. I'm good for you to bandage it now." I didn't want the session to end. I tried to remember the last time someone took such good care of me, and I had to think all the way back to having the stomach flu in 5th grade, when my mom took off work and stayed home with me and we played games and watched movies for a few days. Almost made the sickness worth it for that time with her.

Alice secured the bandages. "Ok, test it out."

I stood up, still balancing on one foot. "I don't want to get it wet. Let's go in and find my shoes."

Alice put my arm around her shoulders and acted as a crutch as we went up the stairs. I was sure I'd be able to manage just fine once I got a shoe on, but I was milking the closeness while I still had the chance. She led me to a chair . . . *the* chair, the one from last night. It was impossible for me to not associate the act of sitting there with the memory of her commanding me to touch myself. She brought me some slip-on sneakers which I'd thought were dorky when I saw them yesterday in my stash of new clothes, but they looked good right about now. She got on her knees and slipped a mini-sock over my foot—we both knew I was fine to put on my own sock, but neither of us was complaining.

"What is that tiny sock thing?"

"It's a no-show sock."

"Are you sure it's not going to show? It looks ridiculous."

"We'll see once your shoe is on. I don't want your naked foot in the shoe with that wound."

Yes, I'd noted her use of the word "naked." After the socks were on, she handed me the shoes. I bent forward to wedge my foot into one and she didn't back away. Our heads were just inches apart and for a moment I felt her breath on my cheek. What if I kissed her? Would she kiss me back now that she was sober? She would, right? She said she was ok with telling HR that we liked each other . . . I tilted my head, and she stayed still. She was looking at my feet, but I could see her chest rise and fall. Her lips were parted. I leaned forward a little more—

The house phone (why the hell was there a house phone?) emitted a ring so startling, obnoxious, and shrill, that both Alice and I jumped, and we smacked our foreheads together.

"Ouch!" She yelped.

"Jesus Christ!" This day had been full of medical mishaps, and it wasn't even noon.

"I'll get it." She rubbed her forehead as she crossed the room to answer the phone. "Hello? Yes, this is the Shoreline Cottage. Ok . . ."

I watched as her face contorted into a look of confusion.

"No, I haven't seen that. Let me ask Mr. Starling." She

covered the mouthpiece of the phone with her hand. "Sebastian, have you happened to come across a box of blindfolds and handcuffs?"

"Excuse me?"

"You know. Bondage equipment? Is it in your bedroom closet or anything? Apparently, that's the one item the bride wants back if we can find it."

"She doesn't want her cock collection?"

"Nope. We're good to keep those."

"Awesome. And no, I've not come across any handcuffs or blindfolds, though they would've come in handy last night."

Alice's face went a lovely shade of bright pink, but she smiled. "I'm sorry," she said into the phone. "We haven't seen those, but is there a number I can call if we find them?" She looked for a pen and paper but gave up and pulled her phone out of her shorts pocket to put the info in her notes app.

"Honey?" I yelled in a stage shout so the caller would be sure to hear. "Did you ask them if we can keep the whips and chains? And what about the ball gag? We can put it in the dishwasher, and it'll be good as new!"

17

ALICE

Sebastian and I were huddled and hiding behind the giant trunk of a 500-year-old oak tree—one wrong move and we'd be discovered.

"Scoot over!" Sebastian pressed his elbow into my ribs. "She's going to see me!"

"*You* scoot over." I pushed him back. "There's more room on your side of the tree and my butt's hanging out as it is."

Sebastian glanced at my ass, gave an approving nod, and slid over a few inches. It was ten minutes until noon, and almost time for our appointment at Scarlet Oaks. We'd arrived early, parked our golf cart, and were walking the perimeter of the grounds when I'd heard the unmistakable twang of Tristan Taber's whiny voice echoing through the woods outside the resort. I didn't want to see her, and didn't want to talk to her, so I shoved Sebastian behind the tree, and there we remained. Tristan had just happened to make a phone call about thirty feet from where we were hiding. It would be too awkward to pop out now, so we were stuck.

"Yes, it went well," Tristan was saying. "I think everything's in line for the sale, and the meeting with Starling is just a formality. The rep told me as much. We're offering more, and the teardown will be about 90%. We're leaving a few original tokens to appease the owner, but it just has a better profile than trying to rehab the place as is. It's a dump."

Sebastian caught my eye and grimaced. Last we'd heard, Oceanview was also proposing rehab and renovation. Maybe I'd been wrong about the Blake family not wanting a faceless corporation erasing their history—maybe everyone wanted a fresh start. If that was true, we were coming in with a losing proposal.

"Yeah, their meeting is at noon. I met with Reggie, so I assume he's doing their meeting too." Tristan said. She'd started walking down a sandy path that led to the golf cart parking area, so Sebastian and I had to shift our position on the tree to remain unseen. "Just the Starling kid and some nobody who used to live on the Island. Alice somebody."

Ouch. Tristan knew my last name—what a little liar. She also knew my middle name, Faye, and she knew my mother chose it because she loved fairies. She knew that I was afraid of worms but not spiders, that chocolate made me break out in a rash, and that I'd only eat the blackberry candy in the Haribo blackberry/raspberry candy pack, even though in our blind taste tests, we couldn't tell the difference between the two when we had our eyes shut.

"No, not Simon Starling. The other one. The brainless pretty boy. Guess his daddy gave him an errand so he'd stay out of trouble." Tristan was further away, but unfortunately for Sebastian, we could still hear her. His face was expressionless, but I bet her words probably stung.

"She's a bitch," I whispered as we rotated another few feet around the tree. "And she's wrong."

Sebastian smiled weakly.

"*Simon's* the pretty one."

That got a real smile, and he grabbed me and pulled me to him, trapping me in his arms. "Take it back or I'll be forced to tickle you."

"What are you, seven years old?" I hoped he was kidding, because if he tried to tickle me, I'd scream, and our cover would be blown.

"Say it," he said into my ear, his breath warm against the side of my neck.

"Say what?" I squirmed, but not too vigorously.

"*Sebastian* Starling is the pretty boy." He touched a finger to my waist ever so slightly as if he was threatening to tickle me there.

"Fine," I whispered. "Just don't tickle me because I'll scream and pee my pants."

"Better say it, then." His voice was low and quiet, and it reminded me of last night when he told me to lift my dress. Shit. This was not the time to get all hot and bothered.

"Sebastian Starling is—" I started.

"Go on. Say it."

"Sebastian Starling is the brainless cousin," I whispered.

"What?" He lowered his face so his lips were on my neck and nibbled at my skin. I took a breath in to cry out, god, that tickled, but he pulled back suddenly. "Shhhh," he said.

What were we listening for? He let go of me and pushed his finger to his lips. I stayed quiet as he let go of me and quickly peeked around the tree.

"She's gone." He tugged on my hand and pulled me in the

direction of the Scarlet Oaks gates. "Time for our meeting. Expect your punishment later, though."

I was so focused on my possible "later punishment" that it took me a second to orient myself after we'd walked through the gates of the abandoned resort. When I was a kid, Scarlet Oaks was the gem of the island. It took up 300 acres on the east side of the island and that included three miles of beautiful beach-front property. But it wasn't alive anymore. At first I didn't realize I was looking at the Grand Hall—what paint was left on its surface was peeling and some windows were boarded up. The golf course just looked like long grass, the pool was empty, and I could only imagine what the stables, the park, and cottages looked like.

"You ok?" Sebastian asked. He was staring up at the Grand Hall with worried eyes.

"I don't know."

"Mr. Starling? Ms. Goode?" A man stepped out from the Grand Hall entrance and greeted us. "I'm Reginald Powers." He offered his hand for me to shake, and then he shook Sebastian's hand. "I'm the representative of the Blake Family." Reggie. This must've been the rep who Tristan referenced. "Do you have any questions before we start our tour? We can do this part on foot and then explore some of the outer acres with the golf carts."

Uh-oh. I felt that pulsing in my stomach. It moved up through my chest, through my throat, and—"I overheard Tristan Tabor say that this sale was a done deal, and that our visit was a formality. I also heard her say that Oceanview was doing a ninety percent teardown, and in the prospect info we were given, it's clearly stated that this was primarily a rehab/restore project, with some teardown where structures were unsafe or rotted." I was getting better at this speaking up thing. Caluska Island was important to me, and that was enough for me not to stay silent.

"Oh, I—" Reggie stammered.

"I know that the Scarlet Oaks property is an eyesore right now, but its history is embedded in the heart of the community. Are we wasting our time here today?"

Reggie and Sebastian both stared at me, their mouths half open. I heard someone laugh. Sebastian hadn't laughed, and neither had Reggie. Sebastian heard it too and looked over his shoulder to find the source of the sound.

"You haven't changed a bit," a man's voice said.

"Who *is* that?" Sebastian turned the other way, still looking for whoever was speaking.

The gatehouse. There, in the tattered remains of the former hub of the Scarlet Oaks entrance, sat a small man. Edward Blake.

Tears pushed at my eyes and there was a catch in my throat. I hadn't seen Mr. Blake since I was a teenager. He used a cane for balance and strength as he stood up, but he looked the same in so many ways, just older. Same dark skin, same generous smile, but instead of black hair, it was now a shocking white.

"Mr. Blake?" I took a step toward him. "I thought you and Mrs. Blake were living in Harborhollow? I thought you couldn't travel?"

"Now, would I let a little something like that stop me from seeing my Miss Lissy?" When I heard my old nickname, I couldn't hold back the tears. I stumbled over to him and collected him into a hug. His shoulders were smaller than they used to be, and he was shorter and slighter. He'd been my grandfather's best friend, and though we weren't related, he was family.

"But why are you here?" I hadn't heard Tristan say anything about Mr. Blake.

"One last look at the place, I guess. Hurts my heart to see it so run down. It's time for it to see new life."

"Did you meet with Tristan Tabor?" I asked. "We saw her on her way out, but she didn't mention you—" No need to admit that Sebastian and I had been eavesdropping on her conversation.

"Didn't chat with Ms. Tabor," he said. "She's mostly hot air, anyway. Not sure I would've got a word in edgewise. I let Reggie handle her."

Reggie nodded in acknowledgment.

Sebastian walked to the gatehouse and held out his hand. "I'm Sebastian Starling. It's nice to meet you, sir."

Mr. Blake shook his hand, and then sat back down on a rickety wooden bench. "Call me Eddie. What do you think of this place, Mr. Starling? What's your first impression?"

Sebastian looked around at the ruins of Scarlet Oaks. I expected him to throw a joke or dodge the question, but he took his time before offering a response. "I think it's magical. And I think it's melancholy."

Mr. Blake considered Sebastian's answer and then nodded his head one time. "I think that's a fair assessment. And you get that just by what you see here?" he asked.

"I get it from what I see here. But I also get it from the photos."

"What photos are those?" Mr. Blake pulled a handkerchief from his pants pocket and dabbed the sweat on his forehead, supporting my original hypothesis that it was usually the old guys who carried those things. Leave it to Sebastian to be the exception to the rule.

"The photos we studied before we arrived." Sebastian retrieved his own handkerchief from his own pocket and mirrored Mr. Blake's forehead dabbing. Was this some sort of manly sizing-up ritual? I half expected Reggie to dip into his pocket next and join the handkerchief gang.

Sebastian pointed out toward the sea grass that swayed over the surface of the former golf course. "That was the 18th hole over there. The approach was up the shoreline, and the hole had a 180-degree view of the ocean, the beach, the pool, and the resort." Sebastian stepped out of the gatehouse and pointed in the other direction. "The guest rooms of the main building are down that way, and the cottages are to the west. The rec center was over there, and the equestrian center was behind the Grand Hall." More sweat dabbing from Sebastian. "I can't shake those images from my head. How these places were filled with families, couples, executives, retirees. It was so alive, and now it feels —" Sebastian stopped, and if I didn't know better, I'd think he was choked up. *Was* he choked up?

"It feels?" Mr. Blake prompted.

"It feels haunted." A gust of wind pushed through the gatehouse as Sebastian spoke and goosebumps bloomed and scattered over my arms.

"It feels that way to me, too." Mr. Blake looked out over the property and sighed.

"Eddie, what's your wish for Scarlet Oaks?" Sebastian asked. "If you could have anything you wanted for this land, with the snap of your fingers, would you want it to return to what it used to be?"

Mr. Blake didn't speak for a minute, and he didn't look at

Sebastian. His eyes were on the horizon. "No one's asked me that before."

"No one's asked you what you want for Scarlet Oaks?" I asked.

"They've asked me how much money I want for it. And they've asked me which buildings I think can be salvaged, and what parts of the property flood, and what do I think about a high-rise on this property, but no one's asked me what my dream would be." He tapped his cane against the wooden floor and looked lost in thought. "I don't think I'd want it to be just like it was," he finally said. "Because the world's not like it used to be." He stood up again, slowly, his hand shaking slightly as he pushed against his cane. "I'd like for people to enjoy this place. Bring their families. Learn something. I'd like the land to be the showcase, not the hotel or the golf course. But I'm not sure that's the biggest moneymaker." His eyes came back into focus, and he laughed and looked at Sebastian. "But you didn't ask me what the best moneymaker was. That's a high rise and a Go Kart track!"

"A Go Kart track?" I squeaked. "No way!"

"I doubt it would happen, but there was one proposal that had one right over there, where the old pool was."

Sebastian leaped out of the gatehouse like he'd stepped on another broken beer bottle. His face was bright, like he'd just thought of something amazing. "Eddie, how long are you here on the island?"

"I'll be here until the weekend. I'm staying with my nephew and getting some of the sea air before I have to go back to the mainland."

"Can we meet with you tomorrow? I have an idea, but I need the day to get some things together for you."

"Reggie, what's our schedule tomorrow?" Mr. Blake asked his representative.

"You're clear after two o'clock."

"Then give this young man your contact information and we'll set up a meeting for tomorrow. Say three o'clock?"

Sebastian nearly jogged over to Reggie, who handed him a business card. "Thank you, Eddie. You won't regret it."

"What's this idea?" I asked him. I'd never seen Sebastian so lit up.

"I'll tell you about it on the way back to the house. I need to make some phone calls and send some emails. Are you all fine if we skip the tour for now?"

"Fine by me," said Mr. Blake.

Sebastian trotted back over to the gatehouse and shook Mr. Blake's hand again. "I'll see you tomorrow." He turned to me. "Ready, Blaze?"

Mr. Blake cocked his head to the side. "Blaze?"

"Oh, it's this silly nickname he has for me—"

"It suits you, Miss Lissy."

My head was swirling with everything that was happening. Sebastian held his hand out to me, and I took it. His palm was warm, and his grip was strong. "See you soon!" Sebastian called to the men as we left the entrance area. We strolled through the gates and back toward the spot where we'd parked our golf cart.

When we were out of earshot, I stopped walking. "What was that about? Are you changing the plan?"

Sebastian ran his hand through his hair and sweat plastered his temples, but he didn't seem to notice. "We're changing the plan. And we're going to see if we can make some dreams come true."

18

ALICE

Yes, I was the handler. I was the one hired to keep Sebastian Starling in line, on track, and above board. When we'd started this project, I wasn't sure about Sebastian's ability to focus on or understand the details of the deal at hand, but then again, I was no expert in heading up corporate initiatives. I'd been a panic-hire.

Sebastian had taken to my style of storytelling and when he understood the history of Caluska island on a more personal level, he'd dialed in to the venture. Now he'd made his own connections to Scarlet Oaks, its history, and its future, and he was off to the races. It was like he'd needed help getting used to the water, but now he was swimming in deep water by himself and staying afloat.

But something worried me: Sebastian had gone off-script, and I had the feeling that the idea was for Sebastian and me to represent Starling Enterprises as warm bodies, not true project managers. This kind of deal wasn't simple, but the project packet Starling Enterprises gave us seemed suspiciously superficial to me. I'd only been at this a few days and it had all happened so quickly, but I had an uneasy feeling that Tristan hadn't been completely wrong when she'd said that Sebastian's father had sent him on an errand to keep him out of trouble. I remembered Mitchell Starling saying in the meeting that the Caluska Island project was a "low-risk" venture. This may have been a throwaway project for Starling Enterprises, or at least one that, if it didn't work out, was no skin off their backs.

I doubted that anyone expected Sebastian to have a great idea and run with it, possibly changing all the stakes. But I wasn't going to stop him. Maybe Sebastian didn't need a handler. He might've just needed someone to believe in him.

"When we get back to the house I'll call in and check with Ethan on the architecture committee. If we can get a rough mock-up for the new plan, and Eddie can see what it could be, I think we have a real chance."

"A chance for what?" I thought I knew what he meant, but I didn't want to put words in his mouth, and I wanted to hear it from him. Maybe he wanted a chance to impress his dad. A chance to shut out Oceanview. Or a chance to make his first official deal.

"A chance to make Eddie Blake's vision a reality and save and improve this little slice of the world."

I couldn't speak. If I'd tried, I would've sounded like a strangled toad. Emotion flooded my chest, my throat, my eyes, and if I made a wrong move, it would all spill out of me. Sebastian kept chatting and relaying his to-do as he drove our golf cart back to the cottage, but I was only half-listening. I was so moved that he cared. He wasn't just here for the money or to impress his dad or to squash the assholes from Orlando—or, if he *had* been here for all of that, something had changed.

Seeing Scarlet Oaks in such poor condition had broken my

heart. And seeing Mr. Blake broke it just that much more. I was so happy to see him, but he was aging and weaker than he used to be, and he was a reminder of what I didn't have: family. At least no living family. Seeing him, hearing his voice, getting to hug him, was almost like making contact with the ghosts of my grandparents. A tear slipped out and toppled down my cheek. I pretended I was swatting a bug when I went to wipe it away. I didn't want to have a meltdown—I didn't want the focus on me, and I didn't want to disrupt Sebastian's train of thought.

"Are you ok?" Sebastian glanced at me with a look of curious concern. Shit. Maybe he'd noticed the tear.

Still not trusting my voice, I nodded.

"You sure?" Now he looked suspicious.

"Yep!" Shit. I sounded worse than a strangled toad. My "yep" came out more like the bray of a suffocating donkey.

Sebastian slowed to a stop on the edge of the beach trail and turned off the engine. The ocean hummed to our right and the cries of gulls echoed in the wind. "Alice."

I gave Sebastian a thumbs up and then turned my back to him. That one tear was a pioneer and had broken the seal, causing my floodgates to open.

"Did you just give me a thumbs-up?"

I felt Sebastian touch my arm, but I didn't turn around. I couldn't hold back, and my shoulders started to shake as I cried harder.

"Alice?" Sebastian got out of the golf cart and crossed over to my side.

I had my face hidden in my hands but there was no hiding that I'd lost my composure. All the stress of the job and the unknown, all the sadness and grief over missing my family, and the intense feelings sparked from returning to Caluska Island—

it had all come to the surface. I waited for Sebastian to ask, "what's wrong?" or "why are you crying?" or to tell me "don't cry," which never helped anyone who was bawling their eyes out, but he stayed silent. I knew he was standing there, in front of me, because I could see his legs through the cracks in my fingers, but he was just quiet and still and waiting. After a minute my tears started to ebb, and I took a deep breath to clear my lungs, but kept my face hidden. I was a mess and I didn't want anyone to see me this way, especially Sebastian.

"Take this," Sebastian said softly. I peeked at what he had to offer and saw a crisp Starling handkerchief fluttering in his fingers.

"How many of those do you have?" I couldn't help but laugh a little.

"As many as you need." He pushed it into my hands, and I wiped my face and turned the other way to hide from him again. "Take your time. I'm going to get you something to drink from the restaurant over there." He was referring to the Oyster Shack, a place that'd been on the island since before I was born. "Any requests?"

Now that he mentioned it, I realized I was seriously parched. "Just water. Or any kind of soda. Anything's fine. But don't you need to get back to the house to make your calls?"

"They can wait. I'll be back in a few." He started to walk away but then doubled back and got back into the driver's seat of the cart. "Let's get you out of the path." He started the golf cart and drove ten feet off the path, pointing me right at the ocean. "There you go. A nice view for you. Sit tight." And then he was gone.

A handful of beachgoers lounged on the shore, but none had umbrellas up because the wind was too strong. Clouds were moving in, so maybe a storm was brewing for an evening arrival. Some golf carts ambled by as I watched the waves churn, but it was a quiet afternoon. My embarrassment faded as my tears dried and I noticed that no one was looking at me. No one was bothering me or bothered *by* me. No one cared that I was weird or crying or sitting there snotty and blotchy faced in a golf cart, staring out at the Atlantic Ocean. I didn't have to hide, and I didn't have to stand out. I could just exist. I could be myself.

It was like I'd been living outside myself for years, my mind and my heart disembodied from my physical form as I tried to fence off parts of myself from one another. Maybe I was afraid of how much I'd feel if all those fragments of me worked themselves together and operated as a whole. But sitting there on the beach after my cry, it was like my soul and my psyche and everything else got stirred up by the ocean breeze and then got dropped back on me all at once. For the first time in so long, I felt whole.

The water. I wanted to be in the water. I wanted the salt to soak into my skin and I wanted to baptize myself in the ocean. I'd immerse myself in nostalgia and memory, and then wash away my past. I'd come out of the water as New Alice. Alice who knew who she was and what she wanted. Or maybe just Alice who wasn't scared to speak up now and again, but either way, I needed to swim.

I looked back toward the Oyster Shack but there was no sign of Sebastian. The water wasn't that far from the cart—he'd be able to see me, and I wouldn't go too far in—just to my knees; I wasn't dressed for a full dip anyway. My eyes were bleary from all the crying, but I made my way down to the beach and up to the water's edge and slipped out of my shoes.

No one else was swimming, a sure sign that the water hadn't warmed up yet for the season.

The cold waves rushed my ankles as I stepped in. Chilly, but bearable for a minute or two. A few more steps and the choppy waves reached my calves. I captured some water in my palm and brought it to my lips, not to drink, but to taste the saltwater I used to cough up as a kid whenever a wave smacked me in the face. The surf rushed powerfully toward me and my feet sunk in the wet sand. The tide was strong today, stronger than I remembered, but when I was a kid, I'd felt strong and safe in the ocean. I lifted my skirt a few inches so it wouldn't get splashed. A few more steps. I closed my eyes and let the memories flood me as the water rushed at my knees. Images flashed before my eyes: Nana, Grandfather, Tristan, our house, the beach, sunsets, card games, boat rides, oysters, fishing. And then new images: Mr. Blake from today, the cottage, Sebastian last night in the living room . . .

Sebastian? I thought I heard his voice calling to me, but I wasn't ready to open my eyes. I wanted a few more moments in the water with just my thoughts before walking out as the new me. But when your eyes are closed, you have no way of knowing if a huge wave might be building and growing and threatening to crash down on you with the full force of nature.

19

SEBASTIAN

A Coke, two waters, and a bag of salty French fries were tricky to hold, but I managed to balance everything as I left the Oyster Shack and headed back to where I'd left Alice. Something salty, something sweet, and some hydration, and Alice should be as good as new.

I wasn't sure exactly what prompted her breakdown, but if I had to guess, I'd say that returning to Caluska Island had brought up a lot of memories and emotions that she'd stuffed down deep. I'd only known Alice since last week, but somehow I was seeing her transform right before my eyes. Maybe I'd just made assumptions about who she was and how she worked, but she seemed both more vulnerable and more outspoken than she had when we first started working together.

I watched my feet and the path ahead of me, looking out for tree roots, sandy pockets, or broken glass. Unlike this morning, I was now wearing shoes, but the memory of stepping on something sharp was enough to make me more cautious about where I stepped. I was almost to the golf cart when I realized that Alice wasn't there.

Alice had been kidnapped. Why that was among my initial thoughts, I had no idea. It was a stupid thought, but it still made my stomach flip and twist to think of someone grabbing Alice and taking her away, scaring her, or hurting her. *She wasn't kidnapped, you idiot; she had to use the bathroom.* That was much more realistic than my kidnapping theory, but the nearest restroom was the one in the Oyster Shack and I would've crossed paths with her; she went for a walk on the beach. Knowing Alice and her obsession with the beach and the ocean, this was the most plausible option.

I dropped the bottled waters onto the seat of the golf cart, stuffed the Coke into the cup holder, and rested the fries in a spot on the console. I scanned the shoreline for Alice, and almost immediately spotted her by the water. She was easy to see because of her gorgeous red hair that captured and reflected the sunlight even when she had her tresses pulled back. Wait. She wasn't *by* the water; she was *in* the water. Why was she in the water? She wasn't that far in, but she was getting deeper with each step. Surely, she'd seen the red flags flying on all of the beaches today: no swimming allowed because of the strong riptides. Alice was used to the ocean, so maybe she knew what she was doing.

"Alice!" I called out, but it was useless. My voice, caught in the wind like a runaway kite, got blown away. Alice couldn't hear me over the rough surf anyway; I picked up my pace and started to jog.

Alice took a few more steps and the water was up to her knees. She had her skirt pulled up to her thighs and she wobbled as each strong wave pushed into her.

"Alice!" I tried again. "Stop!" I felt ridiculous. Alice wasn't a child. She was a grown woman, a good swimmer, and someone who had years of experience around the ocean, but something about it still felt wrong. Maybe it was because she'd seemed so unsteady and raw when I'd left her, and the waters of the Atlantic weren't friendly today. The red beach flags flapped in my peripheral vision as I ran to Alice. Flags. Plural. Why were there double red flags? Earlier, there'd only been one red flag. Alice had to get out of the water, now.

"Alice!" I tried one last time. There was a giant wave coming right at her. Why was she still standing there? There was no way to miss that monster wave unless she had a death wish, or had her eyes closed. I flung off my shoes and stepped into the chilly water. It took a second for the salt to seep in under my bandage and holy shit that stung. Alice was only twenty feet away from me, but it was too far. The current was strong and pushed me backwards with each step I took; I couldn't get to her before that wave did. I watched as it rose up and crested above her head before it crashed down. And then Alice was gone.

The remnants of the wave were so powerful that they caused me to stumble, even though I was only up to my ankles. Panic rose into my throat, and I swallowed the bitter rush of bile as I looked for Alice. There were no lifeguards on this stretch of beach, and the only other people I saw were a family who were chasing after a beach ball that the wind had stolen. More waves were rushing in and desperation took hold. I couldn't see anything except foam and dark water. Alice *had* been kidnapped; the ocean had taken her away from me. "Alice!" I tried to scream, but my voice was stuck, and my plea came out choked and ragged.

"—Bastian?"

I heard someone call half of my name—it had to be Alice.

"Alice?" I didn't see her. I pushed against the waves, trying to get where I'd last seen her when she'd gone under.

"Baz!"

Now *that*, I heard, but it was coming from my right. I turned and saw Alice. Alice standing. Alice alive!

"Baz, get out of the water! Riptide!"

That was rich. *Ms. I almost drowned because I was in the ocean on a double red flag day* was telling me what to do? She was drenched, but upright and walking toward the shore, so I followed her demand and got out of the Atlantic as fast as I could. I ran down the beach to meet her as she emerged from the ocean.

"Are you ok? That's a serious undertow. You could've been hurt!" Alice coughed and wiped her eyes with the back of her hand. "Oh shit, double red." She pointed at the flags.

"Are you kidding me right now?" I wanted to hug her, but I also wanted to yell at her. Instead, I just stood there, soaked, foot throbbing, and freezing.

"What?" She looked truly confused.

"You nearly died. The ocean swallowed you up right in front of me!"

Alice swatted away my argument with a swipe of her hand. "I'm fine. That wave caught me off guard and then I realized I was stuck in the riptide. I just swam parallel to shore until I popped out." She coughed again. "That was stupid of me, though. I didn't notice the flags." She was shivering and her lips had taken on a slightly blue tinge. At least she wasn't crying anymore.

"You're done," I said.

"Done with what?"

"Done with making decisions for a few hours. I'm the boss now."

"Ok, boss," she said, her teeth chattering. "What's the plan?"

"Come with me."

Wet, sandy, and shivering, we pulled up to our cottage a few minutes later. Alice had polished off the fries and slugged most of the coke.

"Drink some water, too," I told her. "And leave our shoes in the golf cart. I'll clean them later." They were sandy from being tossed on shore before both of us had ventured into the ocean.

"We need to wash out your cut again." Alice walked toward the front door and waited for me on the front porch.

"Who's the boss right now?" I entered the code on the lock and opened the door. It was freezing inside—the air conditioning didn't feel great against our wet clothes and cold bodies.

"You're the boss, Mr. Starling," she said as she rolled her eyes.

"Correct. Now go on the porch and wait for me. It's warmer out there."

"Whatever you say, boss." She marched toward the porch, and I couldn't help but stare as she walked away. Her dress was wet and clinging to her every curve. I just wanted to rip it off of her.

I found a robe in her closet, one of several that were hanging up there, maybe for use at the bachelorette party. Luckily it didn't have any stupid sayings on it. It was just white, soft, and hopefully warm. I carried it to the back porch where Alice was standing and looking out at the view.

"I don't know what I was thinking," she said. "The wind had been picking up. The surf was rough. I didn't look for the flags."

"It doesn't matter now. You're ok."

"And so are you." She turned to face me, salty tangled ringlets of hair stuck to her cheek. "I'm glad you're ok, Sebastian. I'm sorry you had to come in after me."

"I figured if I couldn't save you, we'd go to our watery graves together."

She smiled. And shivered. I was standing here, flirting, while Alice was probably coming down with hypothermia.

"I'm glad we didn't drown," she said.

"So am I. Now take off all your clothes."

20

ALICE

If someone had told me last week that today I'd be on Caluska Island, standing in front of *the* Sebastian Starling in my own version of a wet t-shirt contest, and that Sebastian would demand that I strip down naked—I would've politely asked what kind of drugs they were on. It would be even more shocking to "past me" if I knew that when Mr. Starling told me to take my clothes off, that I wanted to. And not just because my dress was wet, and I was shivering and desperate to get into the fluffy robe he was holding; I wanted to strip down because I wanted him to see me naked. I wanted him to touch me. I wanted him to want me. And I wasn't even drunk. What the hell was happening?

"Right here?" I asked him. If he said yes, I'd do it. I'd take everything off. I'd downplayed my tumble in the ocean—I really did panic at first when I got pulled under, but somehow, I swam parallel to the shore and popped out of the riptide. It'd been luck or a guardian angel. However it happened, I was alive, and I was tired of holding back, hiding away, and missing out. New Alice was here.

"I'll step out. I just don't want you to get colder in the house. Put on this robe and I'll get your shower started." Sebastian closed the curtains that hung around the edges of the screens on the porch. They were sheer, but they'd be enough to stop anyone from seeing me as I changed into the robe. "Just come into the bathroom when you're ready." And with that, he went back into the house.

I peeled off my clothes and left them in a wet heap on the porch. I got my arms into the wide sleeves of the robe, closed the front, and secured it with a belt. I untangled my hair from the bun, or tried to, but it was going to take a shower and lots of conditioner to get that mess sorted out. I could just crawl into bed and take a nap, but I was sandy in all my cracks and crevices, and I had to admit that hot water sounded like heaven. The air conditioning unit stopped, and suddenly everything was so much quieter. I could hear birds tweeting and the steady heartbeat of the tide pounding against the shore.

I entered the cottage and headed back to my bathroom where I heard water running. When I rounded the corner, I saw Sebastian in the dimly lit bathroom placing a towel on the hook by the shower door and then he stooped down to straighten out the bath mat. "Oh, hey," he said when he saw me at the bathroom door. "Your water temp should be good. You didn't tell me that you got the princess shower. Two heads! Mine is boring and just has one."

I must've had the master suite if Sebastian had a smaller shower. Mine was one of those extra big walk-ins that had an overhead rain showerhead, and then one that came out of the wall to hit your bottom half. Then there was a bonus wand that you could unhook if you wanted to reach all your nooks and crannies. I'd probably need that one today. "Thank you." I touched his wrist as he scooted by me in the bathroom. "Thank you for everything today."

Sebastian looked at the floor, but he couldn't hide the soft smile that fluttered across his perfect lips. "You're welcome." He moved toward the door. "Just call out if you need anything. I'll wait to take my shower until you're done."

"Why would you wait? You're probably just as cold as—" suddenly the world went a little wonky and I felt like my words separated from my brain and were floating out in front of my face. Time slowed down and I felt woozy for a second, but then I felt normal again. Well, mostly normal, because my robe was half off and Sebastian had his arms around me, and nothing about that felt "normal," really.

"What just happened?" Sebastian was so close that I could feel the heat of his breath on the back of my neck as he held me from behind.

"I don't know. Just felt dizzy there for a second."

"Is there a doctor on the island?" Sebastian's voice was sharp and he sounded worried.

"Yes, there's a doctor, but I don't need one. I probably need more water. Lots of wine last night, not enough water today, and my little near-drowning incident—"

"You said you had the riptide under control!"

"I may have lied," I admitted.

"Dammit, Alice." Sebastian wrapped his arms around me even more tightly. "You can't shower by yourself. My shower is a tub shower. I'm going to run you a bath."

"No." I said, sounding stern even to myself.

"You have to rinse off and warm up." He matched my sternness with his own.

"I will. In here."

"It's not safe." He spun me around to look at me and the look of real concern on his face was endearing.

"It'll be safe if you're in there with me," I said. It was New Alice speaking.

"What do you mean?" His expression of concern had melted into one of confusion.

"I mean that we're both wet, we're both cold, and we could both use a safety buddy."

"I don't know about that." He was looking at the floor again.

I was nervous for a second that he didn't want to get in the shower with me. That what happened the night before was fueled by alcohol for him, and that in the sober light of day, he wasn't into me. Maybe his call to Simon about HR was just to protect him from me claiming that he'd made an uninvited advance. But then I saw the unmistakable bulge in his pants, and I knew that part of him, at least one very obvious part of him, wanted me in the same way that I wanted him.

"You don't want me to fall in the shower, or pass out in the bath, do you?"

Sebastian peeked up at me through his eyelashes. "Of course I don't."

"We're also two consenting adults who've already gotten the HR ball rolling about our situation."

"True." He reached up and ran a finger down the lapel of my robe, getting so close to my breast that a shiver ran through my whole body.

"Then let's go." I dropped my robe on the floor, slid open the shower door, and stepped in. I shut the door to keep in the heat and got under the spray, letting the warm water rush over my body. Sebastian had set the temperature barely above lukewarm, but the drops felt hot when they pelted my chilled skin. *Don't turn around, don't turn around, don't turn around*, I willed myself. I hoped he'd get in with me, but I didn't want to spook him by watching him undress. I also didn't want to get dizzy in the shower and not have anyone in there with me. I'd gotten woozy before if I hadn't had enough to eat or if I was super dehydrated, so maybe that's what happened. I'd eat and have some more water as soon as I was warmed up and cleaned off.

I had my eyes closed and was letting the shower spray my face and hair and as the salt and sand washed away I felt a tension in my shoulders relax and release. I heard the shower door open and felt cold air rush into the stall. Sebastian was coming in. The shower door closed, and the sound of the water changed as if it was hitting against another body along with mine. I was too shy to turn around yet, so I kept my eyes closed and kept rinsing off.

"Hi," Sebastian said, his deep voice echoing off the shower walls.

"Hey." I tried to sound calm, but I didn't feel calm. I felt excited. Nervous.

"Need some help?"

"Yes, please." I didn't know exactly what he was going to help with, but now didn't seem like the time for questions.

"How do we untangle this?" He put his fingers in my hair and I felt little pulls and tugs.

"Conditioner is probably its only hope right now," I said. My heart was beating so quickly that I had to take a deep breath to try to slow it down.

"Shampoo first?"

"Conditioner, then maybe shampoo. Then more conditioner."

"Got it. Can you turn on this side sprayer? It's chilly for those of us not under the main shower."

"Oh god, I'm sorry!" I yanked the second sprayer knob to the left, which caused Sebastian to yelp and jump toward my corner of the shower. "Are you ok? Did I burn you?" I looked at his face but refused to look at the rest of his naked body. Was I really in the shower with Sebastian Starling? Part of me wondered if I was dreaming.

"That shoots out a little cold at first. Should be ok now."

Out of the corner of my eye I saw him reach a hand into the spray, adjust the temperature, and test the water again.

"All good. Can I have the conditioner?"

I handed him the bottle and he took his place behind me again. I turned my water up a few degrees.

For the next five minutes, Sebastian worked conditioner into my matted curls and untangled them piece by piece. He used the wand sprayer to rinse, untangled some more, and rinsed again. By the time he was done, I was so relaxed I wouldn't have cared if I came out of that shower looking like Medusa. And I wasn't nervous anymore. He'd had his hands on me, but not *on* me, and that gave me time to get comfortable with his touch and his presence. I was ready to turn around and face him.

"I think you're good now. Feel for yourself and see what you think."

I raked my fingers through my hair and it felt clean, slippery, and smooth. Perfect. I turned around. "Thank you," I said quietly. "That felt so good."

"My pleasure." Sebastian had his arms crossed in front of him, probably for modesty, but we were beyond that point.

It was either time to get out of the shower, or time for me to make a move. "May I wash yours?"

Sebastian offered me a half-smile. "Sure. I don't think I need as much conditioner, though." He started to turn his back to me, but I stopped him.

"Stay like this."

"I thought I was the boss," he said.

"You can be the boss everywhere but the shower."

He pretended to mull it over. "Fine."

I reached up to his head. pressed my fingertips to his scalp and started to rub. He closed his eyes, dropped his hands to his side, and let out a moan of pleasure. I untangled his hair, which took no extra product, and rinsed out the little bit of sand that had found its way to his head. I stepped closer so I could reach the back of his hair, which meant pressing my body against his. My nipples hardened as they rubbed his chest, and his erection pushed against my belly.

He slid his arms around my waist and rested his hands gently on my hips. His eyes were still closed, and I studied his face. Water beaded on his beard and his mouth was slightly open. I wanted to kiss him so badly. Wanted to taste him and bite his lip and feel his tongue in my mouth.

"Sebastian?"

He opened his eyes and waited for me to ask my question.

"May I kiss you?"

He didn't answer. Instead, he let out a kind of growl and slid his hands off my hips, up my torso, and past my neck, landing with his palms cradling the back of my head. He brought his face down close to mine, waited a beat, and then kissed me.

It was the sweetest, wettest, hottest kiss of my life. Water from the showerhead sprinkled down on us as we pressed our lips together, first softly, and then more urgently. Sebastian clenched his fists in my hair as he opened his mouth against mine and tasted my tongue with his. I caught his lower lip between my teeth and held on for a moment, causing Sebastian to groan again and push his pelvis against me.

I snaked my fingers down his stomach, following the trail of hair that led me down from his belly button to between his legs. There was no avoiding his cock, which was hard and hot to the touch. I gripped his shaft and repositioned him so the length of him was between my legs instead of pressed against my belly. I pulled my face away from his and pressed my cheek against his chest. I wanted to concentrate on how he felt between my thighs as his dick slid across my folds.

Sebastian led me backward a few steps until my back was against the shower wall. The lower sprayer was angled so it shot warm water against our legs, keeping us from getting cold. He traced the curve of my breast with his hand and then let his fingertips linger on my nipple. A surge of pleasure shot from my breast to my clit, and I couldn't help but moan. "Touch me. Please," I said. I took his hand and placed it between my legs. His fingers quickly found my swollen nub and he gently swirled one finger across its wet surface.

I rocked my hips back and forth as he rubbed me, sliding my pussy up and down the length of his cock. Sebastian held himself up with one arm while his other hand was busy touching me, and I slid across him faster and faster as pleasure and pressure built inside me. I was going to come. I could feel the hot sparks swirling and building and I wanted the release. "Don't stop," I begged, my voice ragged. "I'm about to come."

"Yes, Alice, yes. Come on me, Alice. I want to see you come." His voice was rough and full of desire, and hearing the words pushed me over the edge.

I cried out and squeezed my thighs against his shaft as my climax ignited and spread throughout my body. My legs quivered and the wetness of my arousal lubricated our skin. I kept sliding my pussy against him and I could tell he couldn't take much more. His breathing was rapid, and his eyes were closed. "Come, Sebastian," I managed to say. "I want *you* to come."

He cried out and threw his head back as he thrust his cock against my soft folds once, twice, and then a third time. He was so hard and then I felt him shudder as his dick spasmed between my legs. He collapsed against me, his shoulders softening as he released. I felt his come run down my leg in a warm stream as I grabbed his face and kissed him again. He was hungry for me, his mouth biting at me, sucking, prodding, tasting. After a minute we pulled away from each other and we looked into each other's eyes.

"Was that your master plan, Alice Goode?" he teased. He kissed my forehead and traced an invisible line down my arm.

"Never question the boss."

21

SEBASTIAN

So. *That* happened. Me, Alice, the shower. I was no stranger to things moving fast when I was dating someone. It was just last week that Eva and I . . . damn it, was it Ava? I'd never get it straight. It was last week when she and I had that encounter, right before I met Alice. But what had happened with Alice last night, and today—it felt different. I thought it over while I finished my second sandwich.

After the shower, Alice and I had made some lunch and she'd eaten her food in about three bites. Then she'd gone to take a nap while I sent out emails and got working on the revised proposal I wanted to submit to Eddie tomorrow. I was waiting to hear back from some people at the office, and while I knew I should be making notes and formulating a more formal plan, I was having trouble concentrating.

Usually when I'd messed around with a woman, had sex, or whatever we ended up doing, it was nice. Nice, but not necessarily earth-shattering or memorable. I'd started to think that's just how things were—or just how *I* was—that I was destined to a life of casual encounters, casual relationships, casual sex. But nothing about this situation with Alice felt casual to me.

I still couldn't quite believe that I'd actually gotten into the shower with her. She'd dropped her robe and situated herself under the spray, and watching the water run down her tangled hair, over her soft hips, across her luscious ass—I was rock hard and I felt dizzy in my own right, but it was less dehydration and more raging desire. There was no way in hell I could've left her in there alone.

Washing her hair was maybe the sexiest thing I'd ever done, though I did have to concentrate on not stabbing her in the back with my erection. Our climaxes were earth shattering and memorable, for both of us, I think, but the memory I couldn't shake, that I couldn't stop reliving over and over and over, was the kiss. When our lips touched, something changed in me. It felt like every strand of DNA twisted and unlocked as if Alice's name had been written on each cell in my body and our first kiss activated a new way for my body to receive oxygen.

Sometimes kissing felt too intimate for me and I often jumped to the next step with a woman before I got too uncomfortable. But with Alice, I wanted to stay in that kiss for days. Years. Decades. I wanted to taste her. I wanted to bring her essence into me and explore her and unwind her and become a part of her. I wasn't sure what was wrong with me. Maybe there was something in the island air that was messing with me. Either that, or I was falling in—

My cell buzzed and put me out of my misery. Simon's name flashed on the screen.

"Hey Simon, you got my message?"

There was silence on the other end of the line for a few beats. "Yes. I received it." More silence.

"Okay, great. Any thoughts?" I'd sent him a summary of my idea, and I also filled him in on everything I needed from my Starling Enterprises co-workers in case he had to find them in person and make sure they could get me what I needed on such short turn-around time.

"You changed the plan." Simon didn't like change.

"Right. Which is why I let you know, and is also why I need to talk to Cara in design, Jean in planning, Benny in architecture, and—"

"Sebastian." Simon's voice was cold and hard. Not that different from how he sounded on a daily basis, but I was detecting a bit more edge than usual.

"Yes, dear cousin." Maybe some humor would warm him up.

"You changed the plan."

No such luck. His attitude was starting to annoy me. "We've already established that, Simon."

"You did not have authorization to change the plan."

"Okay. Well, it was a spur of the moment decision, informed by my meeting with the client, which is why you sent me down here, right?"

More annoying silence from Simon.

"Hello?"

"We didn't send you down there to change the plan, Sebastian."

"Could you stop using my name when you're talking to me, *Simon*? It makes you sound like my dad when he's reprimanding me." My stomach dropped. Not in the fun bubbly way it'd dropped when I kissed Alice. This was a roller coaster malfunction, knife in the gut, running out of air kind of stomach flip when I realized the answer to my own question. "Oh, I get it."

"You get what, Sebastian?"

"You sent me here to get me out of the way. Or to make me feel like I was doing something important, but really I'm just a puppet and you and my pops are pulling the fucking strings. Is that about right, *Simon*?" I spit out his name like it was poison. I loved my cousin, but if he'd been standing in front of me, I might've punched him.

"Sebastian—" Simon began.

"Stop saying my fucking name."

Simon sighed. "You were supposed to follow the script. This is a first project for you, and we just wanted to see if you could—"

"I understand." I didn't want him to finish his sentence. I didn't want to hear him explain that he and my dad, and probably all the other executives, knew I was a fucking joke and knew that I'd never be a real part of the company, and I'd never amount to anything. I was the playboy, the fuck up, the handsome but ordinary boy who'd never make a real difference in the business, let alone the world. And why should they think anything different? I'd never given them any reason to believe I was anything else.

"Sebastian," Simon tried again.

"Forget it." I disconnected the call and let my phone drop with a clatter onto the table. I dropped my head into my hands and rubbed my forehead roughly with my fingertips.

"Sebastian?" It was Alice, sleepy-eyed from her nap.

"Why the fuck is everyone using my name?" I shoved my chair back, stomped out of the kitchen, across the porch, and out the back door, which I let slam behind me. Anger was blooming in my chest, but it wasn't at Alice. It wasn't even at Simon. Or my dad. I was pissed at myself for getting myself in this position to begin with—for not being better. Thunder rumbled in the distance and branches of nearby trees trembled as gusts of wind swept through. I kept my back to the house and waited for Alice to come out after me, angry and yelling— but she didn't. I stood alone on the sandy grass, barefoot again as the sky grew darkly ominous and flashes of lightning skittered through the air. It wasn't safe for me to walk under the trees or out on the beach. A storm was rapidly approaching, and once again, I'd made the unwise decision to come outside barefoot. I waited another minute for Alice to make an appearance, but no such luck. Time to go back inside and face the music.

The air changed. Something smelled . . . off. My hair felt tingly. Oh fuck. I sprinted to the porch steps and took them two at a time. I flung the door open and nearly threw myself inside, and it was then that I heard the strangest noise, like a gaggle of ghosts ripping invisible pieces of paper—the sizzly snapping sound filled my ears. A second later, the lightning hit.

22

"Are you trying to get yourself killed? What the hell, Sebastian Starling?" Alice's voice echoed through my head, along with the ringing caused by whatever meteor strike or gas explosion that'd just blasted through the backyard.

I blinked, but spots dotted my vision. "Alice?"

"It was just a lightning strike out on the beach."

I was shaken. "Am I on fire? Did it hit me?"

"If it'd hit you, I'd be roasting marshmallows on your hair. It struck out past the tree line." Alice ran her hands over my hair and my face, her fingers lingering on my nose and lips. "It would be a shame if this handsome face got damaged, *Sebastian*." Her heavy emphasis on my name didn't go unnoticed.

"I'm okay, right?"

"You're okay. That was loud and bright, but I don't think you were in any direct danger since you were on the porch."

I was relieved. Relieved that I was unharmed, and that Alice was talking to me. "I'm sorry for before. I was an ass."

"You, an ass? Impossible, *Sebastian*."

I had to let the name thing go, or she'd be doing that

forever. "I'd just gotten off the phone with Simon." My vision had cleared but my ears still felt weird.

"Let me get you some water before we talk about that." She disappeared into the house and came back with a glass of ice water.

"Is this tap water?"

"Don't look a gift horse in the mouth, Starling."

I sipped the water as she ran her fingers through my hair. Being tended to by Alice *almost* made my near-death experience worth it.

"You feeling better?" Alice asked when I finished my water, which tasted fine, even if it did come from the Caluska Island Municipal Water System.

"That just rattled me, that's all. I'm not used to beach storms like that."

"I should've come after you sooner. I knew the storm was getting close." As if to punctuate her sentence, another flash of lightning lit up the sky, followed by a clap of thunder so intense that it rattled the porch. The wind had picked up and I heard the patter of tiny raindrops slapping the trees.

"Let's go inside." I wanted to be away from that storm—no reason to give lightning another chance at me. Alice followed me in, and we settled on the living room couch.

"Do you want to talk about what happened with Simon?" she asked.

"He didn't approve of me changing the plans for Scarlet Oaks."

"Does he have to approve?"

"What do you mean? Do I care if he approves? Not really. But if he isn't supporting me, it's going to be hard to get this off the ground."

"No, I mean, does he have to approve for you to move forward? Does he have authority over you within the organization?" Alice had her hair down, and I had to resist the urge to gather up her curls in both of my hands and press my face into the softness.

I pondered her question for a moment. "Well, not technically. We're both listed as vice presidents, but in reality, he's—"

"You're a vice president?" She laughed and for some reason I didn't feel defensive. "Of what?"

"Sebastian Starling, Vice President of Special Projects."

"Oh dear."

"No kidding."

"But your dad has veto power, I assume." Alice scooted closer to me on the couch.

I put a hand on her knee. Just touching her made me feel calmer and more balanced. "Sure. But it's not like I'm trying to organize a coup. I just wanted to change the proposal for Scarlet Oaks, but the budget would be about the same."

"It would?" Alice asked. We'd talked over the basic plan at lunch, but not the numbers, which I'd run when she went in for her nap.

"Same ballpark."

"And who did you contact?"

"Simon, Cara, Jean, and Benny."

"Did you hear back from any of them?" she asked.

"I'd need to check my email."

"Here's your phone." She pulled my cell out of the back pocket of her shorts. "It had been buzzing and I was about to bring it out to you and crash your pity party, but the lightning got to you first."

I took it from her hand and let my fingers linger on hers for a second. The screen of my phone showed a few missed calls from Simon. I ignored them and checked my email. "Cara says she'll check with the planning and architecture people. No other replies."

"It's four o'clock."

"Yeah." It was getting late in the day. This wasn't going to happen, and I was a fool for thinking otherwise.

"Let me grab my phone." She hopped up from the couch, stretched, and went to her bedroom. All I could see was the memory of what she looked like naked in the shower and how perfect she felt under my hand as she slid herself against me until we both climaxed. How was I supposed to concentrate on work when she was in front of me? I could only play it cool for so long. This must've been one of the reasons it was so dangerous to mix business and pleasure. We were going to have to talk about this after we got our plan sorted.

She was back. "I'm going to call Lacy."

"Lacy?"

"She's my coworker. She'll get this sorted."

"How will someone from the clerical team get this sorted?"

Alice stared at me, and not in an admiring way. She took a deep breath as if she was about to explain an important lesson to an especially dense child. "Sebastian."

I was getting really tired of my own name. "Yes, Blaze?"

Alice rolled her eyes and continued with her speech. "If you're going to be Vice President of Special Projects, you need to understand exactly how those 'special projects'" (Alice used air quotes around the term) "are going to get done."

"Okay. How are my 'special projects'" (I also used air quotes) "going to get done?"

"Really?" Alice looked annoyed, and I felt like I'd missed a step in the process.

"Really what?"

"Sebastian," Alice said my name slowly and gave it four syllables instead of the usual three, "your admin staff."

"My admin staff?" I was still lost.

"Yes. Your admin staff is how you will make all your 'special projects' happen."

"I don't have any admin staff. I barely even have an office."

"Do you come into work very often?" Alice asked.

"Define often."

Another deep breath from Alice. "Perhaps we should define entitlement and nepotism first," she said.

"Hey!" But she wasn't wrong. It was my name that'd earned my title, not my hard work. I came to board meetings and helped with projects, but my time really running the business was minimal.

"There is an entire clerical pool at your beck and call. They are the engine of the entire organization, along with the Executive Assistants, the payroll department, and customer service."

"Not HR?" I teased.

"We don't speak about HR."

"Then it sounds like we need to call Lacy immediately."

"Maybe you have a brain cell in there after all," said Alice. She unlocked her phone screen, called Lacy, and put it on speakerphone. It rang once and then a woman's voice blasted through the speaker.

"Well, if it isn't the missing Ms. Goode. I haven't heard from you in days and I was beginning to think you were dead. How's life with the Starling sex god?"

"You're on speaker, Lacy."

"Fine by me. Let the world hear my proclamations!" Lacy said.

"Hi Lacy," I said.

"Who's that?" Lacy asked.

"Starling sex god, at your service."

"Alice!" Lacy squealed. "You should've warned me!"

"You didn't give me the chance, and you know it," Alice said.

"Good afternoon, Mr. Starling."

"You can call me Sebastian."

"Uh, good afternoon, Sebastian," Lacy squeaked.

"Lace, we need your help."

"Does this mean I can drop this copy job for marketing?"

"The Vice President of Special Projects needs your help, Lace," Alice said. "And we only have a few hours to make it happen."

"What can I do?" Lacy's enthusiasm rang out in her voice.

Alice gave Lacy a rundown of the project and what our goals were.

"I know all about this, and this is a great plan," Lacy told us.

"How do you know all about it?" I asked.

"I'm the one who put the project portfolio together for you. I can make a new portfolio with these adjustments and can easily change out some of the slides in the presentation. I'll check with Cara, and I think Benny and Jean are in a meeting together right now, so I can get them at the same time to get sign-off. One of the architecture interns can work on this tonight to get a quick mock-up rendering, and you should be good to go for a meeting tomorrow."

I must've been sitting there with my mouth hanging open because Alice took one look at me and burst out laughing.

"Thanks, Lacy. Text me or call if you need anything at all, no matter the time. And I'll send you Sebastian's number as well."

"Take me off speaker, Alice."

Alice turned off the speaker and put the phone to her ear. Lacy must've said something because Alice replied, "Yes, his actual personal cell." Another pause. "Yes, you can tell them that you have it, but don't tell them what his number is . . . ok, great. Thank you so much. Talk to you soon." Alice set her phone down on a side table, pulled a hair tie out of her pocket, and swept her hair back into a fluffy ponytail.

"I suppose all the VPs know about the power of the admins?" I asked her.

She put her legs across my lap, making it hard for me to concentrate. "Hardly."

"What do you mean? How can they work there full time and not utilize you and your coworkers?"

"Well, your cousin Simon does. How do you think he gets so much done and is so successful?"

"Right. Of course. Is he an asshole to everyone? Because he's usually one to me, but I still love him."

"No, not an asshole." Alice's shirt had shifted, and I caught a glimpse of the skin on her torso before she straightened the hem and covered back up. "But he's cold. Very down-to-business. Which is professional, I suppose, but everyone is scared of him."

"No one's scared of me." Not that I wanted them to be scared of me, but I didn't like the feeling that they were probably all laughing at me as the playboy airhead.

"They aren't scared of you, but they don't know you. Half of them want to date you. Including the guys."

"Are you part of that half?" My heart rate picked up a little. It didn't really matter, but I wanted her answer to be 'yes.'

"Honestly, you weren't my type."

My chest felt as if a few bees had stung my heart. "How so?"

"You seemed nice enough, but I usually go for the quieter, steady, boy-next-door type."

"You mean like Todd?"

Alice slapped my arm. "Not exactly like Todd. I think I'm just always trying to stay out of the spotlight, and you're in the spotlight—no, you are the spotlight. I didn't think I'd be comfortable in your company, no matter how handsome you are. I'm a little starstruck."

"Starstruck? I'm not a star."

"You're not a regular guy, either."

The fact that she thought I was better than a "regular guy" stroked my ego more than I wanted to admit. "But you're comfortable in my company now?" I asked.

"I am." She pulled a lock of hair out of her ponytail and stuck it in her mouth like she was nervous. "But I'm also not. Because, well. You know."

Maybe we could talk about it now. I stuck my toe in the waters of the conversation topic of *us*. "I'm not sure that I know. Could you elaborate?"

Alice blushed and she fiddled with that strand of hair. "I mean, I like you."

"And I like you," I offered.

"So, I get nervous."

"You didn't seem nervous when you asked me to get in the shower with you."

"Oh god!" Her face was now flaming red, and she brought up her hands to hide behind.

"Don't be embarrassed." I pulled her hands away from her face. "But should we talk about what we're doing here, so we're clear on what each of us wants?"

She tried to pull her hands back to cover her face again, but I held on to them, and she let me. "I don't know what came over me in the shower," she said.

"Well, I came over you—"

"Oh my god!" She ripped her hands out of my grip, drew up her knees, ducked her face behind her legs and covered the top of her head with her arms.

"Sorry, too soon?"

She laughed but remained hidden. After ten seconds she peeked out, and then straightened herself out. "Okay, I'm ready to talk about this like adults."

I had to tell her how I was feeling before I lost the nerve. "I liked what happened in the shower. And I'd like for that kind of thing to happen again. But we also work together, and right now, we're living together, so it's hard to know when it's time to be professional and when it's time to—" I searched for the words.

"—time to get off in the shower?" Alice finished my sentence for me.

"Jesus." Warmth rose in my cheeks.

"Sorry. Too soon?"

"Touché."

"Ok, so, I'd like to, uh, get to know you better, too," Alice said.

"Is that what we're calling it?"

She ignored me and kept talking. "So do you have any ideas on how to make this . . . less awkward?"

I didn't, really, not when we were still staying in the same house together. "Maybe we could assign the hours of eight to six as business hours. And after that, we can move into more personal territory, like we're dating."

"So, blue flag for when we're coworkers and green flag for when it's personal time?"

"Personal time makes it sound like we have to use the bathroom or masturbate in secret."

Alice whacked my arm again. "You know what I mean!"

I laughed, and it felt good to laugh with her. It felt easy. "Do we have any flags?"

"They'd have to be metaphorical flags," she said. "Wait! We might have flags!" She rolled off the couch and scrambled into the kitchen where I heard her rummaging around the pantry. She returned a minute later with sparkly mini flags on poles and pedestals, like they were table decorations.

"Are those—"

"Yes," Alice said, as she shook the pink and purple party favors, "the purple flags are little penises, and the pink ones seem to be glittery vulvas."

"Wow."

"I know."

"So, which one is work time, and which one is play time."

"The penis is work time, for sure," she said.

"Fair enough."

"So, which one?" she asked. "Are we having penis time or vulva time?"

"If someone is listening in to this conversation, we're never going to live it down."

"Good thing no one's listening!"

"While we're waiting for Lacy to work her magic, I suppose it's personal time."

"Great, pink pussy it is!" She shook the flag and specks of glitter fluttered down and landed on her lips. She lowered the purple penis flag on its pole, kept the pink flag raised, and set them both on the coffee table.

"Since it's still personal time, there's something else I'd like to ask you about."

Alice sat back down on the couch, but closer to me, since the pink flag was up. "Sure, what do you want to talk about?"

"You have glitter on your lips." I brushed my fingertip across her mouth and a few shiny specks stuck to my skin. I showed her.

Alice's fingers flew to her lips. "How did that happen?"

"The flag."

"Oh!" She rubbed her lips but I pulled her hand away from her face.

"Leave it. I like it."

Alice tried to keep her face neutral, but I could see a smile threatening to break through. "Is that what you wanted to talk about? The glitter on my lips?"

"No. I'd like to talk about your hair."

23

ALICE

It was a simple sentence, but it took me out at the knees. Nausea rushed over me, I felt woozy, and I started to sweat. *Don't touch it, don't touch it,* I commanded myself, but I disobeyed, and my hands flew to my head and started plucking sections out of my ponytail. Maybe there was just glitter in my hair, too. "What do you mean, you want to talk about my hair?" *Play it cool, Alice.*

Sebastian just watched me. He tilted his head and observed my hands scurry around my scalp like frantic spiders. His brows furrowed and his perfect mouth tilted into a frown.

Shit, I was going to have a panic attack if I kept sitting here. "Want some food? You nearly died an hour ago." I tried to stand up, but Sebastian gently grasped my wrists.

"We don't have to talk about anything you don't want to, Alice. I can see that this stresses you out. I didn't mean to make you uncomfortable." He let go of me.

I slumped back onto the couch and the beginning of tears stung my eyes. "It's a long story," I said, hoping that he didn't have the patience for it.

"That's ok. I'll listen to whatever you have to say."

I took a giant breath and exhaled slowly. I knew my hair was a sore spot, but I'd never told anyone the story of it all, not even myself, really. In my mind, it was just a series of snapshots and feelings that came together to make me insecure and anxious. I'd never constructed a complete narrative about it before. "I don't know where to start." That was the truth. I didn't know how to begin—I couldn't find an entry point.

"How about I ask you some questions, and you answer if you can. We'll see how far we get."

"Okay." My voice was shaky, and my tears were almost on the surface.

Sebastian held my hand, which settled my stomach and evened out my pulse. "What was your hair like when you were little?" he asked me.

A laugh chased away my looming tears. "I was bald for the first year of my life! Apparently, my parents were getting worried that I'd just stay bald, but after I turned one, little red sprouts popped out. By the time I was two I had the most beautiful curls. I guess people used to stop my mom all the time to comment on our hair—hers was red, too, but not as curly."

"I bet you were the cutest baby."

"I was pretty damn adorable." The memories felt good. Or, the stories about the memories—I didn't actually remember that time, but there were photos, and those had become my fill-ins for actual remembering.

"And when you were a bigger kid? Did you like your hair?" Sebastian asked.

"I loved it. I saw it as a connection to my mother. She was gone, but I had her red hair, and it felt like it gave me a superpower."

"When did things change for you?"

This was harder. I knew when they'd changed, but did I want to talk about it? Not really, but I'd try. "It changed here, on the island. With Tristan."

"Did she not like your hair?" Sebastian trailed his fingernails up and down my arm as rain beat down on the roof of the cottage.

"She liked it. A little too much. She was jealous, I realize now. She had straight brown hair that, by the time we were teenagers, I envied. It was so smooth. So regular."

"The grass is always greener kind of thing?"

"Exactly. Tristan and I became friends, but in retrospect, we were more like frenemies."

"I can't see Tristan Tabor being anything but a frenemy to someone, and I only met her yesterday," Sebastian said.

"It was manageable until Graham."

"Who's Graham? Should I be jealous?"

"He was a boy who came to live with his aunt and uncle for a year here on Caluska. All the girls had a crush on him. He was fresh meat. And he was hot."

"Ok, I'm jealous."

I raised and lowered my shoulders and stretched my neck from side to side. The story was getting to the part that made me tense up. "He liked me. And Tristan didn't like that. She told me he'd told her that he liked her better than me, because my hair was too crazy. Hers was prettier. I didn't believe her, exactly, but I was insecure. So, we wrote him a note and gave it to him in History, which was the last class of the day. We wrote that if he wanted to go out with me, he should meet me at Tidal Point, and if he wanted to choose Tristan, he should go to Bay Cove. At 9:00 that night."

"This sounds awful," Sebastian said. "This isn't going to end well, is it?"

"Do you want me to tell you the story as I experienced it, or just an overview of what actually happened, as I came to know when it was all over."

"It's that bad?"

"It's not great."

"Then tell me as it felt to you at the time." He adjusted his legs and folded them under himself. He let go of my hand, propped up his arms on his legs, and rested his chin on the back of his interlaced fingers.

"It was an exercise in masochism. Two sixteen-year-olds fighting for the attention of the same guy, but I'm not sure it was ever about him. I think we were more interested in showing each other up. We even got ready together at her house."

"That's fucked up."

"I know. Tristan said that she had to shower first, because she had to blow-dry her hair, and mine would just air dry because it was curly. She showered, dried her hair, and then she got dressed really quickly and left while I was still in the shower. Her parents were gone for the weekend, so when she left, I was alone in the house."

"Showering in someone else's house when everyone is gone is super creepy."

"It was. I was freaked out." I took a deep breath. A drink would be nice. No, I could keep going. Sober. "I used the shampoo she left me, and then used my own conditioner. But something was wrong." My voice wobbled and Sebastian put his hand on my leg.

"What do you mean?"

"My hair felt weird. Like stiff. Gloopy. All stuck together.

Like I couldn't rinse anything out. After ten minutes in the shower, I finally got out and my hair just felt like straw. It was flat and brittle, and it smelled weird."

"Oh fuck."

"And it was 8:30. I didn't know what to do. I found a baseball hat and put it on, but it didn't go with my dress. I felt ridiculous. I just started crying, so my eyes got all swollen and I didn't have time for make-up, and it was going to take me fifteen minutes to walk to Tidal Point, but I wasn't sure I even wanted Graham to pick me anymore because I looked so awful. But I also didn't want to stand him up, and I didn't want Tristan to win. So I went out. I was running late. I tried to jog, but it was dark and I just had these sandals on, and I was still crying. It was ten minutes after nine when I arrived at the spot, and of course, no one was there. I stood for a few minutes and then sat down and just cried some more. Then I heard a sound coming from out on the water. And I saw Tristan on her dad's little motorboat, and Graham was with her. She had her arm around his shoulder, and they puttered on by and headed toward the cove, and that was that. She'd won."

"I'm sorry. That sounds like an awful night."

"It was bad. But it was worse when my hair started falling out the next day. Tristan had put a chemical relaxer in the shampoo bottle, and it destroyed a lot of my hair. I had to cut it all off, and—" I couldn't finish the sentence, but I didn't have to.

Sebastian gathered me up in his arms. "That fucking bitch. I'm going to kill her." He held me while I let go. Let go of the tears I'd been holding back and all those old emotions I'd kept bottled up for years. I cried for several minutes, which was a release and a relief. Sebastian rubbed my back and murmured softly in my ear. But he didn't say things like "you're ok" or "I'm so sorry." He had a much more amusing repertoire of things like "She'll rue the day she ever messed with you; I'm going to put Nair in her shampoo bottle; She's going to wake up to a horse's head in her bed; Tristan Tabor sleeps with the fishes."

"I appreciate the sentiment, but she's not worth your trouble," I said.

"It's no trouble. I'm going to make her an offer she can't refuse," he grumbled.

"I like you in your Godfather era."

"I need to speak with this Graham dude, though. What a dumbass, choosing Tristan over you." Sebastian slowly pulled out my hair tie and rubbed my head as my hair let loose.

"That's the twist in the story. He wanted to choose me."

"But he was in the boat with Tristan the Terrible!"

"Tristan knew he would probably choose me, and she figured I'd be a no-show with the hair thing. So, she parked her dad's boat at a pier right by Tidal Point. When Graham arrived, he was even five minutes early, she told him I wasn't going to show up and that I was busy hooking up with another guy from our class. She offered to give him a ride home in the boat."

"But surely he found out later what'd happened?"

"I guess he did. But he left soon after. I finished out that last month of school hiding out at home. That's actually when I got to know Mr. Blake really well. He'd come over to play chess with my grandfather every day at noon, and I'd hang out with them while they played. Anyway, Graham left when the school year ended, and I never saw him again. I transferred to a high school on the mainland the next year and lived with some family friends for my junior and senior years."

"And your hair?"

"It grew back. Took a while. But I suppose I never let it fly free much after that. I just had a different relationship with it."

"Did Tristan get punished?"

"Her parents sent her away to an all-girls school for her last two years. So, kind of." My phone vibrated and I grabbed it, ready for a break from all things hair. It was a text from Lacy and I read it aloud to Sebastian. "Green light from all the teams, have a special crew working on this now. I'll text once I email it over, should be a couple of hours."

"I don't even know what to say."

"Telling the team 'thank you' is a good place to start."

"Ok, can you take a video of me?"

"Why?" I asked.

"I'm going to say thank you! Keep up, Goode."

I opened my camera app, focused on Sebastian, and hit record. I gave him a thumbs up to let him know I was recording.

Sebastian leaned forward so he was closer to the camera, dropped his chin, and tilted his head just slightly to the left. He'd transformed from a handsome guy whom I'd like to kiss again very soon, into a goddamn masterpiece, just with a tilt of the head. I wasn't sure I wanted to know how long he'd worked to master that perfect camera presence, but wow, the results were spectacular. "This is a note for Lacy, and all the other employees who've stayed late tonight to help Alice and me with this project. You've gone above and beyond already, and I want you to know that any success we have here with the Caluska Island project will be due to you and your creativity, drive, and generosity. If we get this account, it's your victory. Thank you so much for helping us tonight." Sebastian squinted his eyes slightly and gave a gentle nod before I stopped recording.

"Are you sure you don't want to quit this job and audition for a leading role in a soap opera? You've got the smoldering good looks and you're already camera-ready."

"That's my Plan B. Did you send it?"

I texted the video to Lacy and put my phone on the table. "Sent."

"Hungry?" Sebastian asked?

"Starving."

THIRTY MINUTES LATER, we were back on the couch with food spread out on the coffee table in front of us. We'd found a buffalo chicken pizza in the freezer, and while that cooked, Sebastian made a salad and I washed some purple and green grapes and plopped them in a bowl. Sebastian wanted to eat in the kitchen, but I wanted to watch a movie.

"We can watch the movie when we're done eating," he suggested as he pulled two plates out of the cabinet.

"But the whole fun of it is watching while we eat! Don't you do that?"

"Not very often. I might spill something on my clothes."

"It's a risk you're just going to have to take tonight, Mr. Starling."

"You win." He carried plates and napkins into the living room and turned on the TV. "I can log in to my streaming account. What kind of movies do you like to watch?"

"Romantic comedies. But I just finished my Meg Ryan marathon, so those are out. Lacy and I have a few more movies to finish in our Hugh Grant series, she's British, so I have to watch those with her. What do you like to watch?"

"Horror or—"

"I can do slashers sometimes, but can we skip those tonight? I'd rather have warm-and-cozy than a faces-ripped-off vibe."

"What about a mash-up? I hear the Hallmark Channel has a remake of the *Texas Chainsaw Massacre*."

"Maybe next time," I said. "So what were you going to say after 'horror?'" I snuggled into the couch and put a piece of pizza on my plate.

"Drama. I usually watch dramas."

"What about a romantic drama then?"

"What's an example of a romantic drama?"

"Google it." I bit into my pizza while Sebastian pulled out his phone and typed a question in his browser.

"Ok," he scrolled through a list that had popped up in his search, "at the top of the list we have *The Notebook*."

"Nope. Too depressing. Next."

"*45 Years*?"

"That's the one with the older woman who finds out some of her husband's secrets on their 45th anniversary. Also too depressing. But it's a good movie."

"*Phantom Thread*?" Sebastian suggested.

"Is this a list of 'Top Twenty Romantic Tragedies That Will Make You Wish You'd Never Fallen in Love in the First Place?' Try a new list, Baz."

"Your wish is my command."

"I don't know that one."

"No, I literally meant that your wish was my command."

"Oh, excellent!" I nabbed a second slice of pizza.

"Slow down on that, I haven't had one yet!"

"Not my problem."

"I guess *Brokeback Mountain is* out of the running."

"You'd be correct."

"What about something in Linklater's *Before* trilogy?"

"Yes! That's perfect! Have you seen them?"

"I've seen the first two," he said.

"Let's start at the beginning with *Before Sunrise*," I said. "Then we can watch the next two on some other nights."

Sebastian stared at me.

"Do I have something on my face?" I patted my lips and cheeks, but the coast seemed clear.

He didn't answer, but he sat down on the couch next to me, so close that our legs were touching. He took the pizza out of my hand and put it back on my plate on the coffee table.

"Hey—" but before I could protest any further, he kissed me. Softly at first, and then he pressed his lips into mine with more force, opening his mouth so he could taste me. He pressed his strong palm into the back of my head to bring me closer and suddenly, the movie didn't matter, the pizza didn't matter, and even the storm and the story of my hair didn't matter. All that mattered was the kiss. Sebastian's beard was rubbing against my cheek, his eyelashes fluttered against mine, and his lips made my own lips tingle in a way that was nothing short of magical.

And just as quickly as he'd started kissing me, he stopped. He smiled at me, grabbed my hand, kissed it, and then retrieved my slice of pizza and handed it to me.

"What was that for?" I was still hungry, but now I craved him more than I craved any of the food in front of us.

"That was for saying that there'd be a second movie night for us. And maybe a third." He got his own slice of pizza and took a giant bite. "Ready to watch?"

24

Ninety minutes later, I had no feeling in my right arm and my leg was tingly and cramping. Alice had fallen asleep on me. Literally. She'd scarfed down more than her fair share of the pizza, plus salad, and most of the grapes. Then she tipped over into my lap, and I had zero objections. I couldn't reach the remote control without jostling her, so I was finishing the movie on my own. Watching Céline and Jesse on screen, discussing whether or not they'll ever see each other again, I was overtaken by a sense of melancholy.

This was a movie, but it hit home, because it wasn't far-fetched—it was reality. You had those moments where time stops and something magical happens, and then it's over and you go back to real life. You spend the rest of your life wondering "what if?" I didn't want Alice to be a "what if?" I wanted to watch *Before Sunset* with her, and then watch *Before Midnight*, and I didn't want our time on the island to be some distant memory that I revisited every time I got drunk and nostalgic.

My phone buzzed. Luckily, it was within reach, and I picked it up and saw a text from Lacy on the screen.

> LACY: This is Lacy. Everything's been sent to your email. We'll be on call tomorrow if you need any changes. Good luck!

> SEBASTIAN: Much appreciated. Thank you again.

I texted with my left hand, put my phone down, and then pulled my right arm out from under Alice. It was almost totally numb, but after a minute the tingling came, and it was so unpleasant I almost wished I'd kept it underneath her for an eternity. I moaned as my arm sparked back to life.

"You ok?" Alice popped up, bleary eyed and puffy-haired, and somehow she was still a vision of beauty.

"Just trying to decide if I should amputate my arm or ride out the pain."

"What happened?" She poked my arm which caused me to yelp.

"*You* happened!"

She reached out to grab my arm and inspect it, but I yelped again.

"No touching the arm! It's been dead for a half hour and is in its rebirth cycle."

"Oh no! Céline and Jesse are at the train station! I fell asleep."

"You and my arm both."

"I'm sorry." She sat up slowly and carefully avoided contact with my arm.

"It was worth it. You smell pretty nice." She did. I could've spent all night with my nose in her hair, breathing in the aroma of spiced cotton candy and magnolias.

"It's all that tropical conditioner you put in my hair."

"Then why doesn't my hair smell as good as yours?"

"Because you can't smell your own hair. And I think your brush with death gave you more of the 'campfire musk' vibe."

I grabbed at my hair and tried to sniff it. "Do I smell like I caught on fire?" Maybe I needed to get checked out by a doctor.

Alice giggled and leaned over to sniff my hair. Her face was so close to mine. "Hmm." She inhaled deeply. "I'm getting notes of . . . mesquite matchstick?"

"Shit, really?" My arm had mostly stopped with its tingle torture, and I could use it again. I rubbed both my palms on my hair and sniffed them. Tropical flowers. "You little liar!" I captured Alice in my arms and tickled her ribs.

She squealed like I'd just electrocuted her. "Uncle! I give up! I'm about to pee my pants!"

I released her and she dashed to the bathroom. I turned off the TV, gathered our dishes, and toted them to the kitchen. I was rinsing off a plate when Alice came up behind me and ran her hands up my back.

"Leave those for tomorrow," she said.

"They'll be gross in the morning."

"Sebastian." She wrapped her arms around my waist.

I turned off the water. "There's only a few dishes."

"Turn around."

I started to turn but before I was even fully facing Alice, she put her hands on either side of my face and started to kiss me.

"Oh hey," I said when I came up for air a few moments later. "What's this about?"

"I don't want you to do the dishes."

"You seem to have an adverse reaction to housework," I teased.

"Come to bed with me." Alice's cheeks were pink and her lips were full and soft.

I wanted to go to bed with her, whether it was to sleep, or to do other things. But I didn't want to rush her. I didn't want her to regret this in the morning. "Maybe we shouldn't."

"Maybe we should," she said. "I mean, maybe we already have."

"I just don't want to move too fast—"

"It's fine if you don't want to." Alice let go of me and marched off with such rapid intensity that I almost lost my balance.

"Alice, I want to!" My voice sounded needy and pitiful. I had no idea how to act when the woman in my life actually mattered to me. You'd think it would be easier this way, but for some reason it was exponentially harder. Her bedroom door slammed shut. Fuck. I wanted to go after her, but I didn't want to be that dick who pushed himself into a woman's presence when she wanted to be alone. And speaking of dicks, mine had heard the news that an invitation had been issued and it was at full attention.

I turned back to the sink and yanked the faucet handle. When the water ran hot, I put my hand underneath, almost scalding myself. I washed off a dish while castigating myself. *You're so fucking stupid, Sebastian. You're ordinary and cowardly, and you're only good as a plaything, not a real lover. Let someone else have Alice. Someone better. You're a loser.*

I was used to this kind of self-talk. It was how I punished myself. Kept myself in line. But something was different this time. I kept hearing Alice's voice in my head. What would Alice say if she heard me say those things out loud? Maybe she'd say: *you're not stupid. You're special. You're good. You're enough.* I turned off the water and dried my hands. Fuck it. Tonight, I wasn't going to listen to that shit voice in my head. I'd take a chance and listen to the one that sounded like Alice, instead.

I tossed the dish towel on the counter and strode to Alice's bedroom door. I knocked twice. "Alice?" I waited a few seconds. No answer. "Alice." A statement this time. Not a question. Still no answer. I turned the handle. Locked.

I had three viable options:

1. Keep knocking politely and hope she answers.

2. Respect her silence and walk away.

2.5. Break down the door (that didn't seem like the best idea in a rental, and that might come off as violent and aggressive.) I decided to go with

3. The direct approach.

I pounded three times on the door with my fist. "Alice Goode. Open this door, now. I'm counting to three, and if it isn't open then, I'm breaking it down." I made sure my voice was loud, clear, and commanding. And I wasn't really going to break down the door, so I hoped she wouldn't call my bluff.

I heard some movement in her room, but Alice didn't say anything, and the handle stayed still. "One." I'd give her five seconds between each number. *One-Mississippi. Two-Mississippi. Three-Mississippi. Four-Mississippi. Five-Mississippi.* "Two." Christ, I was going to look like an idiot when I didn't break the door down. I started the Mississippi counting again, but the handle remained locked. "Three!" I said with as much authority as I could muster. "Stand back, Alice! I'm coming in!" I took a few steps back, not knowing what the hell I was actually going to do when I got to five-Mississippi.

"Fine!" Alice huffed as she swung the door open.

Bingo. I rushed forward and scooped her up into my arms.

"What are you doing?" she squealed.

"I'm taking you to bed." I carried her to the bed and softly tossed her onto it, hoping she was into this, because if I gambled wrong, I could fuck up this whole thing.

She was wearing a nightgown. Cream colored and silky with spaghetti straps, it reached to her mid-thighs but was hiked up because of how I'd manhandled her. She stared at me, her mouth slightly open and her chest rising and falling quickly with each breath. Finally, she spoke. Just one word. "Okay."

I leapt onto the bed, landing in a straddle over her torso. I gathered her wrists in my fist and raised her arms above her head. I positioned my mouth next to her ear and whispered, "I'm only going to say this once: If you want me to stop, say 'stop' at any time. But if I don't hear that." I paused to nip her earlobe with my teeth, "I'm going to do whatever I want to do. Okay?"

"Yes, Sebastian," she whimpered. "Yes. Please."

God. She'd said yes. I wanted to do all kinds of things to her, but I hadn't dared to dream that she'd let me. I held my position until my breathing evened out. I had to slow down. Still straddling her, I let go of her wrists, sat up, and leaned back to get a better look at her.

Alice's hair spread out on the bed and her red curls formed a fiery frame around her head. One strap of her nightgown had slipped off her shoulder, leaving the top of her breast exposed. She held my gaze. She didn't look nervous, or tentative, or apprehensive. She looked ready.

I pinched the hem of her nightgown between my fingers and pushed it up. Past her thighs, over her hips, and up her stomach. She wasn't wearing underwear. I paused to kiss her belly button before continuing to push the nightgown up until it was bunched up by her collarbone, leaving her breasts on full display. I hadn't touched her, beyond repositioning her nightgown, and she hadn't touched me, but I was so aroused that if I were to plunge into her right then, I'd probably only last a few seconds before exploding.

I took one of her arms in my hand and stretched it out to the side, and then did the same with her other arm. I slid off the end of the bed and moved her ankles apart until she was spread eagle on the bed in front of me.

Her body. I'd never seen anything like it, in the flesh. She was all curve, all fullness, all rounded edges and softness. Alice was pure beauty, and I wanted to disappear inside her until the end of time. "You're spectacular," I told her.

"Am I?" Her voice was full and raspy.

"What did I do to deserve you?" I trailed my finger along the inside of her calf, down her ankle, and across her foot.

Alice, probably feeling the tickle of my touch, wiggled her foot and tried to escape my finger.

"Did I say you could move?"

"No, you didn't." Alice replied.

I spread her legs further apart so she was more open to me. She gasped. The light in the room was dim, but I could still see her. All of her. I crawled back on the bed, slowly, advancing between her legs. Alice whimpered as my face got closer to her hot center. When I was inches away, I pushed her thighs open even farther, so she fully unfolded before me.

"Your pussy is gorgeous," I told her. Her folds and ruffles waited for me, warm and glistening. I tapped my tongue against her skin and she jolted. I tasted her again, just for a second, causing her to moan loudly. I knelt between her legs and put a hand on either side of her mound, exposing her sensitive swollen nub. Making my tongue soft and loose, I pressed it up against her clit and pulsed.

"Oh my god," she panted.

I pulled back and attacked again, this time catching her clit between my lips and holding it there while flicking the tip of my tongue against her most sensitive spot. She tried to close her legs around my head but I pushed them open and held them there and let my mouth do all the work on her pussy. I went between teasing her clit and pushing into her entrance, until she was writhing and bucking against my face. "Do you want to come, Alice?"

She was so wet that I was covered in her juices and I would've happily stayed there for hours, if she'd let me. "Please," she groaned. "I want to come. Make me come."

I pulled my hands away from her thighs, giving her control again, but she kept her legs spread for me. I slid two fingers inside her while I worked her clit with my mouth and my other hand. It was overkill, but I wanted her to come harder than she'd ever come in her life. She gyrated and squirmed and shivered and thrust her pelvis, but I kept contact with her. She couldn't escape me. She lifted her pelvis, and I slid my hands under her ass and lifted her more until her hips were in the air and her pussy was raised toward my face. Her breasts tilted toward her neck, and she cried out as she came, and came, and came. She was perfection.

Her cries of pleasure quieted, but I noticed she was shaking. I released her hips and lowered her back onto the bed, and she was making noise again. She was crying. Shit.

"Are you ok, Alice? Did I hurt you?" I put my face next to

hers and she turned her head so I couldn't see her tears. I gathered her into my arms and pulled her body against mine. I was still so hard that my dick was nearly throbbing, but I forgot about that when I heard her cry. Wait. Was she laughing? Was she crying *and* laughing?

"You didn't hurt me," she said, when she found her voice. "That was the most amazing thing I'd ever felt. It was just too amazing, I guess. I don't know what happened. The tears just came out of nowhere. Which was also funny. And embarrassing. God."

"You're not embarrassing," I told her. "You're perfect. That was an amazing experience for me, too."

She rolled over to face me and her breasts pressed into my chest. Ok, I was over the crying and was back to my throbbing cock. God, I wanted her. She must've read my mind because she wiggled her hand between us and wrapped her hand around my shaft. It was my turn to moan. Alice squeezed my dick and started to tug at it, stroking me in an up and down motion.

"Alice." I said, though my words came out choked.

"Sebastian." She said back. Her eyes were clear and sparkling and her lips were arranged in a naughty smile.

"If you do that for much longer, I'm just going to come. I'm too turned on." I tried to pull away from her hand, but she had a firm grip on my dick.

"What a shame that would be." She kissed me and started to work my dick more quickly.

"Alice, I can't—"

"Do you like me jerking you off, Sebastian? My pussy was so wet when you fucked me with your fingers. Did that turn you on?"

Fuck. I couldn't escape her hand and the pressure was

building. Then I thought about how it felt to have my fingers inside her and my balls tightened, and heat bloomed from my stomach and my cock spasmed in Alice's hand as she milked me until the rush of my climax overtook me and I'd covered her belly in cum. I dug my nails into her arm as I rode the waves of my orgasm, and she stroked me until I was so sensitive I almost begged her to stop.

"That was so fucking hot," she whispered as she released her grip on me and aftershocks rippled through my body.

I felt totally vulnerable and at her mercy. I slowly returned to consciousness as I recovered from her touch. "I can't believe I just lost it like that."

"I'm just glad I'm not the only one who gave it up too easily," she teased.

"You really manhandled me." I nuzzled my face into her neck. "Are you proud of yourself?"

"Very." She raked her fingers through my hair, which sent goosebumps out in waves across my body. "But I have some bad news for you, Mr. Starling."

"What's that?" I couldn't imagine anything bad after all this good.

"I think we're going to have to take another shower."

25

ALICE

The purple penis was flying high when I walked into the kitchen the next morning. Sebastian was frying up some potatoes and had a container of eggs open on the counter. He smiled when he saw me.

"Want any juice? We've got orange, grapefruit, and cranberry."

"Just coffee, please. And what are you wearing?"

"Oh, this old thing?" Sebastian swiveled his hips left and then swung them the other way so I could appreciate all angles of the apron he was wearing, which had a drawing of a rooster along with the quote "EXPERIENCED COCK HANDLER."

"Is that appropriate attire for 'work time?'" I nodded toward the purple penis flag.

"Work time is about actions, not wardrobe." He smacked an egg against the counter and dropped the yolk and white into a waiting bowl.

"So, you're ok if I eat breakfast in the nude, then?" I slipped my robe off one shoulder.

"No shirt, no service. Wouldn't want any hot coffee to drip on those beautiful breasts, would we?"

I blushed and didn't even try to hide it. "Work time" wasn't getting off to a great start. "I think we've already violated the professional conduct code." I reached out to accept the cup of coffee he handed me. How someone could look so perfect in the morning was a mystery to me. Sebastian's hair fell in perfect waves, with the longest part at the back almost touching his collar. His eyes were bright, his skin somehow tanned for a city boy who hated being out in the heat, and his ass was spectacularly featured in the shorts he was wearing.

"That's your fault," he scolded. "I'm just in here making my lady some breakfast."

My stomach swooped. *My lady.* He'd just called me *his lady.* And even though it seemed completely surreal, he felt a bit like . . . my man. I sipped my coffee as I thought back to last night. How he'd tossed me on the bed and given me the most intense orgasm of my life. And our warm shower after, followed by me falling fast asleep in his arms. But because any woman would be a fool to take such perfection at face value, I had to ask myself: was it *too* perfect? Was I just his island hook-up? And did he know how to touch me like that because he'd touched a hundred women before me? My stomach swooped again, but this time in a way that made me feel nauseous.

"Hungry?" Sebastian slid a plate of food in front of me.

The image of Sebastian with another woman had made me lose my appetite. "After I finish my coffee."

"Egg-cellent." Sebastian sat down at the table with his own plate piled high with scrambled eggs and fried potatoes. "We're good to go for the meeting with Eddie this afternoon. I'm nervous, but I think he'll like what we're bringing to the table."

"What *you're* bringing." I poked at the eggs. Nope. Wasn't ready to eat yet.

"We've both worked on this," he protested. "Not to mention a good portion of the clerical team, architecture, planning—"

I interrupted him. "That's true. But I think you should be the one to propose it to Mr. Blake. I'll be there, but you do the talking."

"I thought we would both do it."

I sipped my coffee. It was strong, and I was grateful. "We can, but I think this would be a good time for you to practice going solo."

Sebastian stabbed a potato with his fork and popped it into his mouth. "Is this a 'push the baby bird out of the nest' kind of thing? Because I know how to fly—I just like having you there with me."

"I'll be there as back-up."

"But—" Sebastian's protest was cut off by the buzzing of my phone.

I glanced at the display to see who was calling. I'd assumed it was Lacy. It was not Lacy.

Sebastian must've noticed a weird expression on my face. "Who's that? Is it your lover calling?" He'd pronounced lover as "luv-ah" as he batted his eyelashes at me.

"It's Todd."

Sebastian's hand stopped halfway between his plate and his mouth, and his forkful of food hovered in the air. "*Your* Todd?"

"He's not *my* Todd. We just went out a few times!" I hissed. The phone kept buzzing.

Sebastian put his fork down and crossed his arms. "You should probably get that."

I cleared my throat and accepted the call. "This is Alice." That greeting was idiotic, but I wanted to sound professional and not like this was a personal call. But for all I knew, it *was* a personal call. Shit.

"Hey there, Alice. It's Todd."

"Hey, Todd." I was trying to sound calm, but Sebastian was on to me.

"*Hey, Todd,*" Sebastian mimed, silently mocking me.

"*Stop it!*" I mouthed.

"*Speaker phone!*" Sebastian mouthed back.

"How are you?" Todd asked. "It's been a while."

"Yes, it has." I didn't want to launch him onto speakerphone until I knew why he was calling.

"Anyway, I'm calling this morning because," he cleared his throat—either we were all uncomfortable, or there were some invasive allergies all up and down the Eastern Seaboard— "I've received a note that you and a colleague would like to start the process of declaring a personal relationship to Human Resources."

Time for speakerphone. "Yes, that's correct. I have you on speaker now, and I'm here with Sebastian Starling."

"Hey, Todd," Sebastian said out loud, and the tone of it was so ridiculous that I threw a chunk of eggs at him, which he dodged.

"Oh, hello Mr. Starling." More throat clearing for poor Todd. "This means one less phone call I have to make this morning!"

"Fewer." Sebastian went back to eating his breakfast.

"Pardon me?"

"One *fewer* phone call you need to make."

"*Stop it!*" I mouthed again.

"Right. That's what I said." Todd continued, "I'll email both of you some forms to fill out, and when you're back in town, we can schedule a meeting."

"That sounds perfect, *Todd*," Sebastian crooned.

"Thanks, Todd. We appreciate the call." I glared at Sebastian, but he ignored me.

"Sure. No problem. Have a great day."

"Ciao, *Todd!*" Sebastian called out.

"Um. Ciao, Mr. Starling."

I ended the call. "You're awful, Baz!"

"Not as awful as *Todd*. And also, I figured out why you can't call me Baz."

"Do tell, Mr. Starling." My eggs had gone cold, so I ate a bite of potatoes instead.

"I realized when I was watching the movie last night as you snored on my chest—"

"I do not snore."

"You sure about that?"

No, I wasn't. Did I snore on Sebastian Starling's perfect chest? "Yep," I lied.

"Anyway, as you slept away the second half of the film, I was thinking about movies and directors, and I thought of Baz Luhrmann." Sebastian stopped talking and stared at me like he was done making his point.

"Go on."

Sebastian threw his hands in the air. "There's nothing else to say! You can't call me the same name as that guy."

"Why not? He made *Strictly Ballroom* and *Romeo + Juliet*."

"But he also made *Moulin Rouge*—"

"If you say one bad thing about Ewan McGregor, we're

done here." I tried to brandish my fork in a way that looked threatening.

"Fine, forget *Moulin Rouge*. But someone has to answer for *The Great Gatsby* and *Elvis*. And he's done weird things to his face. I'm sorry, I just can't stand for it." Sebastian looked serious.

"What about *Australia*?"

"The land down under? What about it?"

"No, the movie!" I said.

"Haven't seen it, don't want to. Is it a musical? Singing kangaroos and all that?"

"No! It has Hugh Jackman and Nicole Kidman, and it's an epic set in—"

"Wait. Let me guess. Australia?"

"Sebastian," I sighed.

"See? So much better than Baz. Let Mr. Aussie have that one all to himself."

"Fine, Bazzy. If you insist."

Sebastian set down his fork again and pushed back from the table. "We just went from bad to worse, didn't we?"

"Be careful what you ask for, Bazzy."

"I'm going to ignore you every time you call me that, Blaze."

"Blaze and Bazzy. We sound like a bunch of lunatics."

"Anything's better than 'Todd.'"

He had a point. "Ok, he who shall not be named, is it purple penis time?"

"Let me clean these dishes and then I'm going to review the stuff Lacy sent last night."

I was not going to argue with a man who kept volunteering to do the dishes. "Do you mind if I go for a quick walk? I love to go down to the beach in the mornings. Then I'll come back and look over everything with you."

"Fine by me. Just wear shoes." I loved that he was watching out for my feet. I carried my plate to the counter and suddenly Sebastian grabbed me from behind. He lifted up my ponytail, planted a kiss on my neck, and then let go of me and went right back to stacking dishes in the sink. I walked out the back door feeling like I was floating.

THE STORMS from the night before had passed and the surf languidly lapped the shoreline. I took my shoes off to walk on the water's edge, but I watched to make sure I didn't step on anything sharp. It turned out I didn't have to worry. Besides seaweed, some driftwood, and a few shells, my path was unobstructed. I walked about half a mile and then turned around to walk back to the cottage. Nothing cleared my head like a good walk by the ocean.

There were a few people out walking and we just nodded at each other as we passed, none of us wanting to disturb each other's peace. This was a sacred time, and we all knew it. A young woman jogged past me and an older couple walked further up on the sand, holding hands. I had the cottage in sight when a man heading the opposite direction gave me the standard nod and closed-mouth smile, and then a "good morning." I did the nod/smile/greet back to him and headed up toward the fluffier sand to put my shoes back on. I should've been more focused on the presentation for Mr. Blake today, but everything felt dreamy and strange and it was like I was a different person than I'd been a week ago, and honestly, I liked this new me.

"Alice?" A man's voice called from behind me. "Alice Goode?"

I turned around to see the man I'd passed a minute earlier. He wore a baseball hat, a Wilco t-shirt, shorts, and was carrying sneakers in his hand. "Yes?" I didn't recognize him, but he seemed to know me.

"I thought that looked like you! I'd recognize that red hair anywhere! It's nice to see you." He took a few steps toward me, and I searched his face for familiar features, but was still coming up blank. "Oh shit, you probably don't recognize me. I'm sorry!" He took his hat off and then I knew who he was. There was no mistaking it. "It's me, Graham."

26

SEBASTIAN

Alice was talking to a man.

I'd gone out to the porch with my coffee after reviewing a few documents and watched the walkers until I saw Alice in the distance. She was wearing white linen pants with blue pinstripes. They were flowy in the legs but nice and snug on her ass, which I appreciated. Her white sweater topped some kind of linen tank top, and she'd gone out with sandals, but was now barefoot from what I could see—naughty girl.

I'd missed her while she was on her walk, which was ridiculous. It was like, what, a half hour? I was restless and antsy, but as soon as she came into view I felt calmer and more focused. I watched her pass a man as she headed back to the cottage and they nodded in greeting, but he stopped as soon as she'd passed him and watched her walk away. If I'd had hackles, they would've been up. Seeing some random dude ogle Alice sent me into Alpha Mode. Fuck that guy.

I set my coffee down on a table and put my hand on the door, ready to push it open if that asshole took even one step toward Alice. He must've said something to her because she turned to him. He took a step. That was enough for me. I shoved the door open so hard it swung and smacked the siding. I didn't give a shit. I jogged down the path toward the beach. I had no idea if the man was friend or foe, but I didn't want Alice to have to find out on her own.

I was a little out of breath when I got to Alice, who'd taken a few steps toward Beach Stalker and was in a conversation with him. "Hey, Alice," I interjected. "Everything good here?"

"Hey, Bazzy!"

I shot her my best look of annoyance, which she ignored, but the good news was that if she was joking around, she didn't feel threatened. That made me less nervous about this guy harassing her, but it opened up room for a different kind of discomfort: was this chump hitting on her? May as well take the bull by the horns. "Sebastian Starling," I said as I held out my hand to the guy, who looked completely average. Boring. Basic.

"Oh wow. *The* Sebastian Starling! Graham Knight. Nice to meet you. Alice and I knew each other back in high school."

Graham. Shit. *The* Graham who Alice had a crush on? The guy she'd lost her hair over? "Oh, yeah?" I said, just to buy myself some time so I could continue to assess the situation.

"I just mentioned you to Sebastian yesterday," Alice said.

"You did?" Graham's face lit up and my hand reflexively balled up into a fist.

"I was telling him about Tristan, who we'd run into, and, well, you know how that story goes."

I watched Graham's face to gauge his reaction. His response to the memory of that fucked up situation was about to display the measure of the man, and I was on guard.

Graham's face fell. "I was actually telling my wife about that situation last night. We're just here for a few days helping my uncle move off the island, and it's the first time I've been back since—" Graham took off his baseball cap, shook it around, and eased it back onto his head. "—since all that happened."

"Yeah. I haven't been back much, either." Alice blushed slightly and stared at her feet. "I guess kids do stupid things."

"That wasn't stupid. It was cruel. And I'm sorry I hid away like a coward. I'm really sorry that happened to you."

Okay, maybe I wouldn't have to punch Graham. The mention of a wife helped his case as well.

"Thanks," Alice said in a hushed tone.

"And you said that Tristan is here? I thought she moved to Florida. I hope we don't cross paths, because I don't know what I'd say to her, but it sure as hell wouldn't be nice."

Fine. Graham wasn't the devil.

"She's here on business. Like we are," I said. "We're both bidding on the Scarlet Oaks project."

"You're on that project? That's actually why I'm here. I'm a contractor and my company wants to get in on some special project bidding, so I thought I'd come take a look. And you two are coworkers? I'd just assumed you were—" it was Graham's turn to blush as he realized he might've put his foot in his mouth.

I slipped my arm around Alice's shoulders and in doing so, I felt taller. Stronger. Better. "We are." What exactly we were, I had no idea, but I said it anyway. "And we also work together. And if you see Taber, I encourage you to speak your mind."

Graham laughed. "What are y'all doing tonight? My wife and I were planning on going to the patio at the Oyster Shack to get a few drinks. Want to join us?"

"Oh, that sounds fun," Alice said. "I don't know what our schedule is tonight, but we'll keep it in mind."

I sighed a breath of relief. I wasn't sure I was ready to hang out with Alice's former crush, even if he did have his wife with him.

"We'll be there at five o'clock. Happy hour. Just look for us if you're in the neighborhood."

"Will do," Alice said as she smiled at him. No reason to go overboard with the smiling, in my opinion.

"Nice meeting you, Sebastian."

"You, too, Graham."

"I hope you crush Tristan's hopes and dreams." Graham said.

"That's our plan."

"Great seeing you again, Alice." Graham held out his arms for a hug and there went my fucking hackles again. Really? A hug? Alice stepped away from my arm and gave Graham a quick hug—thank God it wasn't some weird long embrace. "Have a good morning." Graham held up his hand and waved, and then returned to his route along the beach.

"Did you have to hug him?" I asked her as I reached my hand out to her.

"You aren't jealous, are you, Bazzy?" She accepted my hand and intertwined her fingers in mine.

"He seems nice enough, but he's still on my shit list for not coming to you after what Tristan did."

Alice stopped walking and looked up at me, and after a second, she wrapped her arms around me in what turned out to be a nice, long embrace. When she pulled back, she looked like she might've had tears in her eyes, but she turned her head before I could be sure. "Thank you, Sebastian." She took my hand again and squeezed it, and we walked back to the cottage.

OVER THE NEXT TWO HOURS, I rehearsed my presentation while Alice gave me feedback. I studied the numbers and the renderings and the maps until I had it all memorized. "If he doesn't like the plan, at least it won't be because we weren't prepared," I told Alice.

"You've done your due diligence. And Mr. Blake likes a conversation. Just go with the flow. I think he likes you, so that's a good start. You'll do great."

"I hope you're right. You ready to leave soon?"

"Yes, I'm just going to change clothes. I'll be ready in five minutes." Alice headed to her bedroom, and I packed up our papers.

Lacy had overnighted a presentation packet for Edward Blake, so everything he needed to see was there in the glossy color portfolio. I went out to the porch and paced to pass the time, hoping the sound of the ocean would calm my nerves as I waited for Alice. My phone buzzed in my pocket, and I grabbed it, happy for the distraction. That happiness faded as soon as I saw the text:

AVA/EVA: Hey there. Been thinking of you.

Shit. I didn't want her to be thinking of me. I didn't want anyone but Alice thinking of me. I thought we'd had a mutual ambivalence toward each other, so I hadn't been expecting her to contact me. I glanced toward the door of the house to see if

Alice was ready, but the kitchen was still empty. I wanted to just ignore the text, but that would be shitty. I prided myself on not ghosting people and I didn't want Eva/Ava to get the wrong idea.

> AVA/EVA: I'd love it if you let me have another chance with you. I only got a little taste before and I'm hungry for more.

Fucking hell. That was not an ambivalent text. Time to put her out of her sexting misery.

> SEBASTIAN: I'd like to let you know that I'm seeing someone. I wish you the best.

I looked at the text before hitting send. Was that the right way to say it? Did that come off as cold? Dismissive? I didn't want to be too friendly, but also didn't want to be an asshole. No, it wasn't quite right. I started backspacing so I could rewrite some of the message.

"Who're you texting?"

"Geeze!" I jumped and my phone slipped out of my right hand. I lunged and caught it with my left hand, saving it from smashing into the glass coffee table.

"You're jumpy." Alice, out on the porch and eyeing me suspiciously, pulled her braid over her shoulder, smoothed it down, and flipped it back again. "I still can't believe you don't have a case on that phone. One wrong move—"

"I've never dropped it before." I stuck it in my pocket and prayed that Ava (it was Ava, I think) wouldn't send me another text. I'd have to finish my message to her later.

"Well, you dropped it a second ago. It just didn't hit the ground."

"Right. Ready to go?"

Alice tilted her head and narrowed her eyes. "You sure everything's ok?"

"Absolutely perfect."

27

ALICE

One two, buckle my shoe. Three, four, knock at the door. Five, six, pick up sticks. Seven, eight, lay them straight. Nine, ten, a big fat hen!

As Sebastian and I approached the park where we'd be meeting with Mr. Blake, the old nursery rhyme played over and over in my head. After my parents died, but before I was old enough to go to school, my Nana used to take me to this park every week. She'd pack me my own container of animal crackers—the ones in the colorful box decorated with drawings of elephants, lions, and polar bears, and with a string handle that I'd use to carry the box like a little cardboard purse.

That was the nursery rhyme we'd recite as I hopped over the cracks in the sidewalk on the way to my favorite picnic table under the pavilion. The same table at which Mr. Blake now sat, looking out at the trees that shimmied gently in the afternoon breeze.

Sebastian had been quiet on the drive over, and we'd parked the golf cart in the gravel lot next to the park. Reginald Powers was parked there too, and was busy talking on the phone, so we just waved and headed over toward the meeting spot.

We walked up that same sidewalk Nana and I used to tread on, and I wondered if the cracks were the same ones I tried to dodge all those years ago. They looked smaller. I'd been quiet, too. We were both lost in our separate thoughts, worries, and memories.

"You ready?" I asked him as we neared the pavilion.

"Think so."

"You'll do great."

"Thanks." He reached out and squeezed my arm, and then let go and clutched his portfolio as we approached Mr. Blake, who waved when he saw us, but didn't stand. He looked small as he sat at the picnic table, sipping from a bottle of water. Everything was shrinking, or maybe things just loomed larger in my memory. "Good afternoon, Eddie."

"It's a beautiful day, isn't it?" Mr. Blake asked. "Those storms last night chased away the humidity for a day. They didn't hit you too hard, did they?"

"Aside from the lightning that tried to kill me, we escaped unharmed." Sebastian sat across the table from Mr. Blake.

"You didn't let him go outside during the storm, did you, Miss Lissy?"

"He has a mind of his own!" I said as I sat down at the end of the table, putting a little distance between myself and the two men.

"Sometimes a man doesn't know better. He needs a woman to keep his head on straight. Or to keep him alive."

"I won't argue with that." Sebastian fiddled with the corner of his notebook. "Eddie, I brought you a new proposal with some great new renderings of our vision for the future of Scarlet

Oaks." Sebastian was jumping right in. Not a bad tactic, but there was no way that Mr. Blake would let him do that. I sat back and got comfortable, ready to watch the show.

"Thank you very much." Mr. Blake took the folder from Sebastian and set it next to him on the bench. He studied Sebastian's face for a few moments and then he looked at Sebastian's shirt, and after that he leaned over in an exaggerated way to check out Sebastian's pants. "You're understated today."

Sebastian examined his clothes—black shirt, tan pants, brown sandals—and looked at Mr. Blake with a puzzled expression. "What do you mean?"

"You've got your grandfather's flair for style. Not today, maybe. But usually. You're a chip off the old block."

Sebastian looked at me for clarification, but I shrugged. Maybe Mr. Blake was having some memory problems. I wondered if he meant *my* grandfather, but the style comment wouldn't make sense. My grandfather wore the same pair of overalls every day unless Nana forced him into a button-down shirt for special occasions. "I'm sorry, I don't understand. Did you know my grandfather? My Grandpa Max used to live in Georgia, but I'm not sure he ever made it to Caluska Island."

"Quentin."

"Quentin Maddix? Ah, yes, he was quite stylish. I appreciate the compliment."

Quentin Maddix was Sebastian's famous grandfather. He was the heir to a huge publishing empire, and he was married to Sadie Starling, a ridiculously famous singer and starlet of the 1950s and 1960s. They were the parents of the triplets, one of whom was Sebastian's father, Mitchell.

"He obsessed about his outfits. Planned them days in advance. Would wear one thing to breakfast, another to lunch, had a new ensemble for dinner, and another for drinks. More colorful than any of the birds on the island." Mr. Blake sipped his water.

"Is that right?" A bead of perspiration trickled down Sebastian's temple. His eyes darted over to me and then back to Mr. Blake. I was nervous, too. If Mr. Blake wasn't at full mental capacity, we couldn't ethically go forward with the negotiations.

"He and Birdy knew how to have fun, and Tin-Tin always made the rest of us look shabby." Shit, what was he even talking about?

"Birdy and Tin-Tin?" Sebastian's expression had shifted from confused to shocked. "How do you know their nicknames?"

Mr. Blake narrowed his eyes at Sebastian as if he were trying to figure him out. "They were friends of mine. Seasonal friends. Caluska island was a getaway for famous folk back in the day. They came a few times a year. They were a bit older than me, but we got on well. It's a small island. You get to know people."

"They came here?"

"I thought that's why you had a special interest in this project."

"I—" Sebastian looked at me for help, but I was at a loss. Had we missed something in the initial info packet? No, we'd gone over it several times. We both would've remembered.

"You didn't know this either, Liss?"

"I had no idea that Sebastian had a family connection to the island," I said.

"Hm." Mr. Blake nodded absentmindedly while he thought this over. "Quentin and Peggy got along, too. Birdy wasn't a fan of her, I'm sorry to say."

"*My* Peggy?" I asked. My heart was hopping in my chest. "Nana?"

"Yes, *your* Peggy. It must've been the summer of '55 or so. Birdy was mad at Tin for one thing or another. They were crazy for each other, but they ran hot, which meant their tempers did, too. Quentin always wanted to dance, but Sadie enjoyed more stationary pleasures."

"I've heard she liked drinking."

"You heard right. But most everyone did. She didn't want to follow Quentin around the dance floor that night. I remember because she sang some songs around the pool, and I was starstruck. Quentin found a willing dance partner in the young Peggy, and they danced for hours. I'm afraid it didn't endear her to Sadie, but Quentin had a great time."

"Wait, Quentin Maddix was The Dancing Man?" I felt like I'd seen a ghost.

Mr. Blake chuckled at the memory. "The one and only."

"Holy shit." I hadn't meant to say that out loud, but it just slipped out.

"Peggy didn't tell you the man's name?"

"What's going on?" Sebastian was looking between me and Mr. Blake like he was watching a frenetic tennis match.

"No, she did *not* tell me that The Dancing Man was Quentin freaking Maddix."

"Who the hell is The Dancing Man?"

"Your grandfather!" Mr. Blake and I said at the same time.

Sebastian threw up his arms in surrender. "I have no idea what's happening."

"My grandmother had a story about a handsome man she knew when she was young. Supposedly, he was famous and an amazing dancer, and one summer night they danced for hours, and it was the best night of her life. The story drove my grandfather crazy. If she was mad at him, she'd say, 'Keep it up, Henry, and I'll just run off with The Dancing Man.' Or if my grandfather would fix something around the house, like a leaky toilet, he'd stand back and say, 'Bet your Dancing Man can't do that.' I didn't know The Dancing Man was an actual person—I thought she made him up!" This news made me feel a little dizzy.

"He was as real as this young man sitting here today. Spitting image, if I do say so myself."

"So, you're saying that my grandfather knew Alice's grandmother?"

"Now you've got it."

"Were they, I mean, did they," Sebastian looked a little green around the gills.

"Nothing like that," Mr. Blake reassured Sebastian. "From everything I know, your grandparents were completely committed to each other. But they were big flirts and allowed each other to be their own people. This was all before the triplets, of course."

"I just . . . I don't know what to say." Sebastian looked as bewildered as I felt.

"You carry yourself like him, you know."

"Like my grandfather?"

"Yes. Sometimes when I see a picture of you in a magazine in your funny clothes, it's like seeing him come back to life."

"No one's ever told me that before. Not my dad or anything."

"How could he? He didn't know the young Quentin and Sadie. But he'd have to be blind not to see the likeness."

"I suppose." Sebastian was suddenly very preoccupied with his hands, and his voice sounded thick.

"They passed when you were pretty young, didn't they?"

Sebastian nodded. "I was about four when my grandmother died, and my grandfather died a year later."

"I figured when Sadie got sick and then passed that Quentin wouldn't be too far behind. Some couples just work like that. They don't make sense in the world without each other." Mr. Blake turned to me. "Henry and Peggy were like that, too. And your parents–well–" Now it was Mr. Blake's voice that caught in his throat. "They didn't get the chance to test that theory. Not enough time."

The three of us sat without speaking and listened to the gulls and the waves and the rustling of leaves in the breeze.

After a few moments, Mr. Blake sniffled. "I'd be willing to bet good money that you have a handkerchief on you," he said to Sebastian.

Sebastian reached into his back pocket and produced one of his Starling branded cloths and handed it to Mr. Blake. "You're welcome to keep it."

"I appreciate that." Mr. Blake dabbed his eyes and blew his nose. He tucked it into his shirt pocket. He lifted his wrist to check his watch. "I have about ten more minutes before I need to leave for my next appointment. Want to tell me what you've got cooked up for Scarlet Oaks?"

"Yes, right. Scarlet Oaks." Sebastian cleared his throat, picked up his folder, and flipped through the pages distractedly as Mr. Blake looked on with amusement.

They spent the next ten minutes looking over Sebastian's plan and Mr. Blake did a lot of nodding as he was led through the mock-ups and renderings. Sebastian didn't need my help—he was clear, concise, and convincing.

As Sebastian was finishing his pitch, Reginald approached the pavilion. "Are you ready, sir?" he asked Mr. Blake.

"I am." Mr. Blake stood up and extended his hand to Sebastian. "Thank you, Mr. Starling. Your plan is a compelling one. I'd like you to present it at a town hall meeting tomorrow at 4:00 pm. I have my own preferences for what happens to my place, but it also belongs to the other islanders, and I'd like their input. Will that work for your schedule?"

"Yes, of course." Sebastian's words sounded confident, but I recognized the look of surprise and anxiety on his face. "Where will this meeting take place?"

"Shoreside Hall. Miss Lissy knows where it is. We'll see you there tomorrow." Mr. Blake stood and took a moment to stretch and get his balance, and then he headed out with Reginald.

Sebastian watched them walk away, and then he cocked his head and pointed at Mr. Blake. "Hey, look at his back pocket. He had one of his own!"

Poking out of Mr. Blakes's back pocket was his own white handkerchief.

Sebastian stood and began to gather his papers. I got up and went to his side. I wanted to touch him, and I didn't fight the urge. I rested my hand on the small of his back as he finished picking up.

He stopped moving when my hand made contact with him as if he was soaking up my energy. He closed his eyes and took a long deep breath, and then exhaled. "I hope I passed his test."

I leaned forward and kissed him on the cheek. His skin was

warm and tasted faintly of salt. "I think you did. But now it's the town you have to worry about."

28

SEBASTIAN

I was a convertible guy. Whenever weather allowed, I'd grab one from the family fleet and get out of town as fast as I could. I loved my Porsche 718 Spyder because of how that machine handled the twists and turns of the back roads. The Chevrolet Corvette Z06 was my car of choice when I needed something loud and strong—nothing howled like that American V8.

But my favorite was my 1984 Ferrari Testarossa Spider. Almost nobody had one of those, and I got the most looks when I flew around in that piece of art. Plus, it was fucking fast. It was also flaming red, and I was starting to figure out that red heads had a special hold on me—Alice would look spectacular in the passenger seat next to me, her curls flying in the wind.

For now, we had an island with barely any cars, but somehow, puttering along the beach path with Alice in our Yamaha golf cart at a breathtaking seventeen miles an hour felt just as magical as my drives back home. In fact, maybe even better. "I feel like I need a drink after that meeting." I hit the brakes to allow a mother and her toddler to pass across the path in front of us. "I'm not even sure what happened back there."

Alice pulled her phone out of her bag. "Shit. It's dead. I forgot to bring my mobile charger. Do you know what time it is?"

I glanced at my watch. "Almost five."

"The Oyster Shack's right over there. We could meet up with Graham and his wife for a drink."

I didn't want to be around other people. I just wanted Alice and a G&T on the rocks, and the ocean air. But I also didn't want to be a selfish prick. "Isn't that Loverboy right there?" Graham and Mrs. Graham were headed straight for us. This was my punishment for letting that mother cross the path safely.

"Hey there!" Graham waved as he called out to us. He still had that baseball cap on. Bet he had a bald spot he was intent on hiding. "You joining us?"

"Just got out of a meeting!" Alice called back. "Wrapping up with a few follow-up calls but get a four-top just in case!"

"Will do." Graham and his wife were closer now. "This is Jennie."

Jennie had short blonde hair, a bright blue dress, and a friendly smile. "It's nice to meet you. I hope you can join us."

Great. Didn't see how I could turn down Mr. and Mrs. Nice. "Give us five minutes." At least I'd get some oysters out of the deal.

Alice raised her eyebrows but stayed silent until Graham and Jennie were out of earshot. "Didn't take you for the couples' night out type." She poked me in the ribs.

I grabbed her finger and nibbled on the end of it. "You're the one who told them to get a four-top. But I want that drink. And I'm hungry. Unless you'd rather me eat you."

Alice's cheeks went pink. "I can't say that sounds like the worst idea. But a drink does sound nice right about now."

I hit the gas on the golf cart and started driving toward the Oyster Shack. My phone buzzed in my pocket. "Could you get that? Front right pocket."

"I get to put my hands down your pants? Excellent." She fished out my phone. "Texts from Simon, it looks like."

"Hold it up to my face." She did so and the phone unlocked. "What's he saying?"

"He wants to know how the meeting went."

"Is that how he phrased it?" I pulled the golf cart into a parking space outside the Oyster Shack.

"Well, he said, 'Did you fuck up the meeting?'"

"That sounds more like it. Tell him I hit a home run."

"Do I tell him it's me texting for you, or should I just type it like it's from you?"

"Either way." I turned off the engine, leaned back, and closed my eyes. Maybe this was all going to work. Maybe I'd be able to pull off a good presentation at the Town Hall meeting, maybe my family wouldn't think I was a fuck up, and the best 'maybe' of all, maybe I'd get the girl.

"Who's 'Ava/Eva'?"

Oh no. I hadn't deleted the text from Eva, and I hadn't finished my reply to her. *Please*, I prayed to the texting gods, the beach gods, the island gods, and to the regular white dude in the sky God, *please let my unsent reply be sitting in the text box.*

Just a few seconds passed between Alice asking me that question and me coming up with a reply, but it felt like hours— white hot, nipple-twisting, kicked in the balls hours, while I tried to come up with just the right answer, which would be honest, but not *too* honest. "A woman I went out with once.

There's nothing between us." I'd not been brave enough to look at Alice while I spoke, but I sneaked a glance at her after I'd answered so I could gauge her reaction.

"Really? Because it looks like your dick got between you, judging by all the eggplant and tongue emojis. And—oh god!" Alice's face was flaming red. The brightest I'd ever seen it.

"What?" I grabbed for the phone but she shifted in her seat so I couldn't reach it.

"She just sent a photo. And another one."

"Of what?" My voice broke when I said "what" and I sounded like a pubescent boy who'd just gotten in trouble with his mom.

"Her boobs. And her—wow. She must pay a lot for a waxing job that smooth."

"Let me have my phone!" Adrenaline was coursing through me and my vision had tunneled. All I wanted to do was rip the phone out of Alice's hand and chuck it into the fucking Atlantic.

"What the fuck, Sebastian?" Alice's eyes looked wet but I was guessing those were tears of anger, not sadness.

"I can explain!"

"You can?" Her voice was too calm. Too measured. I was fucked.

"I can! We went out once, and—"

"I get that you've gone out with a lot of women. I knew that from the start. Here's what I don't get."

I snapped my lips together and waited for her next sentence. Maybe this wasn't going to be as bad as I thought. My heart was pounding so fast that I could hear my pulse rushing through my ears.

"Ava/Eva said: 'I'd love it if you let me have another chance with you. I only got a little taste before and I'm hungry for more.'" Alice's voice was still too calm. "And you replied, and let's take a second to note that you sent this reply just a few hours ago: 'I'd like to let you.'"

"I didn't say that!" My mouth had gone dry.

"It's right here." Alice turned the phone so I could see it, and that unfortunate text was right there. I'd sent it.

"Wait! I was deleting my reply, and I didn't delete it all the way and I accidentally sent that!" My words rushed out so fast that I wasn't sure Alice could understand me, but I plowed forward. "I was texting her that I'd like to let her know that I was seeing someone and was asking her to stop texting me." There. The truth. If she knew me at all, she'd believe me.

Alice looked at the phone, looked at me, and looked at the phone again. "To which she replied, 'Can't wait to get my lips on your dick again and this time I'll make you come so hard in my mouth that—"

"Give me that!" I swiped it from her hand. This was bad.

"When did you go out with her?" Alice was staring straight ahead. She couldn't even look at me.

Things were about to get worse, because I wasn't going to lie to Alice. I *was* regretting how careless I'd been with myself and with the women I'd dated. It'd never seemed to matter on any grand scale, and now I'd give almost anything to erase most of those casual forgettable encounters so that Alice didn't have to think about my dick in Eva's mouth. I took a breath. I exhaled. "Last week."

"Last week?" It was Alice's turn to have her voice crack. "*When* last week?"

"Uh, the day I met you. Before I came to the office."

"That's why you were late to the meeting? You were getting a blow job?"

Was that a rhetorical question? I made a judgment call—yes, rhetorical. I kept my mouth shut.

"Sebastian. I don't know what to say."

"It's not like I cheated on you." Oh, goodie. I'd wondered when my defense mechanism would kick in. In a fight or flight situation, I was a fighter. I swung my legs to the left and stepped out of the golf cart. I needed some space. I didn't want to say something that I'd regret. Or, say anything *more* that I'd regret.

"What does *that* mean?" Alice hopped out of the passenger side and walked towards me. Shit, we didn't need two fighters. One of us needed to pull the flight card and get the hell out of dodge before the whole thing went up in flames.

"It means that when I had this meaningless date with a woman I met on an app, and when she grabbed my dick and tried to strangle it, and when yes, I let her, but I didn't love it, I had no idea that an hour later I'd meet you and I'd realize that it was actually possible for me to have feelings for someone that weren't just fleeting and fucking superficial!" I was shouting now. Great.

She crossed her arms and kicked at the parking lot pebbles. "But you told her that you wanted her to do that to you again." A tear trickled down Alice's cheek.

"Alice Goode." I moved close enough to her that I could touch her. I cupped her shoulder with my palm. "Look at me."

Alice tried to shake me off but didn't put much effort into it. She glared at me and huffed a short breath out of her nose like an angry bull. "Why?"

"Listen, I know I can be an asshole. I'm promiscuous. I'm careless. I've made some decisions I regret. I made out with that woman last week, and I wish I hadn't. And it's the truth that this morning I was texting her back to tell her that I wasn't interested. That I had a new woman in my life. You walked out on the porch and startled me, and I never got back to it. That wasn't the text I intended to send. It was an incomplete sentence."

"Really?"

"Really. And I didn't get back to it because I forgot about her. Which confirms my asshole status. But when I'm with you, I don't think about any other women. It's like you erase them from my mind. You're the only woman I want to date, Alice." I dropped my hand from her shoulder and backed up a step.

Alice's eyes bored into my face. It was less like she was looking *at* me than she was looking *through* me. Like her gaze sliced right through my skin and she was assessing my organs, particularly my heart, trying to decide if they were viable and worth taking a chance on.

I squirmed and fought the urge to walk away. I had to stay. I had to face up to this. To her. I had to show up, for once. "I'm not great at expressing myself, but you're different. I'm different when I'm with you. It's all different." I inhaled deeply, hoping to slow down my heart rate. "I'm sorry."

29

ALICE

"I'm going to take a walk." I couldn't stand there any longer and listen to Sebastian. My instinct was to wrap my arms around him and kiss his face and tell him I didn't care what he did last week; that what mattered was today—this moment in the here and now. But I didn't trust myself.

I'd never made good decisions when it came to my heart, which was why I'd found it much safer to stay single. Staying out of relationships or romantic entanglements meant cozying up in my protective bubble, except maybe it wasn't so cozy. More like a cold, industrial warehouse of a bubble where my lone voice echoed off the stark walls and high ceilings. Rom-coms, take-out dinners, and classic TV made my bubble a bit cozier, but if I was being honest, it was still lonely in there.

"A walk?" Sweat glistened in the curls on Sebastian's fore-head. His cheeks were flushed, and his lips were full. He was sexy when he was upset, which was another reason I needed to walk away.

There was a part of me, a big part, that was fantasizing about how hot it would be to crawl into the nearest bed with

Sebastian. This angst, this anger, this mix of jealousy and desire was the perfect recipe for the best sex, and I wanted him. I wanted Sebastian near me, with me, inside me. "I need to think about all of this."

"Please don't leave me." His voice cracked, just like it'd done a few minutes ago. I didn't know if he meant leaving him to take a walk or leaving him for good, but I wasn't going to ask. His sea green eyes looked translucent. A light shone through his irises, but I couldn't fully see what was behind his gaze. Who was he, really?

"It's just a walk. I'll go down the beach a little way, and come back."

"But your phone's dead."

"I won't be long."

"But what about your friends waiting at the bar?" Sebastian pointed to the Oyster Shack.

"I have to get my head straight."

An expression of uncertainty passed over Sebastian's face as if he'd realized he couldn't change my mind, which wasn't exactly true. If he grabbed me and took me into his arms, I wouldn't push him away; I just couldn't bring myself to be the one to initiate the contact.

I waited a few beats to see if he'd hug me. Or kiss me. Or wrap my braid around his fist and pull my head back and press his lips against my neck and suck . . . shit. I really had to go. "I'll be back in a few minutes." My voice wobbled and I knew I was about to cry. I wanted him to keep me from going. I also wanted to be alone. I was a mess. This was exactly why I wasn't fit for love: I was a romantic lightweight.

"Please be careful," he said. He gathered me into a quick hug, kissed my forehead, and then walked toward the Oyster

Shack with his head bowed, shoulders slumped, and hands in his pockets.

I fought the urge to run after him. If I was going to take a chance on Sebastian Starling, it had to be a well-considered gamble, and I hadn't done enough considering. I turned the other way and headed toward the beach.

ONE HOUR. One hour was how long it took me to decide that Sebastian was worth taking a risk on. Walking on the beach acted as a time condenser for me. What might take me days or weeks to think about in normal circumstances could just take minutes on the beach. My mental clouds were cleared out by the ocean breeze, and I could think better.

On my walk I realized that I had a simple choice: I could walk away from Sebastian and throw him back to his sea of casual dates, or I could try being with him. And as much as it ripped out my stomach to think about him with Ava/Eva (what *was* her name, anyway?, it was true that he hadn't even met me when he was out with her. And he and I were moving quickly thanks in large part to me, red wine, and a bucket of dicks. I'd been the initiator of this fast-track love affair, so it wasn't fair of me to punish him for being with another girl last week.

But where was he now? As I crossed the grounds between the beach and the Oyster Hut, I realized that the golf cart was gone. Other carts were parked in the lot along with several bicycles, but none of them were the one Sebastian and I had been using. Did he give up on me?

I'd come up from my beach walk with a buoyant feeling of hope and positivity. I thought Sebastian would be waiting for me, and that I'd put my arms around him, kiss him, and we'd pick up where we left off, but now I was alone.

"Misplace your man?" Tristan's voice dripped with mock sweetness and the shitty grin on her face matched her tone. Her brown hair was down around her shoulders and was, as usual, perfect.

God only knew what *my* hair looked like. I'd been through that meeting, then the fight with Sebastian, and then an hour on the humid and windy beach. I was pretty sure my braid was only holding half my hair, and the rest was probably flying around my face like Medusa's snakes. "Go away." I started to walk back to the beach, but Tristan followed me.

"You don't need to be a bitch, Goodey-two-shoes. And he left a while ago. Loaded up a bunch of oysters, some drinks, and took off. Without you."

I stopped walking and spun around, my shoes making a grinding sound on the pebbles and crushed oyster shells under my feet. "You really don't want to fuck with me right now, Tristan."

"Ooooh." Tristan put her hands out and pretended like she was trembling.

"You're thirty years old," I spat out my words. "Is this really how you want to do this?"

"Thirty-one. Can't believe you forgot my birthday was last week. Some best friend you are."

"Best friend? Are you forgetting what you did to me?" I wasn't into physical violence, but I wanted to shove Tristan, kick her in the shins or punch her right in the middle of her perfect face.

"It's not my fault that your own trick backfired on you."

Tristan whipped her hair around and swept it over her left shoulder. She petted it like you might stroke a long-haired cat.

"What are you talking about?" I was about half an inch from the end of my rope. I didn't lose my shit very often, but I was close to my limit, and after that, there was no telling all the ways in which I'd melt down. I couldn't be held responsible for my actions if Tristan kept pushing me.

"You're the one who tried to put that shit in my shampoo bottle. So I just put it in yours, first."

I had no idea what she was talking about, and I decided that I didn't care. I was done with her. I tried to walk away again.

"That's the only reason I did it! So you'd know what your own nasty prank would feel like!" Her voice had shifted into a higher register and she sounded desperate.

"Are you on some kind of medication that causes hallucinations and memory loss?"

"Jamie Turner told me all about it, so you can stop playing the victim now."

A laugh escaped my chest, making a sound like someone just punched me in the stomach. "Jamie Turner?"

"She told me how you were going to put the hair remover in my shampoo before the thing with Graham. That's why you wanted to take a shower at my house."

"My shower was broken! And I was just going to skip it, but you invited me over, remember?"

Tristan looked up and to the left, like she was trying to recall that night fifteen years ago. But then she just shrugged. "Whatever. I used my Aunt's shampoo for myself and I left a special bottle just for you. And I threw out my bottle that I knew you'd messed with."

Maybe *I* was the one on hallucinatory medication, because

none of this made any sense. "I never put anything in your shampoo. And I never would. Not even today, when you're being such an asshole."

Tristan crossed her arms. "I don't believe you."

"I don't care what you believe. I *do* think it's funny that you went on Jamie's word, though."

"Oh yeah? Why's that?" Tristan smacked the piece of gum in her mouth like she was reverting to her fifteen-year-old self.

"You remember how she made up that story about how your house was infested with fleas and told everyone at school? And how she traded out your carton of milk with one that she'd been saving in her locker for two weeks, just to try to make you barf? And how she told Dylan Barker that you were cheating on him with some guy from Savannah, and that was a lie, too? Should I go on, or are you getting the picture?"

Tristan rolled her eyes. "Whatever." She'd turned into teenage Tristan right before my eyes. Sullen, insecure, needy, and stubborn as shit.

No more wasting my time on people like Tristan. She didn't deserve my attention. "Good to know you're as clueless as ever. Good luck with that—"

Tristan cut me off by shoving me, hard, in the chest. I stumbled backward, lost my balance, and fell onto the rough surface of the parking lot. "You always thought you were smarter than me!" Tristan screeched. She lunged at me, and I covered my head with my hands.

"What are you doing?" A male voice shouted. I peeked up and saw Graham, who'd pulled Tristan back and had her trapped in his arms. Graham's wife, Jennie, stood nearby, her face frozen in a snapshot of shock.

"Let go of me!" Tristan tried to elbow Graham in the ribs, but she whiffed, and just ended up punching the air.

"Are you okay?" Jennie helped me back to my feet.

I was fine except my left palm had suffered a small cut from landing wrong on a piece of oyster shell. "I think so." I was running on adrenaline. Everything was spinning out of control, and as each minute ticked by, I was more and more convinced that Sebastian had truly abandoned me.

Jennie saw the spot of blood on my hand. "Let's go wash that off." She put her arm around my shoulder and started to walk me toward the restaurant.

"That's because she *is* smarter than you," Graham said to Tristan. "You're a grown woman. Get it together and get the hell out of here."

"Nice to see you, too, Graham." Tristan's sarcasm wasn't landing because it was betrayed by the sound of a sob catching in her throat.

"Go away." Graham joined Jennie and me as we walked up the steps to the Oyster Shack, which left Tristan standing by herself in the parking lot. Well, not totally by herself. A few people had gathered around when she pushed me, and there were two teenage girls on the deck above us filming her with their phones. Great. Maybe I'd go viral.

"It's just a little cut. I'm fine. I want to go back to my cottage," I said, and then remembered that I had no way to get there, and that when I did find my way back, I'd probably be there by myself. I didn't even fight the tears that spilled over the rims of my eyes.

"Don't cry!" Jennie hugged me, and I felt ridiculous for crying on the shoulder of a near-stranger. "We'll take you back to the cottage as soon as we wash your hand."

"Sebastian told us to watch for you, and I'm really sorry Tristan got to you before we did. We left as soon as we saw you in the parking lot, but Tristan must've been waiting."

My tears ceased when I heard Sebastian's name. I pulled out of Jennie's hug. "What do you mean he told you to watch for me?"

"He wanted to get a head start at something back at the cottage. He said you didn't have your phone, so he paid for all our food and drinks and asked if we'd bring you back whenever you were done with your walk. We could see the path from our table on the deck, so we were just waiting for you."

My tears were back. "But I thought he left me." I knew I sounded pitiful, but I was beyond caring.

"Oh, Alice," Jennie said, with the tone of a mother soothing her child. "He didn't leave you. I'm under the impression he had something nice planned."

Jennie and Graham hadn't heard our fight, so I wasn't sure she had the right impression, but for the moment, I was willing myself to believe everything she said.

"We'll be right back," Jennie said to her husband, and she pushed open the door to the women's bathroom. I followed her into the restroom where a few sinks lined the wall. It was empty except for us. She set her purse on the floor, turned on the faucet, and got the water set at a good temperature. "Ok, water's ready. Clean that out."

I washed my cut with soap and water and dried it with a paper towel Jennie had collected from the dispenser. "Thank you," I said. "I'm sorry for the tears. It's just been a long day."

"There's no need to apologize," she said kindly. "And if I thought I'd lost track of Sebastian Starling, I might cry, too!" she joked. "But—" she started, but then stopped herself.

My stomach dropped. What did she know that I didn't? "But what?"

"I was just going to say that Sebastian seemed pretty upset himself. We had to convince him that we wouldn't leave until we saw you. And he left us his phone number and made us both call his phone to make sure the connection went through and that we had the number right. He was very worried about you."

That was good to hear, but I felt like she hadn't answered my question. "But why did you say 'but?'"

Jennie bit her lip like she was trying to decide whether or not to say something.

"It's okay," I told her. "Just say it."

"I was just going to say that we might want to fix your hair."

"My hair?" I hadn't even looked in the mirror. I'd gotten into the habit of never checking my reflection unless I had to, so I stepped back to the sink and checked out my reflection. "Oh god." Comparing myself to Medusa had been generous. Far too generous. My hair was a tangled, twisted, frizzy mess.

"My sister has curly hair. I know what to do." Jennie picked up her purse and rifled through the contents. "I have some stuff we can use. Let me tell Graham that we're going to be a few minutes, and we'll get you all fixed up."

30

SEBASTIAN

Rage rushed through my veins like a swarm of fire ants. Graham had texted me to say that there'd been "an altercation" between Tristan and Alice. Fucking Tristan Tabor. I hated that woman.

I had no patience for texting and called Graham as soon as I read his message. He said that Alice was fine, that she was washing up, and they'd have her home soon, but it took everything I had to not rush to her side. Why had I let her walk on the beach? Why had I left her there for someone else to take care of? If she hadn't wanted to call it quits with me before, surely she did now.

My plan had felt right at the time, but now it seemed like too little, too late. Alice had taken time to think, and while maybe a lot of women would've chosen to be with me just because of my name, Alice wasn't most women. For her, that was probably a mark in the "con" column instead of the "pro." I should've followed my instinct, which was to sweep her up in my arms and confess every feeling I had for her. Headlights lit up the tree trunks in the distance, and I prayed that it was Graham and Jennie, bringing Alice back to me.

The text notification rang out on my phone. I'd had my volume on and my ringer on high ever since I'd left the Oyster Shack. I didn't want to miss any calls or messages until Alice was back in my sights.

> GRAHAM: Dropping Alice off where you asked. You should see her in a second.

> SEBASTIAN: Thank you. I owe you one.

> GRAHAM: No problem. Happy to help.

The sun had set but it wasn't fully dark, and the sky was brushed with purple and gold. I'd outlined the path from the tree line to the house with some battery-operated votives I'd found at the cottage, along with a sprinkling of empty oyster shells I'd procured from the restaurant. I wanted to make some kind of special scene for Alice but didn't have much time. It was either that or line the walkway with dildos, and while that would've been funny, it wasn't the vibe I was going for. So to speak.

Alice had her head down and was walking at a brisk pace, but when she came around the bend in the path, she stopped short. I didn't know if it was the line of candles and shells that made her pause, or if it was the sight of me, but either way, she stopped to take it all in, and when she resumed walking, she did so at a much slower pace.

It took me a second to register what was different. Her hair. It was down. When I'd left her at the beach it was in a tattered braid, but now it was loose but tamed and her face was framed in the most stunning dark red curls I'd ever seen.

Shadows danced across the light material of her dress as she walked toward me, and I couldn't help but fantasize about her walking down the aisle as my bride. Just the idea of it sent delicious shivers up my spine and made my heart swoop and swoon.

I wanted to meet her halfway on the path, but I held back and waited. This meant I got to watch her for a little bit longer, and it meant that she could get to me, or not get to me if she chose that, on her own timeline.

I tried to read the expression on her face, but her features were arranged in a lovely but infuriatingly neutral way. I wouldn't be surprised if she told me she never wanted to see me again, and I also wouldn't be surprised if she confessed that she was in love with me. How both ends of that spectrum seemed like real possibilities was confusing to me, but also exciting. This was what I'd been missing. This delicious terror of romance. Feeling sick and elated at the same time, wondering if the rug might get pulled out from underneath you while in the same breath feeling that you might be about to reach ultimate ecstasy. It was my turn to be starstruck.

"Hi," Alice said, when she was about ten paces away.

"Hello. You look beautiful." I noticed that she had on some make-up, too. Her lashes were long and dark and even her mouth sparkled. Glitter lip gloss maybe. She was spectacular.

She smiled with her lips closed and didn't reply. She took a few more steps but stopped walking when she was still five feet away from me. Too far for me to touch without moving.

I held my ground. "Are you alright? I heard you got hurt." God, I wanted her in my fucking arms. But I couldn't grab her. This was up to her.

"It was nothing. Just a little Tabor tussle." Alice held up her left palm which sported a bandage. "You should see the other guy."

I laughed softly but couldn't get out more than that. I was so fucking nervous that I felt nauseous. "I'm glad you're back."

"I'm glad to be back." She took another step forward, close enough that I caught her floral scent. Honeysuckle and vanilla.

"You are?"

"I am." One step closer.

I jammed my hands into my pants pockets to keep from pulling her to me. *Wait, Sebastian, wait for her.* I was terrible at waiting. I usually grabbed what I wanted, whenever I felt like it, and while that supplied me with instant gratification, I'd discovered that it lacked true pleasure and value. I wanted to kiss her. I wanted to strip us both down and let her hair fall on my naked chest as she climbed on top of me. I shifted my hands in my pockets to hide my growing erection. I felt like a fool, fantasizing about her when she could be five seconds away from cutting me loose. "Do you like the candles?" It was a ridiculous and desperate thing to ask, but I was a ridiculous and desperate man.

She smiled again, this time an open, wide smile. "I love them."

Relief hit me so hard and so fast that my legs felt rubbery. I took my hands out of my pockets so I'd be ready to hold her if she took one more step. "I'm sorry, Alice. I'm sorry about—"

Alice took that final step. She was close enough to touch, close enough to kiss. "I'm sorry, too," she said, interrupting me. "If it's ok with you, I'd like to look forward, not backward. Let's start from here. You and me. No Ava."

"I think it's Eva."

"Whatever. You keep those meet-up apps deleted, and I'll consider not dating anyone from HR."

"That's a deal, Alice Goode."

"Care to seal that deal with a kiss, Sebastian Starling?"

I captured her face in my hands, cupping her perfect jaw with my fingers. I tilted my head and leaned forward, and pressed my lips against hers. First softly, with my mouth closed, as I took tiny bites of her lips, teasing her. I slowly opened to her and she responded by grabbing the back of my head, leaning into my body, and letting my tongue meet hers. We were tasting, sucking, biting, searching. It was just a kiss, but it was so much more: it was a devouring.

I wrapped my arms around Alice's torso and lifted her up so our faces were at the same height. She wrapped her legs around my waist and kissed me with a ferocity that turned me on so much I wanted to take her right there on the porch. Maybe I would.

I leaned back against the stair railing for support and snaked my hand up her outer thigh. The heat of her skin just made me think about how warm other parts of her body might be, and the thought made me ache with desire. There was no hiding my erection now, and the light fabric of my pants was no match for my swollen member, and it wasn't helping that Alice had her legs open and her groin pressed against mine.

"I want you," I muttered, my voice sounding strange to my own ears.

"I want you, too," Alice said before kissing me again.

I had to hold her with both arms so I couldn't explore her body with my hands, or my mouth, but my need was blooming into desperation, and I had to have her. "Here? Do you want this here?" I wasn't sure about the logistics, but where there was a will, there was a way, and I knew I'd have no problem finding a way to make Alice completely mine.

"Yes," she moaned. "Yes, Sebastian."

"God, Alice." I'd never wanted anyone like this. Ever. Keeping myself propped up against the stair railing, I reached one hand to the waistband of her underwear and pulled. We'd get these off somehow, but she'd have to help. "Is this okay?" I asked.

"Wait." Alice pulled her head back like she'd just remembered something.

I stopped and waited. "You okay?"

"No. I'm sorry, Sebastian. We have to stop."

31

ALICE

I wanted Sebastian. I wanted him on top of me and inside me or however we were about to make that work with us leaning up against the railing, but there were two problems. First, I didn't have a condom on me, and I didn't know if he did, either. I could ask, but that was going to shift the mood. More importantly, I'd guzzled two bottles of water since Tristan knocked me over in the parking lot, and this was not going to be a comfortable experience unless I could visit the bathroom first.

Poor Sebastian thought I was rejecting him. He stoically and gently set me down and kissed my forehead when I'd told him we needed to stop. "I totally understand. I apologize if I made you uncomfortable."

I needed to put him out of his misery. And I also needed to put myself out of my misery. I crossed my legs and squirmed to try to relieve the pressure in my bladder. "Do you have a condom?"

Sebastian blinked and tilted his head, as if trying to understand what I was asking. "Yes," he said, drawing out the word for a few seconds. "I do. . ." He waited for me to fill in the blanks.

"Great. Can we take this inside, then? And reconvene after I use the bathroom?"

Sebastian's expression shifted from worried and sad to relieved and happy. "Oh! Yes! Of course. I'm sorry." He stumbled up the steps like an overeager puppy and he opened the door for me. "Right this way." God, it was cute to see Sebastian Starling tripping all over himself.

"I'll be right back." I closed myself in the bathroom, and after I'd solved my most pressing problem, I examined myself in the mirror while I washed my hands. Jennie had worked some serious magic on my hair. It was still wild, but in a contained way. In a way that I wouldn't be embarrassed to wear down to work or around town. I stroked a few ringlets—so smooth and soft and curly, not just frizz and fire like usual.

I felt beautiful. Sexy. The woman in the mirror was okay. She had a voice that was worth using and had thoughts that were worth expressing. It was okay to be seen, and I realized, as I stared at myself, that I was the one who had to see the real Alice before anyone else would be able to recognize her. "Hi, Alice," I said out loud to mirror me. "You're looking nice tonight." I smiled and I watched how my face lit up and transformed. I felt like a fool, but at the same time, I felt liberated. "Go on out. There's someone waiting for you."

I FOUND Sebastian standing on the back porch, barefoot and looking out toward the ocean, though it was too dark to see much at all. His right arm was bent above his head and propped against one of the frames of the screens.

"Hey. I'm back."

He swiveled around and smiled when he saw me. "Hey." He crossed the porch until he was right in front of me. With one finger, he pushed a lock of hair off my forehead and tucked it behind my ear. "You alright?"

"Well, I'm hungry. I didn't have any dinner." I was also nervous and while I was confident that Sebastian wouldn't reject me if I just jumped into his arms, I still had some natural shyness to fight against.

"We can fix that." He slid his arm around my waist and walked me into the kitchen. "Have a seat, and I'll put something together." Sebastian motioned to a barstool at the kitchen counter.

I perched on the stool and watched him work. He was a thing of beauty in the kitchen. He sliced cheeses, stacked up crackers in artful lines, turned whole bell peppers into perfect bite-sized chunks, and poured me a glass of wine to sip while he put together our food.

"Maybe you should've been a chef," I told him as I dipped a slice of bread into a dish of olive oil and balsamic vinegar.

"We already have a chef in the family." He poured some vodka into an ice-filled cocktail shaker and added cranberry juice and a squeeze of lime. It was hard to look away from his arms as shook the concoction.

"Are you making a Cosmopolitan?"

"I believe in equal opportunity cocktails." Sebastian poured his drink into a glass.

"So, who's the chef?"

"My cousin Susana."

"She's a chef? I thought she *had* a chef."

"She does. Have one. She *used* to be a chef. She still teaches kids how to cook, and we usually make a meal together on holidays, until I get too drunk, and she kicks me out of the kitchen."

"Sounds about right."

"Hey, I made this spread, didn't I?" He motioned to the impromptu charcuterie board in front of us before popping several slices of soppressata into his mouth.

"It's wonderful. Thank you."

"Want to tell me what happened with Tristan?" He picked up three crackers, handed one to me, and ate the other two.

"Not really. It's boring."

"Try me."

"She saw me walking alone and told me that you'd left me behind on purpose."

"Figures." Sebastian gathered up two strawberries from the platter. "I saw her lurking by the trees when I left. But how did you get into a fight?"

"She told me that she'd thought I was planning on putting the hair remover in her shampoo bottle, so she'd just turned the prank back on me, as revenge."

"Why the fuck would she think that?" Sebastian's righteous anger was endearing. And hot.

"Because another mean girl told her so."

"How many mean girls can one island hold?" Sebastian's nostrils flared. He was truly pissed. "Why did she push you?"

"I basically called her stupid." I raised my wine glass as if making a toast, and then took a celebratory sip.

"You're brilliant," he said, and then he kissed me. That was all it took. To erase Tristan from my mind, to wash away the roller coaster day, and to make me forget that I was ever hungry for anything other than Sebastian Starling. He slid off his stool to get closer to me, and I leaned into his chest. He squatted down, slipped one arm under my knees, and scooped me up like I weighed nothing. "May I take you to the bedroom?"

"Please. Yes." I rested my head in the crook of his neck, and we left our dinner behind in the kitchen as he carried me to my room.

He set me down on the bed gently, as if I was made of glass —a change of pace from when he'd tossed me onto it yesterday. That felt like weeks ago, not hours. And Sebastian was no stranger to me. I'd been more intimate with him in the last week than I had with anyone else, ever. But I was still nervous.

I settled on my back and waited for him to join me, but he just watched me from the side of the bed. Five seconds. Ten Seconds. Fifteen seconds. Sebastian was silent, still, and staring.

I couldn't take the tension. "You ok?" I asked him.

"Take off your sweater."

I was wearing a light cardigan over my dress and slid it off my shoulders and set it aside.

"Put your head on that pillow."

I scooted over so I was centered on the bed and lay back on the pillow.

"Comfortable?"

Unable to find my voice, I just nodded.

In a graceful leap, Sebastian hopped onto the bed and straddled me, landing with his knees on either side of my hips. He went right back to his posture of silent, still, and staring. I stared back as long as I could, holding his gaze until the intensity of it was too much and I looked away. No one had ever seen me like this. It was like Sebastian was uncovering all my unspoken secrets and committing them to memory.

He rose up on his knees, leaned forward, and placed his hands on the edges of my pillow. "Lift your head."

I raised it a few inches and Sebastian slid his hands under my head, gathered my curls in his hands, and fanned them out on the pillow, taking time to arrange things just how he wanted. I reached my hand up to feel what he'd done, but he stopped me from touching my hair.

"Don't move. I want to remember how you look right now. You're perfect."

Heat bloomed in my face, my chest, my belly. Sebastian crossed his arms, grabbed the hem of his t-shirt, and pulled off his shirt in one move. The sight of his bare chest made the warmth in my stomach move down to between my legs.

My dress had spaghetti straps and a scoop neck with elastic trim and Sebastian ran his finger along the neckline, testing the fabric. Using both hands, he grasped the edge of my dress, along with my strapless bra, and pulled. He'd fully exposed my breasts. He tucked the fabric underneath my chest, which pushed my breasts up, putting them on full display. He settled back onto his heels, still straddling me, and let out a murmur of approval.

"Put your hands behind your head and keep them there."

I did as he asked.

Sebastian used his right hand to turn my head to the side. He traced his finger along my jawline, down my neck, and across my collarbone. Making swirly curves with the pad of his finger, his touch snaked down my sternum and over my breast until he finally reached his destination of my areola. I turned my head so I could watch him. His lids were heavy and his eyes were dark. I wanted to kiss him, but he was too far away.

"Oh God!" The words slipped out of me as Sebastian

captured both of my nipples between his thumbs and fore-fingers.

"Do you like that?" He rolled my nipples between his fingers, and they hardened under his touch.

I did like it. I liked it so much. I squirmed and shifted, but he didn't let me escape, not that I wanted to. My desire was just so strong that I couldn't keep my body still. "Yes," I whispered as I closed my eyes and let the sensations overtake me.

Sebastian pushed his legs back and brought himself down toward my breasts. He let go of my nipples and gently pushed my breasts together, forcing my nipples closer to his face. I kept my eyes shut tight. He circled one nipple with his tongue, causing me to gasp. Then he moved to the other nipple, nibbling at it with his lips before going at it with his tongue. It was torture. Perfect, delicious torture. I wanted him to do that forever, and I also wanted him to stop immediately and just fuck me.

"Sebastian?"

He ignored me for a few seconds as he continued to consume my breasts. The wetness between my legs had spread beyond my folds and was moistening my thighs. "Yes, Alice?" he finally responded.

"I want you. Please."

He ignored me again, teasing my nipples with his fingers, lips, tongue, and teeth until I found my full voice and let moans escape. "Do you?"

"I do, I do, I do." I was panting, my words coming out like a chanted mantra.

"Let's see if that's true." Sebastian shifted his position until he was stretched out at my side. My hands were still behind my head, my breasts were bared, and my skirt was up around my thighs, having ridden up with all my squirming. "Keep your eyes closed."

Sebastian's erection pressed up against my hip and it was agonizing to feel how hard he was but not be able to touch him. I wanted to grab his cock with both hands. I wanted to wrap my lips around him and taste the pearl of pre-cum I knew I'd find beading on his tip. I wanted to stroke him, swallow him, bring him to his knees. But instead, I kept still as he tapped his fingers down my rib cage, across my hip, and toward my thighs, putting me in a state of pleasure-filled agony.

"Let's see how much you want me." Sebastian tangled one hand in the curls on my head while he used the other hand to push my thighs apart. He dragged his fingers up my inner thigh, stopping before he made contact with my panty line. "Alice. You're wet here. What does that mean for over . . ." he drew out the word while he slowly, so fucking slowly, moved his hands between my legs. "Here."

"God!" I cried out.

Sebastian just had one finger on the outside of my panties, and he slid it up and down the fabric, which made me writhe and almost hyperventilate. "What do we have here?" His voice was so low and deep that I felt the vibrations of it in my chest. "You're so fucking wet, Alice. You're soaked."

"Please, Sebastian."

"Please what?" He rubbed his fingertip against the fabric that covered my clit, and I bucked to try and meet his hand. I wanted more pressure.

"I want you." I kept bucking, but he kept his touch soft and gentle. Teasing me.

"What do you want?" He slipped his fingers under my panties and just barely made contact with my skin.

"I want you inside. I want—" I could barely speak. If Sebastian would give me any more pressure I'd lose control. I'd come all over his hand. I couldn't find any more words, and a noise that sounded like a sob escaped from my chest. "Sebastian," I cried.

"Oh baby," he moaned. "My sweet Alice. Here I am." He pulled off the rest of his clothes and rolled over so he was back on top of me. He'd pushed up my dress so all the fabric was gathered around my waist. He was naked and I felt all of his heat and hardness against my skin. He kissed me.

I was ravenous. I inhaled his kisses, hoping to consume him completely. I did not keep my hands under the pillow—I moved them to Sebastian's bare ass and pressed him into me. I wanted him inside. "Fuck me. Please." I tore at my underwear, trying to pull them down and give him access.

Sebastian helped me slide my underwear down my legs and he dug into a pocket of his discarded pants and pulled out a condom. He said nothing but looked me in the eye while he opened the package with his teeth. He shifted for a moment as he slid it on, and then he settled back on top of me. I tried to kiss him, but he moved his head back, evading my mouth.

"You ready?" he asked.

"Yes. God. Yes." I tried to kiss him again, but he still wouldn't let me.

"No kisses. I want to watch your face when I fuck you, Alice."

If words alone could've made me come, I would have. I needed him. I spread my legs wide, and he settled between them. I reached down and found his cock. It was so hard, so ready, and so close. I guided him toward my pussy, sliding his tip against my folds. Sebastian took my hand in his, interlaced his fingers in mine, and moved my hand by my head. He did the same with my other hand and then pressed his tip against my entrance. "I'm going to fuck you, Alice."

I closed my eyes, threw my head back, and lifted my hips, trying to force his dick into me. I wanted to fuck him. Now. I wanted him to fill me.

"Look at me," he demanded.

I opened my eyes.

"Yes." Sebastian bit his lower lip and thrust into me. I was so wet that he slid right in and filled me completely. "Oh my god," he said, and he couldn't keep his eyes open any longer. He tucked his face into my neck as he pulled back and thrust into my pussy again. And again. I untangled my fingers from his, wrapped my arms around him, and dug my fingernails into the small of his back.

I moved my hips in circles and rubbed my clit against his pelvis as he fucked me. His teasing had left me so sensitive and aroused that the heavy pressure of his body was the perfect contrast. My cries got louder, and I moved quickly against him. He got louder too, and he thrust into me as my pleasure built and bloomed from my core.

"I'm going to come," I groaned in his ear. "I'm going to come all over your cock." I had no control over my words as I hit my peak, and my climax exploded through my body like fireworks. I seized his hips with my hands and kept his dick deep inside me as my pussy spasmed around him.

"Oh Alice!" he cried out, and he pushed even deeper into me. He bit my neck, made a fist in my curls, pulled my hair back and came so hard that his whole body convulsed in my arms. We were sweaty and slippery and wet, and he was so perfect that

I wanted to cry or never move or stay in his arms for as long as he'd let me.

We were both breathless, shaking, and spent, and Sebastian collapsed on top of me. I loved the weight of him on top of me. When he held me down, I felt like I was part of the earth. I felt real. And if I was real, I could be hurt, but I could also be loved, and that's what I wanted.

Sebastian kissed me on the cheek, slowly pulled out of me, and rolled onto his side. He removed the condom and set it on the nightstand. Then he wrapped his arms around me and settled his face onto the pillow of my breasts. "Alice?" he whispered.

"Yes?" I combed my fingers through his hair, which was damp with sweat.

"You really are perfect. Thank you. Just—" his voice was full of emotion. "—just thank you."

I was still swimming in pleasure as my body rested in the luxurious afterglow of what we'd done. I scratched Sebastian's bare back and he shivered and moaned.

"Sebastian?"

I froze. I hadn't said his name. It was a man's voice. Did I just have an orgasm so intense that I was imagining things? "Did you hear that?" I whispered.

"Shit. I thought I was hallucinating." Sebastian raised his head and we both stayed still and silent, listening to the noises of the night.

"Sebastian?" Louder this time. Definitely real.

Sebastian bolted up in the bed, his eyes wide and worried. "Dad?"

32

SEBASTIAN

No. Nope. Absolutely not. I did *not* just have perfect sex with the perfect woman on the most perfect night of my life to end up with my father busting into my cottage. I *had* to be hallucinating. With an orgasm like the one I just experienced, anything was possible.

"Bash?"

That sealed the deal. I had to be on drugs. That was Simon's voice.

"Sebastian!!" someone else called out.

Alice and I looked at each other. "Was that . . . Indy?" she squeaked.

"I'll be out in a minute!" I yelled to . . . my entire fucking family? I slid off the bed, scurried to the door, and slammed it shut, grateful that it'd only been open a crack. "What time is it?" I asked Alice.

She stretched across the bed to turn the clock so we could see it, and I was so distracted by the beauty of her body that I forgot for half a second that we were being invaded. "Eight thirty-five. What are they all doing here?" Alice jumped out of bed and scrambled to the bathroom.

I pulled my clothes from the bed and quickly got dressed. "I have no idea!" My shoes were in the living room, so I'd have to go out barefoot.

"Maybe there was an emergency?" Alice had the bathroom door open just an inch and all I could see of her was one eye and a bit of red hair.

"We have telephones! We even have a fucking landline." I tried to slow my breathing, but I could feel the anxiety rushing like when I was trying to push against the tide to get Alice out of the ocean.

A few minutes ago, I'd felt like a man. A grown man who'd just made my woman very happy. I didn't feel like somebody's fuck-up son or playboy cousin. I didn't feel like an ordinary loser. In Alice's arms, I'd felt extraordinary. But that feeling was quickly dissolving and anger was moving in. Maybe they thought I couldn't do it. Couldn't make the presentation, couldn't seal the deal. "I'm going to see what's going on," I told Alice.

"Text me if I need to stay hidden in here," she said from her station behind the bathroom door.

"You don't need to hide, no matter what. If you want to come out, please do so at any time. But I'll understand if you want to stay in here."

"Ok. I'm going to get cleaned up."

One more deep breath, and I exited the bathroom and entered what appeared to be a Starling family reunion. My father was in the kitchen, sampling the cheese and crackers and examining the purple penis flag that I'd left on the table. My cousin Susana was looking through the drink tray in the living room.

Indy burst out of my bedroom holding up a few items of clothing they'd sent me and was talking to no one in particular: "maybe these would be good for tomorrow."

And last, but not least, my cousin Simon was on the porch, and I knew exactly what he was going to find out there if he hadn't already. "What the *hell* is going on with these, Bash?" Simon yelled out. Yep. He'd found the container of cocks.

"Stop!" I demanded. "Everyone Stop!"

My father froze, a hunk of gouda in one hand and the pink glittery vulva flag in the other. Susana stopped pouring her drink, and Indy lowered the clothes they were holding. Only Simon ignored me, marching into the kitchen holding a floppy sparkly dildo up like an Olympic torch.

I held my hands out, palms upturned. "What are you all doing here?"

"I could ask you the same thing," Simon said dryly as he shook the dildo in the air.

"We're here for the presentation tomorrow, son!" my father said brightly, returning the vulva flag to the table with its penis flag partner. "We've been keeping tabs on the developments here, and when we heard you'd made it this far, we figured we'd come down to help."

"You can't do this without your stylist!" Indy offered.

Susana shrugged. "Gabe and I were spending a few days in Hilton Head, and when I heard everyone was headed this way, I decided to tag along. Want a drink?" She held up a bottle of gin.

"A strong one, please."

Simon returned to the porch, my dad opened the fridge to

explore other food options, Indy headed back to my bedroom, and Susana crossed the room and put a drink in my hand.

"Sorry about the ambush," Susana said. "I texted you several times, but you didn't answer."

I raised the drink to my lips and gulped down a few sips. "I was busy," I hissed.

Susana looked around as if trying to find the source of my busy-ness. "With what? Planning for the meeting? We can help with that."

"No, not with planning for the meeting. That's taken care of."

Alice walked out of the bedroom right as I finished my sentence. She'd changed into black flowing lounge pants, a black tank top, and a sandy-colored cardigan. Her hair was a little wild, but it looked sexy and dramatic as she made her entrance. Her cheeks had a rosy glow, and her lips were so fucking full and luscious. I didn't know if it was just me, but to my eyes she looked like she'd just rolled out of bed, and not in a sleeping kind of way.

"Oh, shit. *That* kind of busy," Susana whispered.

Indy wandered back into the living room holding two pairs of my shoes. "Which ones are more—" They stopped short when they saw Alice. "Oh God. We're interrupting."

"Ms. Goode!" my dad boomed. "So nice to see you again!" God, was he that clueless?

Simon had just reentered the living room, this time holding Little Richard along with Richard the Twelfth. He took one look at Alice, went pale, murmured "pardon me," spun on his heels, and returned to the porch with the toys.

"I appreciate the support, but the presentation is tomorrow, at the town hall. Why are you *here*?"

Everyone was silent. Even my father, who usually had something to say in every situation. Finally, Simon spoke up. "We thought you'd be happy to see us. Usually, you like a gathering."

He was right. *I* was the one who normally busted in on others, bringing the party with me whether people liked it or not. "True. I just wasn't expecting you." I glanced at Alice, who looked both brave and mortified. I corrected myself: "*We* weren't expecting you."

"Oh!" My dad seemed to have finally gotten the picture. "We can head over to our cottage. We got one just a few houses down. It's the green one with the big front porch." He abandoned his snack and came over to me and put his hand on my back. "What time should we come over tomorrow to help you get ready?"

"With all due respect, Mr. Starling." Alice stepped forward. Her eyes flashed and while I saw a hint of red creep up her neck, she mostly stayed her normal color. "Sebastian is completely prepared for tomorrow. We're grateful that you're here to support us, but all you need to do is show up at the town hall, and we'll do the rest."

A smile spread across Susana's face. My cousin set down her drink on the coffee table and gave me a hug. "Well done, Bash. We'll see you tomorrow." She hugged Alice, too, and stepped aside.

"I'm sure you have the perfect outfit picked out for tomorrow. Just text if you need help," Indy said, setting the shoes down next to the couch.

"Don't be late," Simon added as he eyed me suspiciously. He turned to Alice. "My apologies for the intrusion. I look forward to seeing you tomorrow at the town hall." He gave one of his ridiculous little bows before joining Susana and Indy on their walk out the front door.

Only my father lingered behind. "Are you sure, son? This is a bigger account than you've handled before, and—"

"I'm absolutely sure, dad. I've got this."

My dad pulled on his earlobe, which was his tell. He was nervous. And why shouldn't he be? But I had to push through this, for both of us. "Alright then. If you need anything, just—"

"I'll call you in the morning to check in. But there's nothing to worry about." I hugged my dad and he squeezed me back.

"I'll talk to you tomorrow, then." Another tug on the ear for my dad.

"Goodnight, dad." I put my hand on his back and walked him to the front door.

My dad turned back one last time and waved, and then he got into the four-seater golf cart where Simon was already seated at the wheel, and the others were situated and waiting for my father.

I watched them drive away and then I went back inside the cottage, closed the door, and locked it with the dead bolt this time.

Alice joined me in the foyer and collected me in a hug. "You ok?" she said into my chest, where her face was pressed.

"I think so." I just wanted to disappear into her arms again, but there was work to do. "You know I don't really have everything under control, right?"

Alice let go of me, took half a step back, and smiled. "No one does. But you don't have to say that to them. You're going to do great tomorrow."

"*We're* going to do great."

"You do the talking, and I'll be there for support. I've seen your plan, and I think it's perfect."

"I think you're biased," I said, pulling her back into the hug.

"Who, me?" she asked, right before she kissed me.

33

SEBASTIAN

Alice and I were ready. Ready to win the contract, ready to crush Tristan Tabor, and ready to impress my family. We were also ready to get back in bed, but there was no time for that. We'd flown the work flag all morning at the cottage, and we'd respected the professional time instead of personal. That didn't stop me from getting caught up in fantasies and daydreams throughout the day, but hey, a guy can only take so much.

Having Alice so close was maddening and made it difficult to concentrate. There was early morning Alice in a white bathrobe and curls tumbling over her shoulders, sleepy-eyed and pouring coffee—she made me want to pick her up, carry her back to bed, and not rejoin the real world for a week or so.

There was "down to business" Alice, who chewed on the end of her pencil, piled her hair on top of her head in a bun, and had the most adorable frown lines pop up between her brows when she found something in our presentation that she wanted to change. I wanted to stare at her all day and sit as close as possible to breathe in her scent of rose soap and white tea and grapefruit body lotion.

And then there was bossy Alice, which was what I was getting right now. "You have to memorize that last part! I'll make sure the slideshow is ready to run, but your notes don't cover the closing speech. Do you need me to make a change to those? Sebastian, are you even listening?"

No, I wasn't really listening. I was thinking about how Alice's body felt underneath mine, and was wondering how it would feel on top of mine for a change. Or beside mine, with one leg pulled up so I could move in behind her and—

"Sebastian Maddix Starling," Alice huffed.

"Sorry, what were you saying?"

Alice sighed and shut her laptop. "I guess there's no use in overworking this. If we don't have it by now, more cramming won't help. We need to head out in about an hour." She stood up from the table and stretched, putting her curvy and delicious body on display. So cruel.

Maybe I could convince her to take a break from work time. "I agree. We're ready. Maybe we should put up the pink flag until it's time to go. I bet our minds would be clearer if we released some of the tension—" I grabbed her hips and pulled her to me. My face was at the level of her stomach, and I lifted her shirt a few inches and kissed her belly button.

"Bazzy, we have to keep our focus," she scolded, but she leaned into my embrace.

I ran my hands across her stomach and slid them up to her ribs.

"What is that?" Alice shifted as she pointed to a box labeled "PARTY PROPS" on the top of the pantry shelf.

"Don't know, don't care." I pulled her back to me and tried to resume my exploration of her torso, but she wriggled free.

"I didn't notice this before." She dragged a chair over to the shelf and stepped onto the seat.

"What are you doing? Let me get that." All we needed was some injury or mishap to derail our day. I got up from where I was sitting and crossed the kitchen to be by her side.

"I've got it. It's not heavy." She slid the box off the shelf and shook it, rattling the contents.

"Great, now you just broke the homeowner's prized collection of beach figurines. Give me that."

She handed me the box and used my body as a brace as she climbed down from the chair. Just that small touch sent me back to daydream land. Maybe she'd let me take her right here in the kitchen. I could prop her up on the kitchen counter, and—

"Open it, or give it here." Alice interrupted my fantasy time, once again.

"Curiosity killed the cat, Alice. I'll let you take the fall." I set down the box on the table and backed away.

Alice opened the flaps of cardboard and peered into the box. "Oh my God."

"If there's something dead in there, I don't want to see it." I took another step back. Expired rodents were not my cup of tea, and it was her idea to open Pandora's Box, so I'd let her deal with the mouse carcass if there was one.

"Nothing dead." She reached into the box. Something clanked and clattered. She pulled out something blue and silky.

"What's that?"

"It appears to be—" Alice shook the silky thing, "—a blind-

fold. And these are—" she retrieved a shiny item from the box,"
—handcuffs."

"Holy shit. That really is Pandora's Box!" I peeked into the
box and saw several pairs of handcuffs, a few blindfolds, and a
key on a round ring.

"It's not Pandora's Box," Alice said, "it's just that stuff the
bride was looking for." She took a pair of handcuffs and slipped
one over her wrist.

"Don't do that!" I yanked the cuff off her arm before she
had time to close it.

"There's a key right there, Baz." She plucked the key out of
the box.

"But you haven't tested it, Blaze." I locked the handcuff and
took the key from her fingers and slid it into the keyhole. I
wiggled it around and the cuff popped open.

"See! Don't be such a worrywart."

"*Worrywart?* Okay, grandma."

Alice rolled her eyes. "I'll text the bride and let her know the
stuff is here."

"You can do that later." I set the cuffs and key down on the
table and wrapped my arms around Alice. "I can think of better
ways to spend the next forty-five minutes." I leaned down to
kiss her, and she indulged me with a soft, open kiss, but then
she pulled away.

"Believe me, there is truly nothing I want more than to do
what we did last night, but I don't think I could give it the
proper attention, knowing that we were in a time crunch. I
want to be able to relax and enjoy you." Her hand was on my
waist, and she let it trail down the front of my pants and she
landed on my very obvious erection. "Though, I don't have any

objections to tending to this . . . *issue* you seem to have." She cupped my balls and I couldn't help but moan.

"No, I don't want it to just be for me. I want to get my hands on you." Which was true, but I hadn't been able to pull myself away from her grasp quite yet.

"I'd like to touch you. And that means it would be my turn later, and I'd feel no guilt in letting you take care of me." She slid her hand up and down the outside of my pants, and my dick strained at the fabric. "And, we can make it extra fun." She nodded toward the table.

"You are not using those handcuffs on me," I said, though my desire was strong enough to allow just about anything if it meant Alice continuing with this stroking.

"I didn't take you as the vanilla type." Alice squeezed my dick, and my will to argue was rapidly dissolving.

"I'm just the Alice type," I said, trying to keep my voice steady and normal, but pretty sure it came out breathy and desperate.

"Then go to the bedroom. Your bedroom." Bossy Alice was back.

"Why mine?"

"Because you have the headboard with the rails."

Good god, had she been thinking about this? About tying me up? It was slightly troubling, but mostly so hot that my cock was rock-hard begging to be set free from the confines of my clothing. "Fine. As you wish." I walked into my bedroom, climbed on the bed, and situated myself on my back. The bulge in my pants was like a flashing fluorescent sign advertising my aching need for Alice.

Alice followed me a few seconds later with handcuffs and the key. "I'll do a test again, just to make sure." She closed one of the cuffs, inserted the key, and popped it open. "See? Easy peasy."

"No blindfolds?"

"Seems a little weird to use those. Plus, don't you want to watch?" Naughty Alice had arrived, and I had no objections. "Put your hands above your head."

I raised my hands by the rails of the headboard, and Alice snapped on the handcuffs like she'd been doing this every day of her life. "Jesus, Alice, do you moonlight as a mall cop?"

"No, but speaking of Moonlighting, that's another one of my favorite old shows."

"You're weird, Alice Goode."

She tilted her head to one side. "Maybe, but you're the one who just let me handcuff you to the bed, so I might be weird, but I'm also in charge." She swept up her hair into a ponytail and secured it with a hair tie she'd stashed in her back pocket.

I pulled my hands to test the cuffs, half expecting them to snap open—they seemed pretty cheap, just novelty quality. They couldn't be *that* secure if the bride had ordered them in bulk. But they held tight. I didn't consider myself vanilla, but I hadn't let a lover restrain me before—well, no one had ever asked to do so. There was a first time for everything, and this was definitely my first time having a beautiful woman lock up my hands and look at me like I was a piece of meat.

Alice climbed on the bed and straddled my knees. She yanked on the waistband of my pants and pulled them, and my underwear, down in one sweep. I was surprised, exposed, and very turned on. I liked this aggressive side of Alice, because it felt like a surprise.

As rough as she'd been with locking me up and disrobing me, she was taking the opposite path when it came to touching me. I was so aroused that it wouldn't take much for Alice to put me over the edge, and she was taking her sweet time. She fluttered her fingers around my belly button, my hips, and my thighs, touching me everywhere but where I really wanted her —no, needed her—to touch me. I instinctively moved to put my hands on her shoulders but was quickly reminded that they'd be remaining over my head for the duration of this event.

Alice finally crept her fingers between my legs and touched my shaft so lightly that it barely registered, but also almost sent me over the edge. I wasn't used to waiting, and I wasn't used to wanting—not like this. I craved Alice's touch. I yearned for her closeness. This wasn't about getting off. It was about getting to be intimate with her, and I wanted her, badly.

"This is torture," I said, as I raised my hips, hoping to initiate more contact with Alice's hands.

"Is it?" A wicked smile spread across her face. "How about this, then?" Alice closed both hands around my dick, one on top of the other, and softly twisted her fists in contrasting directions. The sensation was gentle but overwhelming.

"More torture," I gasped, pushing into her fists trying to get more friction.

"And this?" she asked, as she lowered her mouth toward her hands and let her open lips hover just an inch above my tip.

I thrust up again, and she didn't move her head, so she let me push my dick into her mouth just a little. The soft heat of her mouth was perfection, and I needed more. I pushed up again, and again, barely getting the head of my cock to her lips, while she continued to use her hands to drive me insane. On my next push, I met with her tongue, as she'd stuck it out and was waiting for me. I wanted her to devour me, and this teasing was going to destroy me. "Please, Alice," I groaned.

"Please what, Sebastian?" Alice looked up at me, her mouth hovering above my throbbing erection.

I had no pride left. No humility. Only animal desire. If I'd had the use of my hands I would've snatched her up and enveloped her in my arms and sunk my dick into her pussy if she'd let me. But all I could do was squirm and beg. "Please put your mouth on me."

"As you wish." She took me all the way into her mouth in one move, and the sensation of it sent a jolt through my entire body. She pulled back and ran her tongue along the length of me, sucked my tip, and then took my full length again. She massaged my balls in one hand while using the other to stroke me while she licked, sucked, and nibbled.

I was gone. Spent. Had no stamina, no willpower. I squeezed my eyes shut and rode the wave of wetness, warmth, and tenderness, and my climax shot through me like lightning, and I came, and came, and came.

When I opened my eyes, Alice had her cheek against my thigh, and she was stroking me gently as I slowly returned to Earth. I felt like I'd left my body—left the universe, really, but I also felt like I'd been close to Alice the whole time. That hadn't been a solo journey out of the stratosphere–she'd led the way and held me close. "You're perfect," I told her.

"Oh yeah? I thought I was weird?" She let go of me but kept her cheek on my thigh. It was such an intimate pose, but I felt completely comfortable with it.

"You're weirdly perfect."

Alice laughed. "I'll take that." She hopped off the bed, grabbed a box of tissues, and set them next to me. She slid the handcuff key off the nightstand and unlocked my right hand.

"Was that okay?" She bit her lip as she reached over me to unlock my left hand. Regular Alice was back.

I pulled a tissue from the box and cleaned myself off. "Okay?" I laughed. "Alice, that was so much more than okay."

"Oh, good. I just went with it, but I wasn't sure if—" Alice gasped. "Oh fuck."

"What is it?" I craned my neck to see what she was looking at. She was looking at half a key. And the other half was broken in the lock on the handcuff which had my left hand firmly trapped against the headboard railing.

34

ALICE

"Please tell me that the handcuff key did not just break off," Sebastian said. He'd closed his eyes and appeared to be taking some very deep breaths.

"So, do you want me not to tell you that?" I asked. "Because that's what happened."

"What time is it?" Sebastian's voice was low and clear, but not happy. He was pissed.

Leave it to me to bring him to pleasure one minute and crush his soul the next. I checked the clock. "It's time to go."

Sebastian yanked his arm, hard, and then cried out in pain.

"Don't hurt yourself!" I fumbled with the handcuff, looking for a safety latch or some kind of weakness in the metal where I could break it apart. No luck. Those fuckers were stronger than they had a right to be. Except for the key, which apparently was a piece of shit. "I can't get it open." I could feel the tears building. "I'm so sorry."

Sebastian rattled, shook, banged, and thrashed his hand against the railing, but the bed held steady, as did the handcuff.

"If we don't make it in time, then we won't be able to do

the presentation, and your family's there, and I've just ruined everything." The tears started to slip out.

"Alice," Sebastian said sternly.

"What?" I'd felt so powerful and perfect just a few moments earlier, and now I felt helpless and stupid.

"It's purple penis time."

"Oh god!" I looked down at his dick, wondering if I'd cut off his circulation, but everything looked normal. "You look ok." My hands were starting to shake.

"No, not that. Jesus." Sebastian yanked up his pants with his free hand. "The flag. Put on your work brain. It's time to problem solve."

"Right. Ok. Problem solve." I nodded like I was on board with this plan, but really, I was still panicking that I'd hand-cuffed Sebastian Starling to a bed and now he was stuck, and we were going to lose the deal and we'd never, ever, live this down. I could change jobs, but this was a family company for Sebastian. His family would never trust him to be professional and it was all my fault. It didn't matter how many declarations we'd made to HR. I was definitely getting fired, and I deserved it.

"Bring me my phone."

I ran to the kitchen, swiped both our phones off the counter, and brought them back to the bedroom. "What now?"

"I'm going to make some calls. You take the golf cart and head to the town hall. Tabor's going first, so if you're a few minutes late it won't be a deal breaker."

I felt the shivers of a cold sweat run over my skin. "I can't do this without you!"

"You're going to have to, at least for a little bit." Sebastian's jaw was set.

"I'm so sorry, Sebastian."

"Come here, baby." He held out his free hand to me and I took it. He just called me "baby." He pulled me into a hug, and I wanted to collapse on his chest and hide out from the world. He kissed the top of my head. "We can do this. We're a team, and one of us rises up when the other one falls."

I kept my mouth shut even though I really wanted to make a joke about "rising up." I sat up and took a few deep breaths of my own. "Okay. I can do this."

"That's right you can. The bag's in the living room, and the box with the handouts is already in the golf cart."

"What do I tell your family?"

"Tell them I had a work emergency. Or got attacked by a shark. Whatever seems to make sense. I'll be there. Probably before Tristan is done. But I want you there on your own just in case I'm stuck for a while."

"I could call the fire department!" I picked up my phone and unlocked the screen.

"Let's save that for our last-ditch effort. If there's any way this can stay on the down-low, I think that would be preferable."

"Is there anything you need before I leave?" I stood up to go but felt very uncomfortable leaving Sebastian in such a compromising position. I adjusted his pants and pulled down his shirt, so he was completely clothed.

"I have my phone. I'll be fine. You get out of here. I'll text you with updates, and you do the same. It's okay."

I kissed him goodbye and held back the tears. Sebastian was right. We had a job to do, and until he was freed, it was up to me to get the job done. I got my purse from my bedroom, collected the keys from the hook by the door, and stepped out onto the front porch. I could do this.

. . .

OR MAYBE I COULDN'T. I'd pulled into the town hall parking lot and was obviously late. There were so many golf carts already there that I had to park in the grass. But the worst part was that I'd forgotten the bag. The bag that Sebastian had reminded me to bring. The bag that had our laptop, our notes, and almost everything we needed to give a professional presentation. I had the box of handouts that we were going to distribute at the end of our talk, but that was it. God, I was such a fucking loser.

For a minute I considered quitting. I'd just walk to the beach and keep walking until I was far enough away to forget about any of this. But I knew that was ridiculous. I couldn't forget, and I couldn't run away. My hiding era was over. It was time to get on stage, ready or not. I hoisted the box of handouts into my arms and trudged up the path to the town hall.

When I got inside, Tristan was already presenting. She was just at her introduction stage, but I was mortified to walk in late. Never one to miss an opportunity to make me feel like shit, Tristan stopped talking when she saw me, put her hand up to her forehead over her eyes like she was straining to see something far in the distance. "Is that Alice Goode from Starling Enterprises?" All eyes in the hall turned to me. "I thought y'all might've forgotten about us!" A few people laughed and others murmured to each other. Great. Just great.

Tristan went back to her speech, and I scanned the crowd for the Starlings. Shit. There they were, snaking along the side wall and making their way to me. Sebastian's father's face was stern, and so was Simon's, but Simon's face was always stern. Susana followed the men, but her face was neutral. Mr. Blake was sitting in a chair at the back of the room, and he raised his walking stick in greeting. I offered him a weak wave.

"Everything okay?" Jennie had gotten to me before the Starlings, who were slowly getting closer.

"Not really!"

"Where's Sebastian?" she whispered.

"Long story. He should be here soon."

"Anything I can do?" Graham came up behind his wife and his face was lined with worry.

How much would Sebastian hate me if I sent Graham to help him with the handcuff situation? A lot, I assumed.

"We saw one of your crew run out of here about ten minutes ago," Graham said.

"Who?" I whispered back.

"Not sure on the name," Jennie said. "Purple hair. Kilt?"

"Indy!" I said a silent prayer that Indy was on their way to help Sebastian. Indy knew how to be discreet, but I didn't envy the embarrassing situation Sebastian was in.

The Starlings were upon me. Simon jerked his head in the direction of the back door, then turned and headed outside. Susana also went outside, and Mitchell motioned for me to follow Simon, so I did. I had a sinking feeling in my stomach. My days of Corporate Handling were over.

Simon had his arms crossed, and while he always looked tall, he didn't usually look imposing, but right now he looked huge and scary as hell. "Well?" he asked.

Shit. I didn't know what they knew and what they didn't. My strategy: repeat their questions back to them. "Well?" I asked back.

"Is he okay?" Simon stared down at me.

"Is he okay?" I echoed back.

"Yes," Simon said.

"Yes," I answered.

"Indy got the call," Mitchell added.

"Oh, Indy got the call! Okay, good." This echoing wouldn't hold up much longer.

"Something about Sebastian being stuck?" Mitchell Starling furrowed his brow and tugged on his earlobe.

"Yes, he was stuck. But it's a long story, and I need to be inside listening to Ms. Tabor in case she brings up something I need to counter in my presentation. If you'll excuse me—"

"But what exactly happened?" Simon blocked my way with his obnoxiously tall frame.

"Simon, we can talk about that later," Susana chimed in. "Let her go back to the presentations. I'm sure Indy and Bash have it under control."

Simon huffed and rolled his eyes but stepped aside. Susana walked directly behind me as we went back inside, as if to protect me from any more inquiries from her cousin and uncle.

"—so I could go on, but I know your time is valuable, and I'm sure you're ready to hear what the other team has planned for Scarlet Oaks," Tristan was saying. Shit. She'd cut her presentation short. She'd figured out that Sebastian was missing, and she was taking full advantage of the situation.

A few people raised their hands. I breathed a sigh of relief. Questions from the crowd could buy me some time. "How about you save your questions until after the Starlings present. I'll be happy to stay as long as you need to answer each and every one!" Tristan said with false cheer. She spotted me and a malicious smile spread across her smug face. "Mr. Starling and Ms. Goode, it's your turn!"

35

ALICE

Everyone was looking at me. Tristan, the residents of Caluska Island, Mr. Blake, the Starling family—everyone. I took one slow step. And then another. I got to the perch near the podium and stepped up. I turned to face the crowd. Maybe if I moved slow enough, Sebastian would show up. He'd bring the laptop, the notes, the presentation. He'd save me.

Wait. Save me? Maybe I was about to have a heart attack, because a rush of memories overwhelmed my brain. They came in flashes so quick, I could barely distinguish one from the other.

My Nana showing me pictures of my parents and singing me songs at night that my mother used to sing so I could fall asleep. My grandfather walking me to school every day. Mr. Blake teaching me to play chess. Skipping school with Tristan. Swimming in the ocean until my skin was saturated in salt. Moving into my first apartment after leaving Caluska Island. Starting my job at Starling Enterprises. My movie nights and take-out dinners. Sebastian dancing naked at the hotel. Almost drowning in the undertow. Kissing Sebastian. Standing up for myself with

Tristan. Walking alone on the beach, on my island, and feeling at home.

I didn't need anyone to save me. I was enough. I closed my eyes and channeled that feeling that I got when I walked on the beach. Time sped up. My mind cleared. I knew what to do.

"Good afternoon, everyone," I began. "My name is Alice Goode and I can't tell you what a pleasure it's been to return home to Caluska after all these years." Some audience members smiled at me, and a few others nodded. "My associate will be with us shortly, but I wanted a chance to talk to you first, on my own." So far so good. My hair felt tight. I remembered that I'd put my hair back in the ponytail right before my handcuff adventure with Sebastian. I reached back and slid the hair tie out, releasing my ponytail and letting my hair expand into its wild, wonderful self. "Ah, that's better!"

Tristan glared at me from the side of the room.

"I know Scarlet Oaks is important to you," I continued. "I know this, because it's important to me, too. How many people here remember that one crack on the tennis court that came back no matter how many times it was fixed, and for some reason, yellow flowers always grew out of that crack?" A few laughs from the audience. "And who remembers the time the Blakes had the Fourth of July party where they put actual goldfish in the pool for the kids to chase?" Groans from the crowd as hands went up. "I came home with twelve fish that day. Mr. Blake, how many phone calls from mothers and grandmothers did you get after that party?"

Everyone laughed and Mr. Blake pretended to hide underneath his hat. "Never again!" he called out.

"Ms. Tabor had a lovely presentation, and I had one just like it, but I'm not going to show it to you today." I saw the Starlings look at each other in confusion. "We do have a plan for Scarlet Oaks, and I have handouts for each one of you that you can take home and study. But what's most important to us is that you understand the heart of our plan, and no presentation can show you that. Please follow me." I stepped off the podium but hopped back up to add something else. "We're heading out to the beach. Follow my hair if you lose your way, but don't mistake it for one of the red flags!"

I led the people out of the town hall, down the path, through the trees, and out to the beach. I got there first, and turned to watch people walk to join me, and a few others, like Mr. Blake, drove their carts to the spot, because walking was tricky for them. At the back of the line I saw a flash of purple—Indy's hair!—and then I saw an entire rainbow when Sebastian came into view.

Baz had dumped his neutral wardrobe. He was wearing pink shorts, a turquoise linen blazer, and a shirt that had . . . I squinted so I could make out the bright pattern on his button-down shirt . . . parrots. His shirt was covered in parrots.

After a few minutes, everyone was gathered on the beach. It was a group of almost 100 people, and they were mostly Caluska Island residents. The group also included the Starlings, Graham and Jennie, Mr. Blake, Indy, Tristan, and best of all, Sebastian.

"Way to problem solve." He winked at me.

"Are you okay?" I whispered.

"Indy is very resourceful and always comes armed with tools."

"I'll remember that."

"What's your plan here?" Sebastian asked.

"Follow my lead." I walked over to Jennie, who was

standing nearby. "Could you help me with Mr. Blake for a few moments?" I asked her.

"Of course." Jennie followed me as I approached Mr. Blake.

"Could I borrow your walking stick?" I asked him. "I'll lend you my friend if you need a helping hand."

"That's more than a fair trade," he said, and he handed me the stick.

"If everyone could move in closer, please!" I said in my loudest voice. The people on the beach bunched together. I motioned for Sebastian to take the stick from me, and he jogged over and took the stick from my hand. "We're going to draw a circle around you, so stay put for a few moments," I told the crowd.

Sebastian knew just what to do. He put the end of the stick in the sand, and ran in a circle until all the people were gathered together inside the line drawn by Sebastian.

"Caluska Island is about community," I said. "Scarlet Oaks is also about community. It's about having a safe place to gather, and a place that will grow, thrive, and evolve in ways that will keep up with a world that's changing so fast. We want Scarlet Oaks to honor our past but keep an eye to our future. We need comfort in our community, but we also need to embrace growth. That's what our plan offers you, but it's your community, and your circle, so ultimately, it's your choice."

"I'm so thankful that I got to know Caluska Island through the eyes of Alice," Sebastian added. "I'm a city boy at heart, and I'm sure you can tell that by looking at me." The crowd laughed. "But Alice introduced me to Island life, and I can recognize that your community is unique and precious. Thank you for allowing me to be a part of your circle for the last week, and I hope to be a part of the bright future of this place. Thank you so much." Everyone clapped at the end of his speech, everyone except Tristan, but even she didn't break the line of the circle. She stood inside with the rest of us, frowning, but still part of the group.

"Before we break our circle," Sebastian said, "I'd like to say a few words. Alice, to whom this beach is very special, said these words a few days ago, and I'd like to share this little prayer with you."

What was he doing? Surely he couldn't remember my silly beach incantation. Even *I* couldn't remember it.

Sebastian held the walking stick over his head, and he looked part preacher, part model, part Miami Vice actor in his parrot shirt as he gave the closing remarks. "Goddess of the island, hear our call. Guide us as we walk your shifting surface and let our hearts expand to accept the ebb and flow of your tide. Use your salt to soften our rough edges and to expose our wounds. Let us explore your boundaries between earth and sea and help us be brave enough to swim in your deep waters and return safely to your shore once our wanderlust is satisfied. We now break the circle."

He remembered. Word for word.

Sebastian lowered the stick, walked to the edge of the circle, and broke the line.

One by one, people exited the circle, but just through the break Sebastian had drawn in the sand. I joined him as the crowd filed out, and many of the people thanked us or shook our hands.

Tristan was one of the last to leave and she lingered for a second before speaking to me. "I sent Jamie a DM last night, by the way."

"You did?" I was surprised that Tristan was speaking to me at all, let alone bringing this up.

"Yeah. And you were right. She made it up. Guess she couldn't believe I fell for it." Tristan shrugged. "Anyway. Sorry. For the hair. And for yesterday."

"Thanks." It was all I could think to say, and it was all Tristan seemed to need. We'd never be friends again, but it felt like some kind of peace agreement was made. She scurried up the beach and headed back to the town hall.

Jennie escorted Mr. Blake, and Sebastian returned the walking stick to its owner.

"I liked that," Mr. Blake said. "And I like your style today. Your grandfather would be pleased."

Sebastian smiled. "Thank you, Eddie. Thank you for everything."

"Not bad." That came from Simon who was next in line and looking down on Sebastian and me from his high horse.

"Thanks, Si." Sebastian punched Simon on the arm, a little harder than necessary, judging by how Simon winced.

"Well done, Ms. Goode. And you too, son. I didn't expect that, but I was honestly moved." Mitchell Starling patted his son on the back.

"We had some technical difficulties and had to pivot," I said.

"Well, I'm impressed. I look forward to hearing the outcome next week when the final decision is made."

"Great job," Susana Starling said as she followed her family out of the sand circle. "That was really special."

Indy followed a few paces behind and waited to speak until the others were out of earshot. "Next time, use straps. Less risk."

Oh God. "Thank you for coming to our rescue."

"My pleasure. Now I have something to hold over Sebastian's head for at least the next six months."

The last stragglers left the circle, leaving just Sebastian and me. "That was something else," he told me.

"Problem solving, just like you said." I was never great at taking a compliment.

"That was more than problem solving," he said. "That was alchemy."

"Thank you," I said, my face warming with pride.

"We make a good team." Sebastian leaned down and kissed me softly on the lips. He tasted like salted caramel and wintergreen.

"Do you forgive me for the handcuffs?"

"Not only do I not forgive you, but I'm also going to take my sweet time getting my revenge tonight."

Heat rushed through my body, and my stomach flipped. "Is it suddenly hot out here, or is it just me?" I fanned myself with my hand.

Sebastian's devilish smile revealed his dimple. "Buckle up, Ms. Goode. It's blazing."

EPILOGUE

ALICE

"If I'd known that you'd fall more in love with him than you are with me, I never would've let you in here," Sebastian said.

"I'm sorry, Baz. You know I have a weak spot for burly blond guys."

Gabriel Green shook his hair dramatically and puffed up his chest for good measure. "Yeah, Bash. Not everybody falls for the tall, dark, and handsome type."

Sebastian rolled his eyes. "It's one thing to lose my fiancée to a horse, but it would be disappointing if a chump like you caught her eye."

Gabe laughed and then reached up to help me dismount Sandy, the golden Quarter Horse who lived in the stables at Starling Manor.

"Neither of you gents has anything on Sandy's mane," I said as I slid off the gorgeous horse and landed on the soft dirt floor of the stable. "Thanks for letting me ride him, Gabe. It's been a long time since I've been on a horse."

"You rode a stallion last night," Sebastian mumbled just loud enough for me to hear him.

"You aren't jealous, are you, Mr. Starling?"

"Of course not," he said, but he captured me in his arms, lifted me up, and carried me out of the stables.

"Set me down, you beast."

"I thought you had a thing for beasts!"

I tried to reach his ribs to tickle him, but he was too strong.

"We have guests here at the manor, you know. Care to save the antics for later?"

"Hi, Simon," Sebastian and I said in unison. Baz released me and set me down gently. As usual, Simon had entered the scene as silent as a shadow slipping across a wall.

"Once a buzzkill, always a buzzkill," Sebastian said. "Who are those people over by the barn?"

"Finalists in the Starling Enterprises Artist in Residence Program. Susana is hosting a luncheon for them."

We'd all convened at Starling Manor for the long September weekend. We were finalizing some publicity plans for the groundbreaking of the Scarlet Oaks project, which was set to begin in October. The family also wanted to celebrate my engagement to Sebastian at the manor, where we could have some privacy from the media.

Sebastian had stepped more into his role as VP of Special Projects at Starling Enterprises, but he still only worked at the office part-time. He'd promoted Lacy to Director of Special Projects, and she had a small staff with whom she was working on some great new initiatives. When he wasn't in the office, he was splitting his time between apartment hunting for the two of us and being the new face of Eclat Nouveau, a fashion house that chose Sebastian to represent their line of menswear.

I was on the leadership team for the Scarlet Oaks project, from which Sebastian had been entirely removed. It was definitely better for us to not work together, at least from an HR standpoint.

"We're heading out for a drive in a few, so we'll meet back up for drinks at five," Sebastian said to Simon, who was frozen and staring at the barn like he'd seen a ghost. "Simon?"

Simon didn't respond. I wasn't sure he'd even heard Sebastian. He just kept staring at the barn doors where the artists had entered the building for their lunch.

"Cuz. You ok?" Sebastian punched Simon in the arm.

"Ouch! Must you always punch people?" Simon rubbed the spot where Baz had hit him.

"Sorry, Si. Didn't mean to do it that hard. You were just out of it. Something wrong?"

Simon shook his head. "Oh, no. Nothing's right. I mean wrong. Just thought I saw someone I knew. See you at dinner, then. Enjoy your swim." Simon turned and walked briskly back up to the house.

"What was that?" I asked. I'd never seen Simon flustered.

"I have no idea. Something got to him." We both watched him walk up the path toward the manor.

"You two ready for your drive? I'm heading to the garage if you want to walk with me." Gabe wiped some sweat from his brow and brushed some dirt off his tanned biceps. Gabe used to be the groundskeeper at Starling Manor, and even though he was married to Susana now and was the man of the house, he still spent a lot of time in hands-on activities at the property.

Sebastian caught me admiring Gabe and rolled his eyes. "I'm ready, but what about you, my bride-to-be? Need to take in any more scenery, or are you good?" He held out his hand to me.

"I'm good." I took his hand. Gabe was handsome, but no one was as breathtaking as Sebastian, and Baz knew that I only had eyes for him.

We strolled up to the garage where some of the family fleet was stored. Sebastian had some of his favorites transferred here during the summer so we could go for drives on the country roads together.

As we neared the garage, Gabe slowed. "I see one of my gardeners over there. Need to talk to him about plans for a new vegetable garden. Have fun on the drive, and I'll see you later at cocktail hour."

"See you in a bit." Sebastian squeezed my hand as we continued walking. "Excited for our drive?"

"I am. But we still get to watch *Sleepless in Seattle* in the movie room tonight, right?"

"Yes, and even Simon agreed to watch with us. And my dad told me that he has a crush on Meg Ryan, which was TMI."

"Are we taking the Porsche today?"

"We are not."

"Why not?" The Porsche 718 Spyder was Baz's favorite for the kind of roads that surrounded the manor and was the whole reason he'd sent that car to Starling Manor.

"Because we have a new arrival." He hit the code for one of the bay doors and the panel lifted to reveal the most stunningly luscious and sleek car I'd ever seen. It was redder than red, and it made all the other cars in the garage seem like they were painted in shades of gray.

"Holy shit."

"There she is." Sebastian gazed at his 1984 Ferrari Testarossa

Spider with a look in his eye that rivaled any look of lust he'd ever had for me.

I'd never seen the car in person before. It'd been stored at a high security garage outside of the city, and I'd never made it over there. "Hey, don't look at that redhead like that! I'm supposed to be the only ginger in your life."

"I have two redheaded lovers, and you knew this when you agreed to marry me." He approached the car, and I could've sworn he had tears in his eyes. "Riding in this car isn't like driving. It's more like flying."

"Then I guess I need to get to know her. Ready to make our introductions?"

"It would be my pleasure. Scarlet, meet Alice. Alice, this is Scarlet."

"Scarlet? Really?" I loved seeing Sebastian when he was passionate about something, and he was certainly passionate about this car.

Sebastian leaned close to the car and held his hand to his ear like he was trying to hear something the car was whispering. He stood back up. "Scarlet says that she'd be honored to take the future Mrs. Starling out for a ride. You ready?" He approached me and caressed my cheek with his fingers, and then leaned in for a quick kiss. "Don't tell Scarlet," he whispered into my ear, "but you're the most beautiful redhead in the world."

"I won't tell." I raised up on my tiptoes to steal another kiss. "And yes, I'm absolutely ready, Mr. Starling. Let's fly."

ACKNOWLEDGMENTS

This was such a fun book to write, and I hope it's as fun to read!

Thank you to my brother Jon for technical consulting; Sebastian has you to thank for his 1984 Ferari Testarossa Spider. Thank you to the MyJorMega team for your edits, commentary, and endless support.

Many thanks to my friends and family who continue to support my writing journey through all its twists and turns. Love stories matter, especially now, I can't wait to keep writing more for you to enjoy.

Love,
Megan

ABOUT THE AUTHOR

Megan Moores writes cozy steamy romances that combine humor, edge, and happily ever afters. She earned a B.A. in Creative Writing followed by a Master's in Teaching (Secondary English), both from the University of Arkansas. As a mood reader, Megan switches between Literary Fiction, Romance, Nordic Noir, Memoirs, Police Procedurals, and Thrillers. She currently lives in Indiana with her husband, four children, three cats, and one lonely fish.

Website: https://www.meganmoores.com
Newsletter: https://meganmoores.substack.com

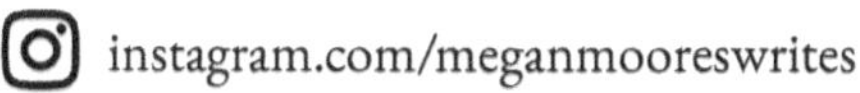 instagram.com/meganmooreswrites

www.ingramcontent.com/pod-product-compliance
Lightning Source LLC
Chambersburg PA
CBHW030150310726
48970CB00005B/1669